Something Blue

Lord & Lady Hetheridge #3

Emma Jameson

For Mary Ellen Wofford, my first true writing teacher.

Chapter One

Anthony Hetheridge, chief superintendent for New Scotland Yard and ninth baron of Wellegrave, would walk down the aisle in three weeks. The day chosen, the twenty-eighth of December, was denounced by most invitees as too soon: a mere two months after his subordinate, Detective Sergeant Kate Wakefield, had accepted his proposal. Not to mention unsuitably close to Christmas! The venue, Hetheridge's home in Mayfair, was condemned as much too small for a guest list of over two hundred. Would the well-wishers be expected to squat in any unguarded space, such as the kitchen or washroom, or else mill about in Wellegrave House's walled back garden?

The wedding's designated hour, five o'clock in the evening, was equally derided. So the ceremony would begin in twilight and end in absolute darkness, except for strings of white fairy lights in the trees or some other such nonsense? Holding a wedding at the dinner hour simply wasn't done. Was the bride, reputedly raised by wolves in the East End's most savage corner, to blame for these bizarre social lapses? Or was Hetheridge himself, who'd recently celebrated his sixtieth birthday, showing signs of early dementia?

Although no stranger to controversy, at least not where his blue-blooded connections were concerned, the vitriol unleashed by his wedding plans surprised even Hetheridge. Around the Yard, men without a family to go home to—at least not a family they cared to spend time with—groused that Hetheridge and DS Wakefield would both "disappear" just after Boxing Day, leaving the less fortunate to sweep up.

"Right, well, what's a little thing like murders and shootings and drugs, when true love's on the line?" Detective Chief Inspector Vic Jackson was overheard to complain between bites of a bacon sarnie. "We'll just have to muddle through, boys. Rank has its privileges. As does a perfect pair of lips, hey?"

Except DCI Jackson hadn't said "lips." And Hetheridge, catching wind of the conversation, as he was surely meant to, had been forced to remind himself that seizing and pummeling a fellow detective was considered bad form. Especially in today's new, improved, more egalitarian Scotland Yard. Still, it would have been satisfying. Rumpled, perpetually unshaven DCI Jackson, still bitter because Kate once spurned his advances, was fortyish, fattish, and better with his mouth than his fists. By contrast, Hetheridge had kept himself up, partly because his lifelong obsession with fencing had never waned. And partly because a beautiful young woman, nearly half his age, was about to become his bride.

Vic Jackson wasn't the only person to broadcast his displeasure over the upcoming nuptials. Hetheridge's nephew and heir, Roderick Hetheridge, middle-aged and the father of three strapping teenaged sons, had responded to the wedding announcement by practically sobbing into the phone. Apparently, Roderick had gotten into the Glenfiddich before deciding to make his "congratulations" call.

"Do you really believe you'll father an heir now? At your age? Never," Roderick had slurred. "You and that tart will

burn in hell for denying me what's mine, Uncle Tony. Burn...
in... *hell*."

"Terribly sorry. No idea whatever whom you're trying to
reach," Hetheridge had said, dropping the old-fashioned
receiver into its cradle. Not long after, he'd traded Wellegrave
House's vintage phones for modern cordless versions, all
equipped to display the caller's identity. He braced himself for
a repeat performance, but his nephew, known to some as
Randy Roddy for his not-so-discreet womanizing, didn't call
again. Either Roddy had thought better of such emotional
theatrics, or his long-suffering wife had changed the locks on
the drinks cabinet.

Even Hetheridge's superior officer, Assistant
Commander Michael Deaver, accepted news of Hetheridge's
impending union with unexpected gravity.

"Marrying a subordinate," Deaver had tutted. "It's
without precedent in the Yard, a superintendent marrying a
detective under his direct supervision. Surely you understand
how this may all play out, Tony. You must know."

"I know what I want. Fortunately for me, Kate feels the
same. I hoped you'd wish us joy."

"I wish all newly married couples joy," Deaver spat,
massaging his temples with both hands. "That personal
sentiment has no bearing on my attitude toward unions that
create professional... irregularities."

"Of course not, sir." Hetheridge sensed the discussion
would intensify after the vows were spoken. But one thing his
long service at the Met had taught him was never to borrow
trouble. DCI Jackson, Roderick Hetheridge, even Assistant
Commissioner Deaver—those responses meant little to him.
Only the disappearance of his longtime administrative
assistant, Mrs. Snell, came as a blow.

The day began like any other Monday. Hetheridge rode
to the Yard in the back of the Bentley, reading the *Independent*
while his manservant, Harvey, navigated London's traffic. As
he took the lift to the third floor, Hetheridge found his
thoughts retracing familiar mental ground. Not the wedding—

thanks to his friend, the iron-willed Lady Margaret Knolls, those details were carved in stone. No, it was the honeymoon that occupied Hetheridge's mind. Occupied it so much, in fact, that when he came upon his office door, he smacked into it. Never before had it been closed, much less locked, when he arrived on a Monday morning.

Hetheridge had hardly finished turning on the lights and booting up his computer before Detective Sergeant Deepal "Paul" Bhar entered, wrapped in the stylish Marc Jacobs coat his mum, Sharada, had given him as a present. Bhar, in his early thirties, was slender and dark, with black eyes and what he bragged was a hundred-pound haircut. Although almost fully recovered from the stab wound he'd sustained during their most recent high-profile case, he still had a tendency to moan or wince theatrically if anyone female, including his mum, lurked within earshot. What with all of Bhar's talk about aches and pains, not to mention the misery of what was predicted to be an unusually cold winter, it was no surprise Sharada had deemed a new coat necessary to protect her only son.

"Where's breakfast?" Bhar cried, stopping just before Hetheridge's desk and turning in a slow circle, as if the usual steaming metal pans of scrambled eggs, fried bread, and beans crouched just on his vision's periphery. "Why don't I see breakfast?"

"Detective," Hetheridge said, striving for something like an equitable tone, "I suggest you use your powers of observation to make a deduction."

"Bloody hell. Mrs. Snell's called in, hasn't she?" Hands on his hips, Bhar pondered the scene. "I can't recall her ever missing a day of work. When's the last time she was too sick to work?"

"If memory serves…." Hetheridge sighed, knowing it always did. "The spring of 1981."

"Oh, really?" Bhar let out an incredulous bark. "So this is a first in my lifetime, is it? We don't have to investigate much to guess which fly landed in Mrs. Snell's particular ointment, do we, guv?"

"Perhaps she's merely been delayed. Let me check my messages," Hetheridge stalled, picking up the phone's receiver and punching in his code.

"Oi! Why's it still dark in the foyer? Nearly walked into a spider plant," Detective Sergeant Kate Wakefield called from the entryway. In the early morning, some women cultivated artful dishevelment, but for Kate, the wild blonde hair and scuffed pumps were merely a symptom of her busy home life. Playing surrogate mum to her eight-year-old nephew, Henry, and her mentally disabled brother, Ritchie, made early mornings a trial. Sometime around noon, she'd look in the mirror, pass a comb through her long hair, give her shoes a polish and put on a little red lipstick. Like most men at the Yard, Hetheridge found Kate equally beguiling either way. But from what he could see, the females much preferred morning Kate to her afternoon reboot.

"It's frigid outside, and I'm famished," Kate said, tossing her long red scarf on a chair. "Hungry enough to gnaw on a—oh! Hang on." Like Bhar, Kate turned in a slow circle, as if the usual morning spread might pop out from behind a coat tree.

One hopes the pair of them are never called upon to solve a murder after missing a meal, Hetheridge thought.

"I don't understand," Kate said. "Where's breakfast?"

Bhar made an outraged noise. "You've *killed* breakfast, you colossal tart! At least I was nice to the mad old bat."

"You weren't!" Kate cried. "Half the time you called her 'Mrs. Smell.'"

"Not to her face. You're the one who stole the guv's heart—"

"Silence!" Hetheridge roared, making a show of pressing the receiver to his ear as his messages began to play. He knew perfectly well Bhar was correct, but admitting the truth would serve no one. When it came to his administrative assistant's antipathy for her much-younger rival, denial was the best weapon. It was absurd, of course, even embarrassing, to find himself the object of an employee's transparent affection. Never tall and never handsome, Hetheridge had passed his twenties and thirties mostly unnoticed by women, unless they recognized him as Lord Hetheridge. But in middle age, he'd grown into his looks, remaining fit and trim with a full head of steel gray hair while most of his contemporaries went soft and bald. And at some point during his long association with Mrs. Snell, she'd apparently fallen in love with him.

Hetheridge listened to his messages. The first referenced an obscure legal defense, dashing all hope to win a minor case. The second confirmed a DNA match on a switchblade, making a conviction almost certain. The third was from Mrs. Snell. When the line went dead, he pretended to listen for another few seconds, trying to decide what to do. Finally, he put on his gravest face, looking from Bhar to Kate.

"The bloody cow's retired," Kate guessed.

"Scratch that. The mad old bat's dead," Bhar said.

"*Mrs. Snell*," Hetheridge emphasized in a tone he'd learned from his own chilly father, "finds herself unwell. She's…." He mumbled deliberately. "So I shall go visit her, of course. Both of you should—"

"Sorry, guv." Bhar's missing breakfast was clearly forgotten; his black eyes, usually snapping with good humor, widened as if he had a winning lottery ticket in hand. "Did you say she's *taken to her bed?*"

Hetheridge gave Bhar a curt nod.

Bhar hooted with laughter. Kate joined in, slapping Bhar on the back. Hetheridge let them get the mirth out, and then silenced them with one loud, theatrical sigh.

"For a woman of Mrs. Snell's generation, not to mention a man of mine, the phrase is hardly unknown. Given her long years of dedicated, tireless, and apparently unappreciated service, the least we can do is call upon her at home."

Hetheridge smiled, waiting for the full meaning of this last to sink in.

"*We?*" Bhar burst out. Kate looked stunned.

"Yes," Hetheridge said. "We three form a unit. We interact with Mrs. Snell throughout the week and depend upon her help. Surely we should visit her bedside together, to emphasize how much we care?"

***

They took the Bentley, which Harvey brought back to the Yard in record time, since morning gridlock had allowed him to progress only a few streets away. Hetheridge, ever-conscious of public impropriety when it came to Kate, took the passenger seat, leaving Kate and Bhar to spread out in the Bentley's leather-upholstered, wood-paneled interior. They did so in mutinous silence, clearly missing their accustomed morning orgy of carbohydrates, caffeine, and fat.

"I don't feel guilty about disliking her. She's racist," Bhar announced as the Bentley drew within sight of Mrs. Snell's neighborhood, Muswell Hill.

"Hah!" Kate laughed. "Everything she says and does sets women back a hundred years. That makes her sexist, too."

"Mrs. Snell," Hetheridge said, not bothering to turn his head since his voice projected easily within the car, "is neither racist nor sexist. You misunderstand her hostility. She detests the two of you as human beings."

"Here we are, sir," Harvey said. He had a gift for speaking up at precisely the right moment. Now he slid the long, black Bentley to a halt outside a row of neat, well-kept red brick houses, each with matching white trim, triple-stack chimneys, peaks, and gables. Despite all the changes the world had seen in the last fifty years, despite the spillover of riots just a summer ago, this little corner of Muswell Hill looked as delightful as ever.

"Thank you, Harvey. We'll meet you back here at about—half-eight, let's say?"

"Very good, sir."

Hetheridge waited until Harvey pulled away from the

curb. Then he turned to his team, both of whom seemed poised to argue against the wisdom of such a visit.

"Since you've both aired your opinions of Mrs. Snell time and again, there's no need for you to revisit them here, practically on the poor woman's doorstep." Hetheridge gestured at no. 129, a house identical to all the others, except for white lace curtains in the front window. "So let me say this. Our goal is to encourage Mrs. Snell to return to work as soon as possible. Should either of you prove less than convincing, I'll have no choice but to enact certain changes. For one thing, I'll require all reports to be turned in on deadline, no more extensions, to assure proper turnaround. For another, I'll expect you both in the office for a half-day every weekend, no exceptions, to cover the basic fact-checking formerly entrusted to Mrs. Snell. As for breakfast, you'll find it served only in the canteen. Do I make myself clear?"

Bhar and Kate exchanged glances. Any leftover rebellious impulses appeared to be fading fast.

"Yes, guv." Bhar examined the pavement.

"Sure, guv." Kate's hazel eyes were trained on her manicure. Hetheridge pretended not to notice the lack of enthusiasm. It was possible that sometime that evening, he'd pay for pulling rank. *Could* man and wife work together within Scotland Yard's rigid hierarchy, one answering to the other? No doubt they'd find out. And if Hetheridge found himself in a spot of trouble with Kate later that night, well—he bit back a smile. Behind closed doors, that sort of friction made the eventual reconciliation all the sweeter.

An old woman, at least eighty, answered the door after Hetheridge rang the bell a third time. Judging by her prehistoric peplum house dress and the rollers in her thin white hair, callers were not expected.

"Who're you meant to be?" She squinted at Hetheridge. "Got cataracts. Can't see properly when the sun does that." The old woman gestured toward the east as if inconvenienced by the sun's habit of rising. "Are you the man who flogs satellite TV?"

"Indeed, I am not. My name is Anthony Hetheridge. Chief Superintendent for Scotland Yard. I'm told Vera was taken ill?"

Behind him, Hetheridge heard a suspicious intake of breath. Without turning, he suspected Bhar had laughed to hear his nemesis called "Vera," and Kate had silenced him with an elbow to the ribs.

"Scotland Yard. Oh, my heavens. I'm Vera's mum." The old woman, perhaps five feet tall, raised on her toes to peer straight up Hetheridge's nose. "Never thought you'd come. Not with all those murderers about. Whole world's gone to the devil. I told Vera, come off it, my girl. You could die up there and the Met would go right on without you. Nothing special, my Vera, no matter what airs she puts on. And now she's made you take time away from the sort of thing that really matters," the woman, apparently Mrs. Snell's mother, sniffed. "Pakis buying up all the corner shops. Jamaicans thicker than Jews in some parts. Muslims everywhere on motorbikes...."

"With bombs hidden under their burkas," came a familiar voice just behind Hetheridge. Then another muffled *oof.*

"I don't doubt it," Mrs. Snell's mother agreed, missing Bhar's cheerful sarcasm entirely. "Well, I'm sorry you've wasted your time, but our Vera's headstrong. When she says she's well, she's well, even with a fever of a hundred and two. And when she says she's sick and won't see anyone, there's naught you can do but go about your business, I expect."

Hetheridge was considering his next approach when he heard the sound of a throat being cleared. Behind the old woman, up the flight of stairs but still hidden on the landing one floor above, someone had made her presence known.

"Did you hear something?" The old woman clutched at the neck of her housedress. "Not safe in your own home these days...."

"Mum. I'll see him." Mrs. Snell spoke quietly, still concealed on the landing.

"Sounds like voices." Mrs. Snell's mother looked wildly

from side to side. "Lord help me, have I got tinnitus now?"

"*Mum!* I said I'm well enough to receive the chief superintendent!" Mrs. Snell snapped.

"Oh. It's only our Vera." The old woman shrugged at Hetheridge. "Risen from the dead, as it were. Come in, let me take your coat. And who are all these?" she asked, squinting at Kate and Bhar.

"My team. Detective Sergeant Kate Wakefield and Detective Sergeant Paul Bhar."

Mrs. Snell's mother accepted Bhar's Marc Jacobs coat with obvious suspicion. "What sort of person are you, young man?"

"Black Irish. Named for St. Paul," Bhar said, putting on an accent thicker than a leprechaun's.

"Irish," she repeated, frowning at the coat. The reassurance didn't stop her from hanging it on a hook, as if placement on the coat tree next to Kate's and Hetheridge's was a bit more ethnic fraternization than she was willing to permit in her own home.

To Hetheridge's relief, Mrs. Snell's mum chose to put the kettle on rather than follow them upstairs. Over the last thirty years, his long-widowed administrative assistant had been almost entirely closed-mouthed about her personal life, including her relationship with her mother. But it didn't require a detective's training to deduce, when it came to issuing friendly encouragement, the old woman in the violent pink hair curlers hadn't the foggiest notion how.

"In here," Mrs. Snell called as Hetheridge gained the landing. "First door on the left."

The bedroom, neat and spare, was nothing like Hetheridge had imagined. Of course, Bhar had long claimed Mrs. Snell was the love child of Dame Edna Everage and the Queen, a mysterious, unnatural being with clothing from 1960 and a mindset from 1690, if not before. Unable to deny such accusations, at least as far as Mrs. Snell's wardrobe was concerned, Hetheridge entered her room expecting tea cozies, vintage dolls, and porcelain kittens. Instead, he found himself confronted by white walls dotted with framed black and white photos. The bookshelf held a collection of guides for the self-taught photographer. On Mrs. Snell's bedside table sat an alarm clock, a silver pill box, and what he suspected was a top-of-the-line Nikon digital camera.

"Chief Superintendent, I deeply regret causing such a disruption to your day," Mrs. Snell said. Wrapped in a faded pink dressing gown, she sat propped up against pillows, covers pulled to her waist. Her gray hair was permed as tightly as ever; her horsey face seemed to have picked up an extra line or two. Behind her thick spectacles, hugely magnified eyes flicked toward Kate and Bhar. "No doubt you could all be far better employed."

"You really must return. We can't go on without you, Mrs. Snell," Bhar blurted.

Hetheridge found himself smiling. It was what he always did when Bhar stopped skirting the edge, usually to topple off face-first.

"Not until you're better, of course," Kate said, filling the breach in her most earnest tones. She, at least, knew how to make a humiliating concession without sounding like a complete nutter. Or, worse, a standup comedian. "We just want you to know how important you are. Is there, er, anything we can get you?"

Mrs. Snell stared at Kate, unblinking, until even Hetheridge felt a tickle of unease beneath his collar. Not that anything so trivial could unnerve him; over the course of his long career, he'd stood his ground against psychopaths, murderers and gunmen with nothing to lose. Probably Harvey had gone overboard with the fabric softener again.

"Is there anything you might bring me?" Mrs. Snell said at last, restating Kate's statement to more genteel effect, though her tone was frigid. "No. I think not. But thanks all the same for considering me."

Hetheridge dug under his collar with a forefinger. Fabric softener wasn't at fault. And the more he allowed Kate and Bhar to thrash about issuing ridiculous sentiments, the more

11

fiendish this knot would prove in the end.

"DS Wakefield. DS Bhar. I do believe our hostess mentioned putting on the kettle? Please go down and join her for tea. I'd like some time with Mrs. Snell alone."

Kate and Bhar hurried out like schoolchildren unexpectedly freed from detention. Not for the first time, Hetheridge reflectéd that in his line of work, having children was unnecessary. Overseeing detectives was remarkably similar, with one exception—detectives never seemed to grow up.

"Vera." He smiled. "May I sit?"

Mrs. Snell nodded.

Although a chair was positioned near the bookcase, Hetheridge eased onto the bed, careful not to jar his administrative assistant in case her illness wasn't entirely put on.

"We've worked together for a long time."

She sniffed, eyes widening alarmingly, as if she might shed a tear. "I've worked for you, I think you'll find. With the greatest pride and contentment. Best years of my life."

"Best years of my life, too, most likely." Hetheridge smiled. "I'm on the downhill route now, I know. But there's still some fight in the old man. And still some fight in you, unless I miss the mark."

Sniffing again, Mrs. Snell looked toward the window.

"May I speak freely, Vera? Not as—you know. But simply as Tony Hetheridge."

Meeting his gaze, Mrs. Snell nodded, lifting her chin with a stoicism he'd witnessed many times in his nanny, dead forty years now. Not to mention his mum's housekeeper, his father's gamekeeper, and even his first fencing master at Eton. The expectation was pain and disappointment, yet the bearing was brave. Strong. Braced to endure.

"I fear I've offended you by proposing matrimony to Kate. I know she joined my team under a cloud of suspicion, but that was Vic's doing. As for the bit with the gun, it wasn't her fault so much as mine. Surely she redeemed herself at Halloween, did she not? Paul and I both stayed alive, even if he took a knife to the shoulder."

"One would never know that young man had any training in self-defense."

"Indeed." Hetheridge chuckled. "You'd perform better in the field, wouldn't you?"

Mrs. Snell was startled out of her incipient tears. "Me? Nonsense."

"At his age, you would have, as you very well know. Opportunities were different then. Paul is still fighting the racism almost everyone swears has ceased to exist."

"Not to mention delusions of his own cleverness."

"Yes. Whereas Kate fought her way up. She has no notion of gentility, much less cooperation between women. The outcast is her natural role."

"I would argue there's nothing natural about taking on such a role." Mrs. Snell's gaze slid back to Hetheridge. "It's thrust upon certain women, no matter how hard they fight the label."

Hetheridge took that in. Then, before he could stop himself, he leaned closer, taking one of Mrs. Snell's hands in both of his. "Vera, please understand. I fell in love. I didn't think it was possible, but there it is. Kate's not what my mum or dad would have wanted. Had my elder brother lived, he would have chosen properly, no doubt. He was reared to the barony. I took it by default."

Mrs. Snell didn't pull away. "Your brother wasn't better than you," she said, a wealth of emotion in her usually controlled voice. "There's no one person better than another, not in the sight of almighty God or the universe. The barony of Wellegrave came to you because it was meant to be yours."

Hetheridge smiled. "What would I do without you?"

Mrs. Snell sniffed. A tear dropped; she did her best to wipe it away unobtrusively.

"My point is this. When it comes to Kate, I fully expect to pay for my choice of what people will call the wrong woman. The incorrect woman."

"No one has the right to call her that."

Hetheridge fought back a smile. It was the first kind word Mrs. Snell had ever given Kate. "Believe me, I know it. She's the best thing that ever happened to me, and I don't give a damn what my relatives think, or society at large. But at the Yard—well. You know better than anyone, Vera. Over the years I've made enemies, and they'll be coming for my head. I may succeed in keeping my place. I may fail. But no matter how it ends, I beg of you. Don't make me face the bastards alone."

***

"Isn't this snug?" Hetheridge said upon entering Mrs. Snell's kitchen, which lived up to every preconceived notion he'd ever entertained. Crocheted oven mitts, placemats, napkin rings, and tea cozies were everywhere; a porcelain cat salt shaker sat beside a porcelain dog pepper mill in the breakfast area. All that was required to complete the scene was a garden gnome, and Hetheridge, turning to smile at Mrs. Snell's mother, saw she'd tied on a gnome-patterned apron. The white-bearded imp gave a double-thumbs up, perhaps ironically, or perhaps as a sincere affirmation of English middle class culture.

"Afraid I don't have any Irish breakfast tea," the old woman told Bhar as she filled his cup, a BBC item commemorating the *Pride & Prejudice* miniseries starring Colin Firth.

"It's all right. I've heard Irish breakfast tea is mostly Kenyan these days. Lots of dark blokes in Kenya." Bhar dropped two sugar cubes into his cup. "Except for Obama, obviously."

"This is what they had on special at Tesco," Mrs. Snell's mother continued, filling Kate's cup, which featured a somewhat unflattering photo of Jennifer Ehle, the actress who'd played Elizabeth Bennett in the 1995 broadcast. "Care for sugar?"

"Detective Sergeant Bhar takes two sugars," Mrs. Snell

14

announced, striding into the kitchen with pink dressing gown belted tight and chin held high. "Let me do this, Mother. I know the needs of Chief Superintendent Hetheridge's staff better than my own."

"Fine. I'll handle the entertainment, as always. With your demeanor, you could chase the grin off a skeleton." Locating the remote, the old woman pointed it at the flat screen television mounted above the breakfast table. "I adore the twenty-four hour news cycle, don't you, Chief?"

"I find it a necessary evil." Hetheridge nodded over her head at Mrs. Snell, who gave him a controlled smile in return. It was a relief to see her on the job again. For a moment, the outcome had been in doubt.

"Fancy a bit of CNN?" Mrs. Snell's mother asked. But before Hetheridge could say he preferred the BBC's news channel, the old woman had already snapped it on.

"... authorities already decline to call the death a natural occurrence," CNN's female newsreader said. "Now we'll go to UK correspondent Clive Penvensy, outside Hotel Nonpareil in London's fashionable West End. Clive, tell us about the victim. Michael Martin Hughes was a figure steeped in international controversy, was he not?"

"He was, Jennifer," Clive replied enthusiastically, as if getting paid by the number of teeth flashed. "In Green and ecological circles, Michael Martin Hughes was the devil, or as near as made no difference. The Peerless Petrol crude oil spill, still unresolved, happened on his watch. Worse, as CEO of Peerless Petrol, some thought Mr. Hughes refused to shoulder the blame. His statement three days after the ecological disaster, which read in part, 'I'm ready to move on and enjoy my life,' was seen by many as a betrayal of environmentalists, not to mention the thousands of people impacted by his company's oil spill, the worst in history."

"Thank you, Clive. Here's the question everyone in the U.S. is asking: was Michael Martin Hughes murdered?"

Hetheridge drew in his breath. Almost at the same time, Bhar and Kate did the same, tea cups halting halfway to their mouths. Only Mrs. Snell, lately on her deathbed, seemed energized by the broadcast.

"I believe the three of you should get back to the Yard. I'll see that a late breakfast is delivered, or failing that, brunch. My intuition tells me this situation will soon involve Chief Superintendent Hetheridge."

Chapter Two

According to travel guides, no list of London's ugliest buildings would be complete without Hotel Nonpareil. Built by an American businessman who fancied himself a forward-thinker, the structure, a tower with a bulbous glass top, was balanced by a smaller, asymmetric pyramid. According to the London *Telegraph's* architecture critic, who'd once called London's City Hall a "glass gonad" and the Blue Fin Building "the end of civilization," Hotel Nonpareil was "loathsome, senseless, and almost pornographically foul."

Apparently, this last insult rang true with the average Londoner, many of whom had begun calling it Hotel Knob-in-Peril. If one squinted, very little imagination was required to perceive the pyramid as a scalpel blade and the tower as a certain male appendage. Still, aesthetic scorn aside, Hotel Nonpareil was a roaring success. Frequently playing host to conventions and charity events, the hotel was triumphantly in the black, boasting a year-round occupancy rate of seventy-seven percent.

"God in heaven," Hetheridge muttered when Bhar, studying briefing details on his phone, read the statistic aloud.

"Three hundred rooms, guv." Bhar sounded bleak. "Assuming the hotel is three-quarters occupied—"

"Double occupied," Kate broke in as Harvey guided the Bentley toward Hotel Nonpareil's entrance, now police-barricaded and ringed with panda cars. "Not many people travel alone."

"Double occupied, that brings the number of potential witnesses and interviewees up to—"

Hetheridge's mobile chimed. Relieved, he waved Bhar into silence. "Hello, Michael," he greeted the assistant commissioner.

"Tony. Good to find you on the job already." Deaver sounded only mildly suicidal. For Hetheridge's glass-half-full-of-hemlock superior, that was a good sign. "I've already called the DI in charge and buggered him blind. His slow response time will have us crucified on the ten o'clock news. The precise moment homicide was suspected, you should have been consulted."

"I'm flattered, of course, and happy to assist. But, sir, from what I've been told, Michael Martin Hughes was a self-made man. I was given to understand he resided mostly in New York and Dubai. Did he have some link to London society of which I'm unaware?"

Deaver's chuckle was not reassuring. "The prospect of matrimony must be rattling you to the marrow, old boy, for you to even ask. Hughes was killed during the biggest fundraiser Peerless Petrol's ever thrown. It was the company's attempt to show the UK, not to mention the rest of the world, they're working to do something about the oil spill. When you examine Hotel Nonpareil's guest list, you'll find a virtual *Who's Who* of pedigreed names. Hughes himself may have risen from common stock, but at least half your witnesses will quite likely be upper class."

"Splendid." From long habit, Hetheridge managed to sound neutral, but inside, his mood turned nearly as black as Deaver's default outlook. Any bluebloods he found himself obliged to treat, even briefly, as suspects would find it easy to retaliate. They could wreak social vengeance on the soon-to-be Lady Hetheridge for decades to come.

Is this to be the pattern of my married life? Hands tied in every major investigation unless I'm willing to subject Kate to eternal unpleasantness?

"Splendid, is it?" Assistant Commissioner Deaver issued one of his humorless chuckles. "Then this final tidbit should gratify you even more. Two of the distinguished personages currently lodged at Hotel Nonpareil are none other than Lady Isabel Bartlow and her brother, Sir Duncan Godington."

Hetheridge bit the inside of his cheek. When receiving truly unwelcome news, it was the only physical response he permitted himself. Twice now, in his capacity as a detective, he'd crossed paths with Sir Duncan: first, in the triple murder trial which had made the baronet a figure of unexpected public sympathy, and then again, after a Halloween bash turned deadly. With the wedding day closing in, the last thing Hetheridge wanted was another cat-and-mouse game with Sir Duncan. Like the proverbial feline, Sir Duncan enjoyed playing with his quarry as much as he enjoyed killing it. And when it came to mind games, even between intellectually well-matched players, Hetheridge knew the amoral player would always have the advantage.

"I see," he told Deaver. "Well. It's unfortunate, and I'll do what I can to expedite their processing and dismissal, of course."

"Good God, Tony. I appreciate a stiff upper lip as much as the next man, but this isn't stoicism. It's rigor mortis."

"Rubbish, Michael. I can't die. Our honeymoon plane tickets are entirely non-refundable. Put Sir Duncan out of your mind," Hetheridge said. "At least until I canvass the scene and form a few impressions."

Despite Hetheridge's outwardly calm reassurance, Sir Duncan's presence at the fundraiser rang alarm bells inside. The man was rich, but far from idle. Fossil fuel companies, especially those embroiled in environmental disasters, were precisely the entities Sir Duncan, an outspoken conservationist, worked against. Why would he agree to appear at a fundraiser thrown by Peerless Petrol? Had the disgraced company promised the sort of green concessions that would earn Sir Duncan's approval?

"Fair enough, Tony. One more thing," Assistant Commissioner Deaver said. "If Sir Duncan becomes a suspect, you may have to reassign DS Bhar."

"Bad connection, sir," Hetheridge said serenely. "Sorry. All this cloud cover…."

"Tony—"

"I'll ring back as soon as I'm able." Hetheridge disconnected, and then turned off his mobile for good measure. Although the habit frustrated his junior officers, Hetheridge, like most of his generation, scoffed at the notion he should be phone-accessible 24/7. In his experience, many a police career had been saved by an unanswered phone call or unfinished letter. Kate and Bhar's generation, spouting off daily via text, Tweet, Facebook, or email, suffered repercussions that Hetheridge, equally hot-headed in his youth, had avoided. It was difficult, after all, to maintain righteous fury when one's superior officer pretended, via his secretary, to be out of the office. And the effort of actually typing a vitriolic letter, signing it in black ink, and sealing it into an envelope, had twice saved Hetheridge from dire consequences, had such a letter actually been posted.

"What was all that about?" Kate's voice from the Bentley's interior roused Hetheridge from his thoughts. "Some kind of bombshell from the AC?"

"Potentially." Turning round in his seat, Hetheridge met Kate's eyes. "When Hughes was killed, Sir Duncan Godington was a guest in the hotel. He's still there, awaiting his preliminary interview along with his sister, Lady Isabel."

"Sir Duncan?" Kate sounded disappointingly neutral. Hetheridge, aware that it was ridiculous to envy such a man, felt a stab of emotion that was surely not jealousy. Kate and Sir Duncan had met at a society function. Kate had been ravishing in a ball gown; Sir Duncan had looked handsomer than ever in evening dress. Not to mention clearly attracted to Kate, a fact Hetheridge preferred not to dwell on. Ready for a scorching outburst from Bhar, he looked back and received a groan instead.

"I knew it. The Grim." Bhar massaged his temples.

"The what?"

"A big black dog. The Grim. Omen of death." Eyes wide, Bhar sounded aggrieved that he had to explain.

"Oh, good Lord." Kate looked ready to slap him. "He means Harry Potter, guv."

"Harry Potter?" Despite his reputation as a dinosaur, Hetheridge had seen the J. K. Rowling book series displayed in shop windows; the premiere of each movie adaptation had been an occasion of widespread national pride. But when he read for pleasure, it was never fantasy, or even novels. He heard enough fiction from confabulating witnesses and guilty parties desperate to shift the blame. These days, Hetheridge most often read history. Currently at 50% on his ereader: a new biography of Richard the Third, about as modern as Hetheridge cared to get.

"Paul," Hetheridge said. "Do you refer to those books meant for small children?"

"Oh, please, everyone's read them," Bhar said. "And I wasn't going to mention it, but yesterday evening I saw a huge black dog crouched at the end of my street, watching as I locked up the Astra. It wasn't a neighborhood dog. Flashing eyes. Growling, too. When I got to the door, I looked back and it was gone. Vanished, like an evil spirit."

"I don't believe him," Kate told Hetheridge.

"You don't believe Paul saw a stray dog?"

"I don't believe he wasn't going to mention it." Punching Bhar's upper arm, Kate grinned at his yelp. "Here you go, throwing another wobbly. Why don't you don't bring Mummy on the job, so she can make the world safer for little Paulie?"

"Stop hitting me! Did you see that?" Bhar turned to Hetheridge. "She's always hitting me."

Shutting his eyes briefly, Hetheridge chose to otherwise ignore the complaint. "I've never heard of a 'Grim, ' but I've heard of the Black Shuck, a spectral figure of doom that haunts churchyards. Usually described as a hostile dog. Is that what you think you saw?"

"I *know* I saw it." Bhar shot Kate a sidelong glance. "And what happens to me the very next day? Yet another case where Sir Duncan Stab-a-Fork-in-His-Eye Godington turns up. This time, he'll ruin my career for certain. I suppose the AC wants to fling me off the case? Fruit of the poisonous tree and all that?" Bhar was referring to the perception that once a police officer and a suspect interacted negatively or unethically, all subsequent dealings must be assumed tainted. In Bhar's case, it meant, since he'd once dated Sir Duncan's ex-girlfriend, telling her details about the triple murder case that were leaked back to Sir Duncan himself, members of the public might infer Bhar would thereafter seek vengeance. So even if he discovered legitimate evidence against the baronet, the presumption might be that such "fruit" came from a poisonous tree and could not be trusted.

"Yes, well, lucky for us, 'fruit of the poisonous tree' is an American legal issue, not an English one. No matter how many Brits enjoy *CSI: Miami*, we need only concern ourselves with the realities of the Crown court."

"The AC cares about the court of public opinion, guv." Bhar sighed. "All those campaigns to improve the public's trust in the police service—he'll see me on this case as a guaranteed tabloid headline, once the snouts from the *Sun* get wind of it."

"Let me handle the Assistant Commissioner," Hetheridge said. "Kate, based on your prior interaction with Sir Duncan, you have the best chance of getting a straightforward interview out of him. If you can see your way clear to release him early, by all means, do so. If not, tread cautiously."

"Ever known me not to?" Kate asked seriously, and then winked. "Kidding. I'll be professional."

Hetheridge had a feeling Sir Duncan would expect

flattery, nervous apologies and outright arse-kissing, but kept the suspicion to himself. Since joining his team, Kate was growing into her role, but she had yet to fully accept that rich, titled, and self-consciously upper class people expected far more than a competent detective. They expected Scotland Yard's agent to behave like a personal concierge, shielding them from unpleasantness and offering frequent expressions of gratitude, some of them tangible. More than once, Hetheridge had been the target of abusive screeds because, after an investigation, the witnesses had been offered no compensation, not even flower arrangements, theater tickets, or paid dinners. As F. Scott Fitzgerald had so famously noted, the rich were different. And one of those differences was a willingness, at least among some of them, to seek a *quid pro quo* arrangement for time spent, even during a murder investigation. Bhar had learned this the hard way; Kate would, too.

Bhar still looked troubled. Ludicrous as his story about glimpsing the Grim or Black Shuck was, he obviously believed it. Hetheridge, who'd suffered two near-death experiences on the job, understood Bhar's stabbing had affected him more deeply than Kate perhaps realized. The solution wasn't to indulge his fantasies, but to immerse him in reality.

"Paul, you'll accompany me to the murder scene."

"I don't see the point if the AC—"

"That was not a request."

"I only mean if—"

"Nor is this. Say nothing. Not another word until I give you leave."

Eyes wide, Bhar stared at Hetheridge in consternation, lips pressed together.

Kate looked equally startled, lips tight, but for a different reason. When push came to shove, she was loyal to her colleagues. In this case, loyalty meant doing her best not to laugh.

Hetheridge faced forward as Harvey drew the Bentley alongside Hotel Nonpareil's entrance. No one spoke.

Hetheridge knew he'd better enjoy the silence. It was unlikely to last long.

***

"We held the scene for you, sir," the uniformed PC said, opening the Bentley's door and quickly stepping back to stand more or less at attention. Junior officers often behaved that way around Hetheridge. At Scotland Yard, he was never called Lord Hetheridge, except as a peculiar form of reverse snobbery—as if he'd inherited the role of Chief Superintendent, just as he'd inherited the barony of Wellegrave. But when it came to the Met's unformed officers, the opposite was true. They often treated Hetheridge with exaggerated respect, stammers, even an occasional bow.

At Hotel Nonpareil's grand entrance, another uniformed PC opened the glass door for Hetheridge to stride in, unquestioned. Behind him, Kate and Bhar were stopped, obliged to flash their warrant cards to secure entry.

"The Assistant Commissioner told Mr. Garrett to expect you," the PC said, leading Hetheridge toward the hotel's gilt-edged reception desk, where a short, conspicuously perspiring bald man waited. Doubtless this was the manager. And the musclebound, blue-uniformed hulk beside him could only be Hotel Nonpareil's head of security.

"I'm Leo Makepeace," the little man said, mopping his forehead with a handkerchief. "This is Bob Junkett, the hotel's security chief."

"Pleased to meet you." Hetheridge, accustomed to sizing up men at a glance, shook hands with both and tried not to judge. If he did, Makepeace was a frustrated sap and Junkett, an unfulfilled meathead. But that was too easy. And indeed, one of the attractions of detective work was surprising, even shocking insights into human nature. "Did you say Dr. Garrett's on duty? Thank heavens."

Hetheridge had known Divisional Surgeon Peter Garrett for more than twenty years. The man's work was impeccable, his instincts, phenomenal. He understood the requirements of the Met better than some junior officers, yet remained a fierce advocate for the dignity of the dead, never allowing a corpse be exposed to ridicule or tabloid reporters simply for the convenience of law enforcement. If Garrett had agreed to let the body of Michael Martin Hughes, discovered sometime after midnight, languish at the crime scene until Hetheridge arrived more than eight hours later, there could be only one reason. Garrett believed the scene, surely already photographed and videoed, might contain hidden details no one but a detective could ferret out. And only if that detective was permitted to view the murder scene intact.

"Yes, sir, Mr. Garrett's waiting for you inside suite 800. With the body."

Hetheridge and Bhar followed Junkett into the lift. At the same time, Kate steered Makepeace, still dabbing at his forehead, toward a quiet corner. If raw nerves were any indication of guilt, the poor little man should have been jailed straightaway. But in Hetheridge's experience, transparent fear early in an investigation indicated nothing, except an indication of personal neuroses. Deep down inside, many people were quivering masses of guilt, perpetually braced for an accusation. This didn't make them culpable. At least not when it came to murder.

One side of the lift was paneled with mirrored tiles. Bhar took the opportunity to preen, straightening his tie and smoothing his hair. Junkett, apparently unaffected by physical vanity, stared straight ahead. Giving himself a reluctant once-over, Hetheridge met his own pale blue eyes. Who was this old man, mad enough to torpedo his quiet existence and walk down the aisle at age sixty?

The doubt, though painful, was fleeting. Not because Hetheridge doubted he was too old for Kate—he knew he was—but because he'd lived long enough to abandon notions of perfection. Yes, in an ideal world, Hetheridge would be forty, not sixty, and Kate would work with a different unit, lessening the perception of unprofessional conduct. But in that perfect world, a corporate bastard like Michael Martin Hughes wouldn't exist. And even if he did, murder would be off the menu, since killing one's fellow creatures for love, money, or vengeance was far from ideal. No. Better to accept reality, warts and all, and simply get on with it.

"We've restricted eighth floor access to police and hotel security only, of course," Junkett said. "Naturally, we've prepared a list of everyone who was lodged on the eighth floor during the approximate time Mr. Hughes died. The moment I heard you'd be leading the investigation, I took the liberty," Junkett said proudly, "of emailing you, care of your office. Just some remarks from yours truly on the character of each relevant guest, Lord Hetheridge. I'm sorry, may I address you as Lord Hetheridge? Or do you prefer Chief Superintendent, milord?"

"Chief Superintendent will do." Hetheridge forced a smile as the lift doors parted. The head of security's oily enthusiasm was worse than off-putting. It rang warning bells. "How did you find out I'd be leading the investigation?"

Junkett tapped his nose like an old school crook. "Friends in high places."

"I see. Tell me, Mr. Junkett, were you affiliated with the Metropolitan Police Service at some point?

"Indeed I was, sir. Indeed I was!" Junkett beamed. "Had to resign five years back. Injured in the line of duty, don't you know. Broke up a designer drug ring. Ran down a bloke with a shooter and took a bullet meself. Still, no regrets. And it's quite the treat for a former copper like me to be remembered by a chief."

Hetheridge, unable to differentiate Junkett from Adam, confined himself to a vague nod before following the beefy man along the eighth floor corridor. It wasn't surprising to discover a major hotel's head of security had started his career in law enforcement. But Junkett's enthusiasm, not to mention his assumption of personal memorability, was troubling. Of course, former lawmen caught up in a murder investigation occasionally proved indispensable, using their specialized knowledge to help the police. But from time to time, disgruntled or mentally unstable former officers, desperate for the limelight, committed murder themselves. Afterward, they lurked on the investigation's periphery, not only to exonerate themselves, but to earn praise by "assisting."

Someone tapped Hetheridge on the shoulder. Still lost in thought, Hetheridge jumped, only to find Bhar grinning like the Cheshire cat. The detective sergeant had been uncharacteristically silent for so long—nearly three minutes—Hetheridge had forgotten his presence.

"Good God, man. What?"

Blinking daintily at Hetheridge's tone, Bhar placed a finger against his lips. Pointing at his leatherbound notebook, he showed Hetheridge his first notation:

Check J.'s Met file

Hetheridge forced a nod. Perhaps this edict of silence would prove more trouble than it was worth.

The door to suite 800 stood open. Blocked by a diagonal strip of blue and white police tape, it was guarded not only by a female PC, but by one of Hotel Nonpareil's uniformed guards.

"I took the liberty of providing extra backup, milord. Pardon me—*Chief Superintendent.*" Junkett 's chest puffed. "Couldn't allow the scene to be disturbed before your arrival, hey?"

Drawing in a deep breath, Hetheridge allowed the silence to stretch out uncomfortably before speaking. "Mr. Junkett, I'm surprised at you. Not to mention disappointed. I certainly hope you've not also taken the liberty, as you put it, of placing another of your own subordinates *inside* the crime scene."

Junkett visibly deflated. "No, sir. I wanted to, sir. I mean, I was prepared to, but the divisional surgeon wouldn't allow it."

"Then I owe him a debt. May I presume Mr. Garrett also lodged an objection about the placement of your employee"—Hetheridge indicted the uniformed security guard—"just beyond an open door? Since the entire hotel staff is, at this early juncture, routinely considered under suspicion?"

"Oh, aye." Junkett's cheeks reddened. "But I reminded Dr. Garrett the crime scene is his patch. The rest of the hotel is mine. And he needed to respect my authority, same as I respect his."

"Of course. No disrespect whatsoever, Mr. Junkett." Hetheridge allowed his tone to put the lie to that statement. "Nevertheless, I require you to escort this guard back to your office. Wait with him there until you're summoned for interviews. And from this moment forward, I'm afraid I must insist—leave police work to the police."

"But chief. I only meant to—" Junkett broke off. If Hetheridge's words hadn't penetrated, his expression apparently got through. The big man's sulky look was better suited to a small boy than a six-foot-two, seventeen stone giant.

"As you wish. *Sir.*" Spitting out the honorific, Junkett and his red-faced subordinate stomped back toward the lifts. But just as Hetheridge bent to duck beneath the crime scene tape, someone tapped his shoulder.

Silently, Hetheridge counted to five. When he turned, he found Bhar's notebook held at eye level, a single word twice underlined.

Smackdown!

Most days, Bhar's irrepressible humor amused Hetheridge. Today it made him long for an age when punching a junior officer was considered not only acceptable, but inevitable.

Yet another proud macho tradition that ended when women were permitted to join the police force. Which was renamed the "service" not long after. I'll have to throw that in Kate's face, when next I feel like courting my own destruction.

"Paul. It's curious to see Sir Duncan turn up on the periphery of not one, but two investigations," Hetheridge said seriously, hoping the younger man would listen. "I'd like your input for as long as possible. Frankly, I need it. So speak, if you must. But remember this. A joke or ill-considered remark at the wrong moment may get you relegated to some other, lower-profile case. If this cloud over your career is ever to be dispersed, you need to begin conducting yourself like a sober, competent detective. Not a clown."

Bhar winced, but the smile which followed looked not only contrite, but genuine. "Understood, guv. And thanks."

Hetheridge patted Bhar on his uninjured shoulder. Then he turned, lifted the blue and white police tape, and led the way into suite 800.

Chapter Three

During his years with Scotland Yard, Hetheridge had entered a multitude of crime scenes. The venue of murder could, as the saying went, range from the sublime to the ridiculous. Nevertheless, Hetheridge was unprepared for the sublime ridiculousness of Michael Martin Hughes's suite. In a decade of global recession and belt-tightening, Peerless Petrol's embattled CEO had surrounded himself with opulence.

The gleaming marble floor was littered with India rugs. Gold velvet sofas, loveseats, and poufs were positioned here and there. Oil paintings hung from lavishly papered walls; an enormous crystal chandelier glittered overhead. At the suite's center, a baby grand piano was positioned directly opposite the formal dining room, which contained a table long enough to seat twenty. Potted tropical trees towered in the corners; bowls of flowers, pink and orange and direct from the hothouse, were everywhere. No matter where Hetheridge turned, he spied something black-lacquered and gold-tooled, adorned with velvet, tassels, or both. Aggressive displays of affluence made Hetheridge, whose personal fortune numbered in the eight figures, uncomfortable. He had nothing against luxury. But this was style for the graceless; lavishness for the criminally unconcerned.

"Right. Perfect. Bloody perfect," Bhar said.

Hetheridge turned, brows raised.

"Come on, you know. Just yesterday, the *Sun* called Hughes a modern-day Marie Antoinette."

Hetheridge said nothing. How had he missed that?

"Didn't you hear? A reporter told Hughes schoolchildren are worried the oil spill means the Gulf of Mexico won't be around when they grow up. And Hughes said, 'Well, I reckon they'll have to holiday in Vegas, now won't they?'"

"I remember," Hetheridge lied, surprised at himself.

"I should hope so. It was world news for at least forty-eight hours," Divisional Surgeon Peter Garrett said, appearing from one of the vast suite's many inner rooms. A tall, spectrally slim man, his white overalls covered him from collar to ankles. Filmy blue booties were stretched over his brogues; a face mask hung around his neck.

"Then again." Garrett flashed his trademark death's-head grin. "This close to the big day, I suppose a lifelong bachelor looking down the barrel of matrimony barely knows his own name. I notice you've also managed to forget your protective gear. This isn't the days of yore, Tony." Garrett wagged a finger. "Dripping DNA all over the scene has become bad form."

Hetheridge groped for excuses, but found none. In the boot of the Bentley, he kept a box of standard Met gear: overalls, booties, masks, eye shields, and the Met's latex-free gloves. Available in one size, those gloves mysteriously managed to fit no one, male or female, large or small. Yet with his mind on the Assistant Commissioner's news about Sir Duncan, not to mention Bhar's potential reassignment, Hetheridge had forgotten to bring the necessary items upstairs.

By God, I wish this was over. I'd marry Kate tomorrow if I could.

But it wasn't that simple, it could never be that simple, and balancing certain details, even with Lady Margaret's help, was more distracting than Hetheridge liked to admit. Now some new problem niggled at him, jumping and waving on the sidelines of his mind like a third division footballer desperate to snag the attention of....

Staring at Garrett's sunken eyes and toothy smile, Hetheridge suddenly understood what, besides protective gear for himself and Bhar, he'd forgotten. A wedding invitation.

"Speaking of matrimony." Hetheridge winced. "I-I've turned up some irregularities in the guest list. Unintended oversights. I do hope you didn't think—"

"Tony. Don't trouble yourself. I'm only teasing." Garrett sounded genuinely unoffended. "To be perfectly honest, seeing you discombobulated is sweeter than any slice of wedding cake. And good news about the scene," he added, clapping Hetheridge on the back. "It's already been photographed, filmed in 360 degrees for posterity, and SOCO-swabbed. Besides, unlike you princes of Scotland Yard, I always carry extra booties and gloves for the unprepared. Let me fetch them. Once you're kitted out, I'll take you to our victim."

"Sorry, guv," Bhar said, forcing his hand inside a sticky, overly-small glove as they donned Garrett's protective gear. "I should have taken charge of the small details. Next time I will."

Hetheridge blinked. Although an excellent detective, Bhar tended to play fast and loose with certain procedures, especially those he disliked.

"I haven't been replaced with an imposter. It's just... we all know you have a lot on your mind." Bhar sounded even more apologetic.

Hetheridge bit back a tart response. The skill, long ago ingrained in him by family, schoolmasters, and his superiors at the Met, was second nature to him now, rarely requiring conscious effort. But the mere fact he was sufficiently on edge to nearly bite Bhar's head off, not for irresponsibility but for helpfulness, proved Garrett's point. The wedding plans were taking their toll.

"It doesn't matter," Bhar whispered loyally. "Even distracted, you're better than most."

"Thanks for that," Hetheridge forced himself to reply. No more distractions. Hadn't he just cautioned Bhar? From now on, the same went for him. After all, every murder victim deserved an advocate, even if the dead man had been as repulsive as Michael Martin Hughes.

"Well done," Garrett said when Hetheridge and Bhar were acceptably garbed. "Gentlemen. Follow me."

Hughes lay on the suite's kitchen floor, near the free standing bar and trio of barstools. Seeing the body, Bhar gave a low whistle. Even Hetheridge drew up short, secret notions dashed. Given how much self-induced notoriety Peerless Petrol's CEO had suffered after the oil spill, Hetheridge had expected a gunshot to the head, self-inflicted but mistaken for foul play. Instead, an altogether different scene faced him.

"Poison," Bhar said, summing it up in a single word.

"Indeed." Mindful of getting too close, Hetheridge knelt at a safe distance from the corpse, ignoring the twinge in his arthritic left knee.

After the oil spill, Hughes had frequently been accused of smiling too much, beaming at TV cameras and throngs of booing protestors. Attractive, if rather less than handsome, with curly brown hair, blue eyes, and prominent cheekbones, the man's insistence on meeting every accusation with a capped-tooth smile had been lampooned in political cartoons all over the world. Now those cartoons had become literal truth.

In death, Hughes's lips, dark blue, were stretched in a frozen, maniacal grin. His eyes bulged; dried white froth decorated the edges of his mouth. His hands were locked around his neck, as if he'd spent his final moments trying to claw his own throat out. But what had inspired Bhar's guess of poison was Hughes's body position. Called the opisthotonic death pose, it was also seen in drowning victims. Back arched and entire body hyperextended, Hughes was mostly off the floor, hideously balanced between the heels of his feet and the crown of his head.

"Still in full rigor, as you see," Garrett said. "Another

reason I didn't mind keeping the corpse here so many hours. I hoped it would start to fade. Some press vulture is likely to spy the body bag's shape and snap photos. From all I can gather, the man was a right prat. Still. He doesn't deserve to be publicly humiliated in death. Not if I can help it. Now." Garrett looked from Hetheridge to Bhar. "Here's your question. Which poison is most apt to produce cyanosis of the lips, frothing around the mouth, and proptotic eyes, not to mention a body shaped like a boomerang? Answer correctly, and I'll buy the first round when next we're down the pub."

Bhar glanced at Hetheridge, who nodded for the younger detective to go first.

"Ricin. Most toxic substance in the world. A single gram of ricin could wipe out a city, something like 30,000 people. Plus it's hard to detect and exotic. Found in Africa." Bhar's eyes gleamed. "So it would be instructive to check on any hotel guest who's visited the continent lately or maintains ties there."

Hetheridge knew Bhar was referring to Sir Duncan Godington, who had spent long stretches of his life in jungles, including those in Borneo and the Congo River basin. Hetheridge also knew Bhar's guess at the poisonous agent was wrong, though he allowed Garrett to deliver the correction.

"Ricin tends to be anyone's first guess in a homicide poisoning these days. Sounds rather impressive, doesn't it? If it can kill a small city, it can certainly knock off a single unlucky punter, or so the reasoning goes. However," Garrett flashed that avid death's-head smile again, "the plain fact is, ricin can take almost a fortnight to kill its victim, who will surely seek medical help long before his or her death. Mr. Hughes didn't have a fortnight. He died quickly and horribly, probably within half an hour of ingesting the fatal substance. Besides, ricin needs to be injected. I believe Mr. Hughes drank the poison, probably concealed in whiskey." Garrett pointed to an empty double Old Fashioned glass sitting alone atop the bar. "What substance goes down easy, yet kills rapidly?"

"Strychnine," Hetheridge said.

"And the first round's on me." Garrett sounded pleased.

"Nice to find someone listened to my last lecture, even whilst the younger set texted and Tweeted and generally blanked me all-round."

"Strychnine?" Bhar sounded appalled. "But that's so... so—"

"Old-fashioned?"

"Easy to detect. Someone went to all the trouble of getting Hughes alone and poisoning his drink," Bhar said. "Why not use ricin and just wait a few days? Sure, Hughes might have gone to hospital, and the docs could have realized it was ricin, but they couldn't have saved his life. They might even have misdiagnosed Hughes and written off his death as natural. Too bad," Bhar huffed. "Whatever else our killer may be, I doubt he's a master criminal. Probably a bit of a thickie."

The genesis of Bhar's irritation wasn't hard to guess. Sir Duncan Godington was many things: rich, egotistical, handsome, popular, and obsessed with animal rights. He was also, in Hetheridge's opinion, an evil man with an incestuous fixation on his half-sister. Defining Sir Duncan exhaustively might be impossible. Determining all the things he was not came easier. And one thing Sir Duncan was not, and had never been, was a bit of a thickie.

"Using a simple poison like strychnine might be a sign the murder was planned in haste, especially if the killer had easy access to it," Hetheridge agreed. "It could indicate an unsophisticated killer operating on pure emotion. Or...." He paused, lifting an eyebrow at Bhar. "The choice of something so easily detectible could indicate arrogance."

"I thought the same," Garrett said, seeming curiously expectant.

"That double Old Fashioned glass," Hetheridge said, pointing at the item. "I suppose it's already been dusted for fingerprints?"

"Of course. I'll carry it out with me in a bag so it may be entered into evidence, along with the transfer attempts," Garrett said. "According to the technician, there were no prints. It was wiped clean."

35

"Alas." Hetheridge found himself taking in the scene again all at once, looking from the granite worktops to the gas cooker to the stainless steel refrigerator, all of it spotless and looking brand new. The area around Hughes's corpse appeared clear, at least to the naked eye. And any cloth fibers or hairs would have been removed by SOCOs some hours before.

"There's a bit of filth, just there," Hetheridge said, noting a faint smear that was nearly invisible against the marble tile's dark gray swirls. "A bit there, too," he added, indicating a rung on one of the bar's twin stools.

"Indeed," Garrett said. "SOCOs collected most of it for chemical analysis, but left traces for your inspection. The original area was photographed from several angles. No discernible shoe print, I fear."

"Not that they've ever done me much good." Three times in his career, Hetheridge had tried introducing a shoe print into evidence, only to have the match thrown out as too flimsy. Only on American TV programs could an entire conviction be assembled around a shoe print, and those gifted sleuths managed the feat in just forty-two minutes, if one subtracted ad breaks.

"Looks like we've scored an arse print, too." Bhar pointed. One of the barstools, upholstered with crushed velvet in a particularly indefensible shade of yellow, had been flattened by a guest. The person who'd left dirt on the floor and rung had left a more subtle, yet unmistakable, impression on the cushion.

"Someone heavy visited Hughes," Bhar said.

"Or someone of standard weight pulled up a stool and sat upon it for at least thirty minutes," Hetheridge said.

"To make sure Hughes finished his poisoned drink?"

"Perhaps. Or else." Hetheridge considered. "To watch every tremor and contortion as Hughes died right in front of him."

Bhar made a choked sound. "Now we're heading into Sir Duncan's territory. Someone decorated a Christmas tree with his poor old dad's entrails. I don't care what the jury said, we all know damn well Sir D—"

"No!" a woman shrieked from behind them. "Michael! *Michael!*"

Chapter Four

Spinning on his heel, Detective Sergeant Paul Bhar saw a female PC dart into the kitchen just behind the intruder.

"I'm sorry, sir!" the PC told Hetheridge. "I said no entry, but she pushed past me!"

The intruder, a fair-skinned, green-eyed woman, wore ethnic garb in a riot of opposing colors: dark red *kurta*, billowing green palazzo pants embroidered with flowers, and bright yellow clogs. When the PC seized the intruder's hands, beginning to recite the standard police caution, the woman kicked with both feet, sending one of those wooden clogs sailing through the air. Bhar ducked. When the shoe struck the floor, he saw it was painted with the Dutch emblem, the windmill.

"Michael! What have they done to you?" the woman shrieked, fighting wildly.

"Guv?" Bhar looked at Hetheridge, who shook his head.

"Officer!" Hetheridge addressed the PC in his most commanding tone. "Release that woman."

Startled, the PC did as she was bid. Drawing herself up, the intruder took a deep breath.

"You'll be hearing from my lawyer," she announced to no one in particular. "I'm an American, so when I say 'lawyer,' prepare for shock and awe."

The PC looked insulted. For his part, Bhar concentrated on keeping a straight face. It wasn't every day a Yank burst into a crime scene and started issuing threats half-barefoot. For that matter, it wasn't every day a presumably ordinary citizen came upon a corpse as grotesque as Hughes's, yet managed to focus on personal one-upmanship.

"Everything's quite all right, I assure you," Hetheridge soothed the PC. "You were correct to attempt restraint. Please, return to your post. Call for immediate backup to better secure the scene and use my name if need be."

Bhar could see the PC found Hetheridge's tolerance inexplicable. Over time, however, he'd come to understand his guv's preference for unstudied first impressions. Why permit their intruder to be taken into immediate custody, giving her time and opportunity to repent her impulsive actions, or perhaps even dream up a plausible excuse? This woman was loud, aggressive, apparently well-acquainted with "Michael," as she called him, and naïve enough to imagine she could behave however she pleased. She was, in short, the case's first person of interest, and for once that person had come calling on Scotland Yard, instead of the other way round.

"I'm Chief Superintendent Hetheridge. This is Detective Sergeant Bhar and Divisional Surgeon Garrett," Hetheridge said smoothly. "I take it you knew Mr. Hughes. My deepest sympathies. You are…?"

"Riley Castanet." She stared at Hughes's contorted body. Her eyes, wide and long-lashed, were free of tears, but her lips were twisted. Either Riley Castanet was a natural actress, or the sight of Hughes's corpse caused her genuine pain.

"Ignore the Spanish last name," Riley continued. "I'm my mother's daughter, and she's full-blooded Comanche. Child of the earth."

Bhar, who'd nearly forgotten his pen and old-fashioned

notebook were still in hand, jotted that down.

Claims ethnic mix, Spanish/Native Amer. Yet pale skin, pale eyes, light brown hair....

"Comanche? How extraordinary," Hetheridge said. "And how did you know Mr. Hughes?"

"The whole world knew him! But why is he twisted like that? Was he electrocuted? Did he have a stroke?" Dropping beside the body, Riley reached out, apparently determined to examine Hughes herself.

"Madam." Hetheridge raised neither his hand nor his voice. Nevertheless, Riley jerked as if struck.

"If you wish to remain at liberty and perhaps assist the police with our inquiries, you must obey our rules," he said. "Touch nothing. Answer our questions. Or be taken into custody for tampering with a crime scene. A consequence, I assure you, not even the American Embassy can prevent, should Scotland Yard deem it necessary."

Riley emitted a little huff. For several seconds, she goggled at Hetheridge, hardly seeming to breathe. Then her mouth twisted into a parody of a smile.

"Listen, Mr. White Privilege. I've had about all the Protestant Anglo-Saxon colonialism crap I can take from this broken-down, rinky-dink little country. I happen to be Michael's personal assistant. I know more about him than anyone on the planet, including his lawyer, his mother, and his soon-to-be-ex-wife. If Scotland Yard would like the *opportunity* to interview me and discover everything I have to offer, you'd better start by getting out of my face. Hook me up with an officer I can actually respect. Like him." She pointed at Bhar.

"I will not be dictated to." Hetheridge's tone was uncharacteristically bombastic. "Ms. Castanet, I am in authority here. You will submit to my questions or find yourself—"

"It's all right, guv." Bhar cast aside the polished dialect he'd adopted—the Received Pronunciation of TV actors, newsreaders, and the Queen—for the slightly more relaxed cadence of Clerkenwell, his boyhood home. "I'd be glad to get this sorted for you."

"Deepal. Absolutely not. Out of the question." Hetheridge glared at Riley.

"*Deepal* and I will do very well." Tossing her head, Riley floated toward Bhar. "If Scotland Yard wants an interview, it's him or no one. Go on, Mr. White Privilege. Arrest me if it makes you feel two inches taller. I'll let my lawyers do the talking." She thrust out her wrists as if daring Hetheridge to snap on the handcuffs.

"Guv. It'll be fine," Bhar said. "Just this once. Give me a chance, why don't you?"

"Very well. But only because this... *American* gives me no choice."

Bhar nodded. By unspoken accord, he and Hetheridge had fallen into the quintessential good cop, bad cop routine, and Hetheridge appeared to be playing his bad-cop role with unprecedented relish. Bhar bit back a smile. It seemed that falling in love with Kate had loosened up the guv in unexpected ways.

"Yes, sir. Right away, sir." Bhar strove to sound properly downtrodden. "Ms. Castanet—"

"Please. Call me Riley."

"Riley. Let me take you someplace private, perhaps an office in the lobby. Somewhere away from Mr. Hughes's remains."

"That's very nice. Thank you, Deepal." Riley sniffed, dabbing at her eyes, though Bhar detected no actual tears. As they exited the suite, he glanced over his shoulder at Hetheridge. And with a nod and a smile, the guv saw him off.

***

Hotel Nonpareil's manager, the still-copiously perspiring Leo Makepeace, dithered a bit when Bhar requested a quiet place to talk with Riley Castanet. Bhar assured the little man anywhere was acceptable. This was, after all, a pre-interview, simply a way to determine if Riley knew enough to be considered a bystander, witness, or suspect. If Riley struck Bhar as a witness, he would use his professional judgment on how to proceed. If Riley became a suspect, he'd fall back on time-honored habits to secure what might prove crucial testimony: a private room at the Yard with a second detective present and a digital recording of the interview. No one, with the possible exception of Hetheridge, understood how Bhar's errors on the first Sir Duncan Godington case still haunted him. He never wanted to find himself in that position again, guilty and miserable, trying to defend the indefensible.

"I think it's best if you just use my office," Makepeace said, fumbling to fit his key into the door lock. "I'll get a soda and wait outside."

"Maybe something not caffeinated?" Bhar asked, watching the manager's hands shake as he fought to make the lock release.

"I never drink caffeine." Makepeace shot Bhar a surprised look. "Causes cancer."

"Does it?"

"It must. Everything else does." Grasping the stuck key with both hands, Makepeace agitated it so violently, the door's glass pane rattled in its frame.

"Give me that." Riley slapped Makepeace's hands away. "Oh, gross. The entire key ring is greasy. Bet you live on trans-fat and high fructose corn syrup. Probably haven't had a high colonic in ten years, am I right or am I right?" Gritting her teeth, she clutched the knob with both hands, opening the door by main force. Then she extracted the sweaty keys, tossing them at Makepeace. "You're a wreck. At the very least, you need an aura cleansing."

"I—I had a colon cleansing last month," he muttered, mopping his forehead with that silk handkerchief again.

"Yeah, well, the crap backed up in your intestines is nothing compared to the BS clogging your soul." Riley gave the little man a wide, superior smile. "I can help you. Figure out which chakra is laying down on the job and get everything flowing again." Her gesture, a dramatic downward flourish of both hands, made Bhar think of those commercials advertising a yogurt that reputedly kept women regular.

"Chakra? Is that an organ?" Makepeace asked.

"A spiritual organ. And I'm a spiritual practitioner." Riley, who'd retrieved her missing shoe before going downstairs, had nonetheless chosen to carry her shoes and continue barefoot, soaking up surprised glances as she strolled alongside Bhar. Now she shifted her clogs from right hand to left, digging in the pocket of those flower embroidered palazzo pants. Coming up with a handful of business cards, she passed one to Makepeace. "Careful. If you sweat too much, the ink will bleed."

"'Riley Castanet. Seer, Earth Mediator, and Pagan Priestess. Special Assistant and Adviser to Michael Martin Hughes, '" Makepeace read aloud, voice lifting to a squeak on the last three words. "Oh! Ms. Castanet. I'm so sorry for your loss. You must be devastated."

"Of course not." Riley adopted a grave, portentous tone. "Death is only a transition. It can never separate soul mates. Michael may have departed this world in body, but he's still with us. Right now," she added, glancing around Makepeace's office as if his overloaded desk, overflowing rubbish bin, and bare walls constituted a spectral haven.

"He's here? Are you quite sure?" Makepeace peered at a cobwebbed corner.

"Of course. Spirits are nowhere and everywhere at once." Grinning, Riley tapped the front of her business card. "There's my mobile and my email. Call for an appointment about that aura cleansing. And don't wait too long. I'll be back in southern California sometime next week."

"Er." Bhar coughed. "Not necessarily. Not if you're needed to assist with police inquiries."

Riley blinked. "But I told you. I'm an American."

Bhar restrained himself from informing her that hailing from the United States didn't amount to a "Get Out of Jail Free" card. Particularly in the midst of a murder investigation. Rules, restrictions, and facts seemed to irritate Riley, and since he needed to keep her talking, he refrained from correcting her.

"Thank you, Mr. Makepeace. We'll make use of your office as briefly as possible." Shutting the door, Bhar indicated a chair positioned before the manager's desk. As Riley seated herself, he decided to take the chair beside her. No sense seating himself behind Makepeace's desk, which would put them face-to-face and make the discussion needlessly adversarial. Besides, sitting in Makepeace's chair would force Bhar to peer at Riley over what appeared to be reams of unfinished paperwork. Either Makepeace didn't believe in digital archives, or Hotel Nonpareil's nervous little manager kept a hard copy of every document he touched.

"Now. Riley. Let me introduce myself properly." Bhar gave her his most charming smile. "I'm Detective Sergeant Deepal Bhar. I—"

"You must be miserable night and day," Riley interrupted, dropping her clogs on the floor and propping her feet on Makepeace's desk. Her toes were French-manicured. Of course, London was an international destination, and Bhar had met many Americans. But never had he encountered any suspect, British or otherwise, who worked so relentlessly to keep herself the center of attention.

"Miserable?" he repeated, trying not to focus on all those bejeweled silver toe rings.

"Working for that arrogant jerk," Riley said. "You should move to the USA, where people believe in a little thing called equality. Well, at least on the west coast. The south is just as bad as England. I'll never understand how a country as small as this one can manage to stay on a constant ego trip."

"It's a mystery, the confidence certain people exude." Bhar kept up his wide, innocent smile. "Tell me. How did a, er, spiritual practitioner like yourself end up working for a big oil CEO like Michael Martin Hughes?"

"Okay. First of all, I object to the term, 'big oil.' Strike it from your vocabulary. It's a nasty buzzword invented by zealots like Greenpeace to demonize legitimate businesses."

Bhar was startled. Based on Riley's garb and

44

metaphysical interests, he'd imagined Hughes hired her post-oil spill to help him understand the protesters and activists demanding his resignation from Peerless Petrol. To hear her characterize Greenpeace as radical was wholly unexpected.

"Very well. But tell me, Ms. Casta—Riley. How did a person like you, given your particular expertise, decide to—"

She cut Bhar off with a loud, self-conscious laugh. "There you go again. 'A person like me?' There's only one person like me, Deepal. Let you in on a secret. I don't consider myself human."

It was Bhar's turn to blink. "You don't?"

"Nope. Some people consider themselves human beings put on this earth to have a spiritual experience. Other people say they're spiritual beings born to have a human experience. Me?" Riley smiled, green eyes flashing. "I'm a horse having a human experience."

"A what?"

"A horse." Still smiling, Riley allowed Bhar an additional moment to absorb her statement. "I already told you, my mother is full-blooded Comanche. I have flashbacks to my past life on the reservation. I was a horse called Tintonha. An Appaloosa who birthed the finest equine members of the Horse Nation. And the Horse Nation will rise again, mark my words, when this world returns to honoring what really matters."

Bhar realized he wasn't taking notes, just staring open-mouthed. Riley didn't seem insulted by his reaction. If anything, she seemed to feed upon it.

"Er. Right." Bhar cleared his throat. "So, what, er, really matters?"

"Only you can say that." Riley seemed to be going for a tone of timeless mystery, which was difficult to achieve with her bare feet propped on Makepeace's desk. "But I can tell you what doesn't matter. Stocks. Bonds. Designer clothes. They're all meaningless. Me, I survive on very little." She lifted her chin. "I give more than I get to everyone I meet, every day of my life. And you know what? Because I give unselfishly, the universe takes care of me. I'm a spiritual teacher, and there's nothing the cosmos values more. My bills are paid, my bed is soft, and my path leads to the sunset of immortality."

"Right. Well. Let me jot that down," Bhar muttered. For once in his life, he couldn't think of anything clever to say— nothing that wouldn't get him sued and/or demoted to detective constable, at least. What had Hetheridge said? Time to be the sober professional and stop playing the clown.

Focusing on his notebook, Bhar wrote in a quick, jagged hand: *Keeps avoiding saying exactly what she did for Hughes… grandiose… Appaloosa in past life… in one breath, cash/objects = meaningless… next breath, brags she has it all.…*

"Need me to repeat anything, Deepal?" Sitting up straight, Riley stared into his eyes with seductive intensity. Either she believed what she'd said about Hughes's soul being nearby, approving of everything he saw, or she felt nothing over her former employer's demise. Nothing negative, at any rate.

"No, thank you, I have it." Bhar closed his book before she could see what he'd written. "Forgive me, but can we get back to Mr. Hughes? You called yourself his personal assistant. I presume your duties were just that, of a personal nature? They never coincided with his career with Peerless Petrol?"

"Why would you assume that? Michael and I had no secrets. I was involved in every single facet of his life."

That was difficult to imagine, unless Big Oil had more of a tolerance for barefoot New Age mediums than Bhar had previously suspected. "You worked beside him at the office, accompanied him to board meetings, etc.?"

"Of course not." Riley waved a dismissive hand. "He was at it like a Hebrew slave, working from dawn to dusk. Most days, I don't get up before noon."

Desperate for one straight, simple, run-of-the-mill response, Bhar pointed his pen at Riley. "As Mr. Hughes's assistant, what was your single primary duty?"

She groaned. "Well, since I foresaw his death, it was to help him avoid it, of course."

"You foresaw Michael Martin Hughes's death and told him it would come to pass?"

"Um, hello? The first word on my business card is 'seer.'" Riley flipped one such card at Bhar. "Of course I knew he was going to die. I didn't want it to happen, but the universe is in control. Michael isn't angry because I couldn't save him from his preordained fate. In fact, I can feel him watching us right now, letting me know he's okay. He's transitioning into a higher state."

"Well." Bhar capped his pen. "Thank you. That's good to know. We'll take a break. Regroup. Then continue this conversation at Scotland Yard."

"What do you mean?" Riley looked spring-loaded to pitch another fit.

"It's standard procedure. Ordinary witnesses – unimportant, garden-variety witnesses—are interviewed on site." Bhar sold the lie with every ounce of charm he possessed. "Special witnesses are interviewed at the Yard, where we have the resources to process what you tell us for maximal effect."

"Oh." Riley ducked her head coquettishly. "Well. If you put it that way, Deepal... I'm all yours."

Chapter Five

D espite Hetheridge's desire to have Sir Duncan Godington interviewed and—if possible—released from suspicion as soon as possible, Detective Sergeant Kate Wakefield couldn't resist gathering a bit of background first. Of course, there were protocols designed to assemble, check, and recheck the murder timeline. Although Hetheridge was always the senior investigative officer in any case that required his direct involvement—cases that touched on high society, the peerage, or England's wealthiest citizens—this did not mean he also supervised the Incident Room, as it was still called, despite the fact the "room" was, more and more, simply a digital compendium of facts and files. Just as the case's scientific branch would consist of Dr. Garrett, an Exhibits Officer responsible for preserving all physical evidence, and SOCOs (what Americans would call CSIs), the Incident Room would consist of fact checkers and administrators, all of them charged with assembling the most accurate timeline possible. Nevertheless, Kate didn't like the sensation of flying blind.

"Maybe you can help me," she said, stopping Hotel Nonpareil's musclebound head of security, Bob Junkett, as he emerged from the lift with a uniformed subordinate in tow.

Shooting her a sullen glance, Junkett lumbered toward a door behind the concierge desk marked PRIVATE.

"It's quite all right to talk to me, I'm with Scotland Yard," Kate said, digging in her purse for her warrant card. "You just showed my guv upstairs—"

"Too right I did." Junkett pivoted, moving with surprising speed for such a big man. "Not that he appreciated my efforts to help. Don't imagine you will, either, so push off. Find someone important to annoy."

There was any number of ways Kate could react. With warrant card in hand, the most obvious choice was to remind Junkett, politely but firmly, that he addressed a Scotland Yard investigator capable of arresting him for obstructing a police officer. Another approach was to play the needy female, giggling at her own ineptitude and asking a big, strong man like Junkett to ride to the rescue. During the course of several murder investigations, Kate had used both approaches multiple times. She was paid to get results, after all, and sometimes the best way to reap them was a bit of post-feminist performance art. But her copper instincts told her Junkett would respond better to something different.

"Do me a favor," Kate snapped, letting the unmistakable East End bray come through loud and clear. "I happen to know you're the big bloke 'round here. 'Charge of security, am I right? I'm not some bleeding nancy, just ponced in from the West End. Test me and see if I mean it!"

Junkett stopped walking. Kate saw what she wanted in his face. A dollop of surprise—and a much larger portion of dawning respect.

"Go on through," he told his subordinate. "Take an early lunch, I don't care. Just keep yourself available in case you're wanted for questioning."

Addressing Kate, the burly head of security inclined his head, full cheeks turning pink. Whatever else Bob Junkett was, he was quick to blush, at least when dressed down by an attractive female.

"Sorry, luv. Rude of me. Of course, you got a job to do, and it's my place to help. Born in Manchester. City all the way," he added, referring to the football team he supported. "Moved to London when I was fifteen, but the damage was done. You?"

"Newham till I was eight. Then Bethnal Green. Now the South End." *Until the wedding*, Kate added mentally. *Then I'll be poncing through the West End with the best of them.*

Junkett's blush deepened even as his grin widened. Yes, he was on the hook, making Kate glad she'd foregone wearing her engagement ring while on the job. At first, Hetheridge had been miffed. After all, the brilliant cushion-cut diamond, set in platinum and bookended with two spectacular sapphires, was a family heirloom, not to mention a potent symbol of his feelings for her. But Hetheridge was too much of a pragmatist not to acknowledge that in many situations, a woman like Kate possessed far more leverage if apparently single. The same wasn't true of men—in many cases, a visible wedding ring seemed to increase their personal desirability—but that curious imbalance was an issue Kate had no time to ponder.

"Follow me to my office, luv," Junkett said, pronouncing "my" as "me." An opportunity to revert to his home dialect without censure seemed to please him.

"Why not?" In situations like these, Kate channeled her elder sister Maura, who charmed working class men the way eastern mystics charmed snakes. Or she had, once upon a time, before her mental illness and subsequent sectioning: committal into a psychiatric hospital.

"I can make tea," Junkett said, unlocking his office door and holding it open for Kate. "How d'you feel about PG Tips?"

"Love it. Got any biscuits?"

"Indeed I do. Digestives: plain or chocolate, your choice." Plugging in a white plastic kettle, Junkett switched it on. "So how might I help such a far more compelling and, I must add, far more *professional* member of Scotland Yard?"

Kate, who doubted her professionalism would ever

match Hetheridge's, kept up what she hoped was a sweet smile. Taking offense at slights on Hetheridge's character, however it might demonstrate her loyalty in the short run, would prove counterproductive in the long run. "I'm meant to interview Sir Duncan Godington. He's the most famous, or should I say infamous, guest at this hotel, so tackling him first was my guv's choice."

"Oh, of course. Sir Duncan." Junkett sighed. "I could understand the thought process behind such a choice, if it wasn't so bleeding obvious. Not to mention incidental. Before I decided earning a good living was more important than prestige, I used to be a police officer. I know the difference between a true lead and a red herring."

This early in the investigation? That makes you a psychic, not a detective, Kate thought. "Go on."

"Sir Duncan's just an easy avenue, innit?" Junkett's blush faded. Safe on his own patch with a pot of tea brewing, he rapidly grew more comfortable, even expansive. "A man falsely accused, railroaded by the system, backed into a corner by lesser men desperate to solve a crime. Believe me, Ms.—" Junkett stopped, stymied by lack of a formal introduction.

"Wakefield. Kate Wakefield," she said, deliberately omitting her title.

"Right. Pleased to make your acquaintance. Call me Bob." Placing two mismatched mugs on his desk, Junkett gathered several packets of sugar and, from his mini-fridge, a carton of milk. "When you work for a hotel as exclusive as this one, you get to know toffs from the inside out. Mr. Hughes wasn't here for three hours before he'd complained about the view, screamed at the concierge, and threatened a maid. I had to go up to his room with Mr. Makepeace and counsel the bugger myself."

"What did you tell him?"

"Same speech I give pop stars, footballers, and MPs. Save your tantrums for home, no one here is your dogsbody, and bear in mind, the service this establishment offers works both ways. Yes, we enjoy your business. But unless transferring your gala to the Holiday Inn sounds nice, don't tempt us to fling your arse out."

"There's quite a nice Holiday Inn in Mayfair," Kate said, testing Junkett's allegiance to his place of employment.

"Of course it's nice, but tiny. Blokes like Hughes only care about optics. To them, the best planned gala for the most relevant cause in the world is worthless, less than bloody zero, if not held at an *exclusive destination*. That's where Hotel Nonpareil comes in." The kettle clicked, signaling it was done. Filling Kate's mug, Junkett asked, "Shall I sweeten it up?"

"I'll do it." Kate tore open a packet of sugar. Officially, she'd gone off carbs, determined to shrink a bit before her wedding gown's final fitting. Unofficially, after missing breakfast, she was fortunate to merely dump the sugar into her mug, rather than pour the granules directly into her mouth. "Why did Mr. Hughes scream at the concierge?"

"Because the front desk booked two perfectly legitimate guests. Griffin Hughes, his son, and Thora Hughes his wife. Not yet divorced, no restraining orders, no red flags to alert the booking staff. How were we to know Mr. Hughes didn't want the woman who was still legally his wife, not to mention his adult son, on the premises?"

"Were they lodged close to Mr. Hughes?"

"On the same floor, the eighth. Along with Mr. Hughes's assistants, Ms. Castanet, and Ms. Freemont. And with the hotel so full, it was impossible to move them."

"Of course." Allowing herself only a swallow of tea, Kate withdrew her mobile, preparing to text notes to herself. Later that night, she'd type them up properly and submit them to the Incident Room. "Let's see. Son—Griffin. Wife—Thora. Both are still on these premises awaiting pre-interview by the Met, I assume?"

"I believe so." Junkett, thoroughly comfortable, was digging into a fresh packet of chocolate biscuits. "Care for one?"

"Lord, yes." Kate was surprised by the tiny spark of guilt she suffered. Junkett's brown eyes were avid, his smile embarrassingly earnest. He was on the hook, all right. And her not three weeks from matrimony in front of God, Ritchie, Henry, Bhar, Lady Margaret, and two hundred of Hetheridge's so-called closest friends.

"So despite the fact Mr. Hughes objected to their presence, his estranged wife and grown son were permitted to remain lodged at Hotel Nonpareil. Was there any problem?"

Junkett snorted.

"Is that a yes?"

"Some drama between Hughes and his wife in the lounge. By the time I arrived, both denied it. And an ugly moment when Griffin beat on his dad's door for ten minutes. Threatened to kill himself if Hughes didn't open the door."

"Did Hughes open up?"

"Nope. Threatened to use the suite's panic button, which summons the police in five minutes or less. Then called me. I escorted Griffin away myself. Mind you." Junkett paused, clearly enjoying Kate's attention. "The last thing Griffin shouted at his old dad was, 'Maybe I'll kill you!'"

"Did you find the threat credible?"

Junkett laughed. "Never."

"What about Peerless Petrol's fundraiser? Did Thora and Griffin attend?"

"Well." Junkett chewed his biscuit so lustily, he reminded Kate of her workplace nemesis, DCI Vic Jackson, defiling a powdered doughnut. "They weren't invited, that I know for sure. Head of Security always has the official list. I reckon Griffin has been disinherited, though I can't prove it. They crashed the gala around nine. Griffin didn't make any trouble. Thora was a different story. Confronted Hughes and his new lady friend on the dance floor. My staff called me straightaway. I escorted Thora Hughes out of the gala and back to her room myself."

"What about Griffin?"

"I asked Mr. Hughes if he wanted the boy removed, but he said no. I guess one ugly scene was enough for him, and the kid didn't cause trouble. Seemed like Billy no-mates to me, just drifting about looking sullen."

"Mr. Hughes had a new lady?" Kate asked, rapidly texting notes to herself. Her personal shorthand was so hard to follow, the transmissions were virtually encrypted.

"Oh, yes. Hughes weren't what you'd call discreet about it. Ms. Arianna Freemont is his head of PR and future wife, according to everyone I talked to. Opened the gala with him. Danced every other dance in his arms."

"Are there CCTV cameras in the ballroom?"

"Yes."

"And in every hotel corridor?"

"Yes." Junkett had stopped making eye contact.

"Of course, the footage from the eighth floor on the night of the murder is critical. May I review it now?"

"All in good time." Junkett finished his biscuit in one huge bite. "There's a right mountain of footage to get sorted, but I'll put someone on it. In the meantime, take it from me, Ms. Wakefield, there's more to good police work than relying on camera footage. Foolish to put all your eggs in that basket. Most of the time you reap nothing but back-of-the-head shots or pictures snapped at such a high angle, it's pointless to—"

"I understand all that. How soon can I review the footage, Mr. Junkett?" Kate felt an unpleasant suspicion rising.

"As soon as possible, as I've said." Fiddling with the biscuit packet, he stared fixedly at his mug. "Sacked our head of IT not long ago. Had to put in a request to our new IT service to iron out any technical issues. Of course, we can't invite them onto the premises until you lot declare the scene secure, but in a few days—"

"Mr. Junkett." This time, Kate's east London bray returned by instinct rather than design. "Why do you anticipate technical issues?"

His eyes lit briefly on hers before flicking away. "Because someone seems to have, er. Tampered. With the, er, camera."

"Why do you say that?"

"Because the only images it transmits seem to come

from the Royal London Zoo. Specifically…." He cleared his throat. "The Gorilla Kingdom."

Chapter Six

The what?" Bhar shouted when Kate excused herself to ring him up with the news. "How's that even possible?"

"I don't know yet." Kate had gone into the women's room to make the call, unable to find another place where Junkett or the manager, Makepeace, wasn't lurking nearby, obviously hoping to overhear. "Most high quality security cameras send the data directly to a central computer via wireless connection. That way, even if someone knocks the camera down or steals it, all the pre-vandalism shots will still be transmitted. I've heard of people using bright flashes or strobe lights to dazzle the camera—make it send back nothing but frames of white. But this is the first time I've heard of someone hacking the feed to re-route it, or swapping one fixed camera's data for another."

"And from the gorilla cam in the London Zoo, no less. Cocky little hacker, eh?"

"Definitely. And maybe trying to send a message."

"Meaning?"

"Well, for starters, the head of security, Junkett, is a bit of an ape. I'll bet he has plenty of disgruntled employees.

Maybe one of them wanted to embarrass him." Even as Kate said it, she tried to put the preconceived notion aside. Assumptions were inevitable, but it was much too soon to give any one notion automatic credence over another. Not unless she wanted to become as biased and sloppy as DCI Jackson. "But Paul, put me in the picture. Why are you heading back to the Yard so soon?"

"The interview of the century. You're dealing with apes and I'm about to debrief a horse. An Appaloosa, to be specific." Bhar explained Riley Castanet's unusual views in detail as Kate chuckled.

"Please tell me she's not riding in the Astra with you."

"Not bloody likely. I—crikey, a little warning!" Bhar cried, no doubt addressing the infamous London traffic. "I don't know which is worse, the taxis or the cyclists. Two did their best to collide right in front of me. And Victoria Street is closed again. Another burst water main, which means the detour could cost me half an hour."

"I gave up my car because of the congestion charge. Why bother with a car if I have to pay extra fees just to drive it round the city? Got myself an Oyster card and now it's public transport all the way," Kate said virtuously.

"Yes, well, you'll be trading those Tube queues for the Bentley soon enough, won't you?" Bhar shot back. "As for Ms. Castanet, I put her in a cab. Being alone with a suspect like that is a guaranteed sexual harassment charge. I'll conduct the interview with at least one female detective in the room at all times. And possibly a horse, just to be safe."

"And to think, just a few hours ago, you saw the Grim." Kate laughed, visualizing the illustration from the Harry Potter series with ease. They were some of her nephew Henry's favorite books. "First a big black dog, then an Appaloosa, and now gorillas. This is shaping up to be an animal-themed case."

"True. So perhaps it's time to interview Britain's most notorious animal lover? The man who once lived in Borneo with the bonobos?"

"Orangutans." Kate's amusement drained away. "You

know what? You're right. Sir Duncan it is."

***

Kate wasn't surprised to learn Sir Duncan Godington and his half-sister, Lady Isabel Bartlow, had booked Hotel Nonpareil's most exclusive suite, the penthouse. According to Leo Makepeace, Sir Duncan had temporarily moved into the hotel two weeks before Peerless Petrol threw its ill-fated fundraiser. After the Halloween ax murder briefly cast suspicion upon him, Sir Duncan had decided to sell his Chelsea house and build a new dwelling in Knightsbridge, flattening a grand old Victorian to make way for something better, or at least more current. In the meantime, he'd made Hotel Nonpareil his home, reputedly redecorating the penthouse to better suit his tastes and entertaining his half-sister, Lady Isabel, for days at a time.

They certainly don't trouble themselves about all those nasty rumors, Kate thought as one of the hotel's lifts sped her toward the penthouse. *If I ever heard folks thought I was shagging Ritchie....*

She cut off the thought, too repulsed to continue. Her brother Ritchie, older by two years, was mentally retarded, a medical term that had fallen so out of favor, Kate had begun to say "mentally disabled." It didn't matter to her what anyone called it, so long as the words were spoken with respect. Ritchie lived a singular sort of life. Most schoolwork beyond letters and a few numbers eluded him, though he seemed to have an instinctual gift for three-dimensional art, especially art rendered in Legos. He couldn't support himself, or even look after his basic needs, without supervision. For Ritchie, earning a living was out of the question; he existed slightly askew from most people, aware of them, craving their company, yet never quite *with* them, really. Nevertheless, Kate thought Ritchie loved her. And whether or not her brother did, according to her personal definition of that emotion, she loved him. He was a part of her, a bit of gentleness and mystery in a life that was often cool, scientific, and all too cut-and-dried. Ritchie reminded Kate that even things that didn't make sense to her intellectually still possessed intrinsic value.

In light of her relationship with Ritchie, Kate found Sir Duncan's and Lady Isabel's bond, either unusually intimate or outright incestuous, particularly troubling. But fortunately, she didn't need to empathize to investigate. All she had to do was take down the facts, enter them into the case's greater context, and let the logical conclusion speak for itself.

Tony would be proud of me, Kate thought. Since their engagement, she'd given up calling him "the guv," at least in the privacy of her own mind. *He never confuses his feelings for a situation with the facts of an individual case. And he trusts me and Paul to do the same.*

Strange, how he seemed to trust so easily. Was that part of being an aristocrat? The deep certainly that people will behave and do their best, because once upon a time, the peasants behaved and did their best? Or was she indulging in a too-rosy look back at the bad old days?

For Kate, trust had always been tricky. Taking it on faith that some other flawed human being, tempted by circumstances and fate, wouldn't turn away at the worst possible moment, making Kate the fool. She trusted Ritchie. He was more than her brother, he was someone who'd also suffered their mum's non-benign neglect, a man who now desired nothing more than a quiet, simple life. And she trusted Henry, her eight-year-old nephew, refugee from his mum Maura's wild life; her descent into untreated schizophrenia, a disease worsened by street drugs until residential care was her only option. Fate hadn't been especially gentle on Henry. Portly, bespectacled, and over-enamored of reading, the boy was bullied in school and falling behind in maths class. Not long ago, on Hetheridge's encouragement, Henry had stood up to his tormentors, proving he was willing to fight for his dignity. But there would be many more battles until the war was won.

Henry trusts Tony. It's not just the desire for a male role model. Henry's soul is more trusting than mine ever was. Can I become someone like that? A woman who doesn't walk down the aisle waiting for everything to blow up, who doesn't say "I do" while expecting the roof to fall in?

"Here we are," Leo Makepeace said, ushering Kate from the lift to the penthouse's front door. "Sir Duncan and his sister. Half-sister. I don't know. It's none of my business who they are or what they do inside that room." He wrung his hands, grinning horribly like he might keel over from discomposure at any moment.

"Thank you," Kate said, pushing a strand behind her ear and smiling at the little man. "May I ask you a question?"

"W-well. Yes. O-of course."

"On a scale of one to ten, with ten being perfect and one being perfectly dreadful, how would you rate Sir Duncan Godington? Off the record, of course."

"I—I—I'd have to call him a none. I mean, a nine. A nine is fair," Makepeace said, shooting a longing glance at the lift.

"A nine?" Kate repeated, ignoring Makepeace's spasms of discomfort. "Not a ten? What made you deduct a point?"

"He—he frightens me," Makepeace gasped.

"Why? What does he do?"

"Looks me in the eye. Smiles. Calls me 'Leo.'" The manager shuddered. "That can't be right."

"Of course not," Kate said, recalling her own close encounter with the man. On a chilly October evening, on a balcony in the very best part of London, Kate had stood in her rented ball gown and borrowed jewelry, feeling like an utter fraud. Sir Duncan, that scion of the upper class, had appeared, making her feel at ease. Was there anything more dangerous in all the world?

As Hotel Nonpareil's manager at last escaped her clutches, Kate made a fist, lifting it to rap against the penthouse door. But before her knuckles connected with wood, the door swung inward, revealing a smiling woman. Kate, stranded with fist in the air, brought it slowly back to her side, trying to match half the grace and confidence that faced her.

"Sergeant Wakefield!" Lady Isabel Bartlow came toward Kate with open arms. Before Kate could protest, retreat, or do anything other than stiffen into an ironing board, she was embraced, then air-kissed on both cheeks.

Still smiling, Lady Isabel drew back, holding Kate at arm's length. As far as Kate was concerned, Lady Isabel was the perfect young aristocrat, not only in demeanor but physically, too. Tall and slim, ever-so-slightly boyish, with a long torso, high cheekbones, and wide brown eyes, she wore her dark hair swept up like Audrey Hepburn or, more recently, Anne Hathaway. Whether viewed through a prism calibrated in the 1960s or the 2010s, Lady Isabel was elegant, gracious, and kind. Kate knew Lady Isabel had married young, then divorced, the details never divulged. Society gossip blamed Sir Duncan for the split, claiming excessive meddling, unwholesome or otherwise, had driven a wedge between Lady Isabel and her university sweetheart. But no matter what caused the divorce, she was a free agent now, most often photographed on her dashing half-brother's arm.

"I can't believe you remembered my name," Kate blurted, unable to stop herself. Now she sounded as foolish as Leo Makepeace, undone by mere recognition of her existence.

"I didn't," Lady Isabel confided, making the admission sound like an inexplicable failing on her part. "Dunc did. The penthouse comes with its own security cameras." She gestured toward a viewscreen mounted near the flat screen TV, where four separate views were displayed simultaneously. "He saw the poor little manager—what's-his-name—escorting you and said, 'By Jove, there's Detective Sergeant Kate Wakefield.' So I hurried over to greet you."

Kate had the feeling Lady Isabel was too good to be true, that she was made of spun sugar and might dissolve after the first hard rain. "Lady Isabel, did your brother really say 'by Jove?'"

Lady Isabel laughed. "Of course not. This is what he said." She whispered the rest in Kate's ear. In spite of herself,

Kate laughed.

"That sounds more… believable."

"As long as you understand he wasn't being vulgar in reaction to you personally. Dunc simply enjoys vulgarity," Lady Isabel said. "Flouting convention makes him feel powerful."

Kate considered that. "I don't mind. I barely know him. But do you mind, Lady Isabel? If people misinterpret Sir Duncan, particularly in regard to his relationship with you?"

"I don't." Lady Isabel's tone was serious. "He's my blood. He matters to me, his happiness, his well-being. The gossips of this world will come and go. They'll never suffer agonies to defend me. Never suffer a sleepless night worrying over me. So I turn my face toward the people who truly care and simply pretend the liars don't exist."

"Whenever the word 'liar' is uttered aloud, I find myself obligated to appear," Sir Duncan Godington said, entering the penthouse's living room. He smiled, wide mouth stretching to push up those high cheekbones, making him very handsome indeed. "Having admitted such a compulsion, it's no lie to say I'm glad to see you, Detective Sergeant Wakefield."

"Oh. Well. Ta. And—same to you?" Kate hoped she didn't look as idiotic as she sounded.

Never breaking eye contact, he crossed the room in three long strides. Taking Kate's hand, he squeezed it gently while inclining his head. For a moment, she thought he would kiss her hand, and her heart thudded wildly at the potential embarrassment. That would be taking the piss and no mistake, as her mum used to say. But Sir Duncan did no more than shake her hand and bow his head. The action was expansive, wildly flattering, but not outrageous enough to be a veiled form of humiliation. Still, that moment of dizzying uncertainty was pure hell. Classic Sir Duncan.

"I see you're charming as ever," Kate added, willing her heart to slow down.

"Of course. The devil has to be charming. Otherwise, no one would ever invite him inside." Sir Duncan flashed that cannibal smile, the one the tabloids had delighted in showing off via full-color photos during his trial. At one point during the Crown's prosecution of Sir Duncan for triple murder—his father, brother, and butler—the tabloids floated the rumor that Sir Duncan, like the fictional Hannibal Lector, might have dined on his victims, explaining certain missing body parts.

"Good point." Kate had no idea if Sir Duncan had cannibalistic tendencies. She only knew that after his exoneration, he was generally safe from being tried a second time for the same crime, despite the repeal of England's medieval double-jeopardy laws. A teasing private "confession" of the sort to which she'd been privy, uttered at a party where all were consuming alcohol, wasn't enough. Only new evidence introduced into Crown court and judged to be compelling could trigger a second trial.

"Let me guess," Sir Duncan continued. "You've come to see me because that oilman was murdered. I'm notorious enough to merit quick attention from a crack Scotland Yard liaison, and the oilman was rich enough to merit a visit, albeit posthumous, from the great Lord Hetheridge himself." Sir Duncan pronounced Hetheridge's name in a theatrical whisper, widening his eyes and pretending to shiver. "Arriving in state, no doubt. I realize we're still in love with the class system in this country, and heaven knows I've benefitted from the magic of a title, even one so pathetic as 'baronet.' But Kate, please, you're a rational working class woman. Don't you find it odd, if not obscene, that modern folk are expected to bend the knee to Hetheridge just because some ancestor of his did something unspeakable to six peasants and a pig, once upon a time?"

"Eight."

"What?"

"I have it on good authority, Sir Duncan." Kate smiled. "Eight peasants and a pig. Not six."

"Ah, well. Fair play." Sir Duncan shrugged. "You know me. I only give a damn about the pig."

"What about Michael Martin Hughes, Sir Duncan? Did you give a damn about him? Were you acquainted?"

"And from a snippet of pleasant conversation to ice

cold business, just like that. If you ever give up policing, Kate, you'd do brilliantly on one of those home shopping channels. From a friendly gibe with a co-anchor to a hard sell on a two-bar electric fire, just like that. Do sit down." Sir Duncan indicated the long white sofa.

Like the rest of the penthouse's furnishings, it was sumptuous but modern, more functional than luxurious. All told, the penthouse's understated décor surprised her after Bhar's description of Hughes's suite. If rumors that Sir Duncan had redecorated were true, he clearly preferred simplicity over wretched excess.

Sir Duncan draped himself on one end, leaning against the sofa's arm to better face her, body language so open as to be intimidating. After a split second's inner debate, Kate chose to sit just past the middle, close enough to be cordial, but still beyond Sir Duncan's reach. The man exuded a startling energy. He always seemed on the verge of eruption, like a jar of lightning improperly sealed. Kate's instincts told her not to ignore that subliminal clue or take her eyes off him for a minute.

"Am I meant to leave the room?" Lady Isabel asked. "Is this a secret interrogation?"

"Oh, no, far from it. It's just a conversation," Kate began, but Sir Duncan cut across her.

"Izzy! What luck you're still on your feet. Didn't the caterer leave us a tray of emergency nibbles? Break-glass-in-case-of-unexpected-guest sort of thing? I bet they'd go down a treat with a spot of tea. That is, if you can find it in your heart…."

Lady Isabel laughed. "I'd send you to fetch them yourself, my dear, except I know you're much too lazy to lift a finger. Oh, I'm afraid it's true, Kate. Even in Borneo, he taught the locals to serve him. This includes the primates. I'm told at least one orangutan pre-chewed a bit of fruit and tried to feed it to Dunc."

"Untrue. Milo didn't try to feed me. He succeeded in feeding me," Sir Duncan said. "Never look a gift orangutan in the mouth. Not even a pre-adolescent, comparatively docile male."

Kate heard herself giggle. Quite literally giggle, as if she'd taken leave of her senses. Thank goodness Hetheridge wasn't within earshot. The last time he'd crossed verbal swords with Sir Duncan, the considerably taller, considerably younger man had almost taken a swing at him.

"So you'll fetch us those nibbles?" he asked Lady Isabel.

"Yes. Only because I don't want poor Kate to starve." Lady Isabel disappeared deeper into the penthouse, presumably heading toward the kitchen.

Looking pleased, Sir Duncan scooted closer. Now he *was* within arm's length, and there was no way Kate could evade him without potentially giving offense.

"Alone at last," Sir Duncan said. "But I sidestepped your question, didn't I? You asked me how I felt about Michael Martin Hughes. Well, I hardly knew him, socially. Nodding acquaintance at best. Then Peerless Petrol did its level best to destroy the Gulf of Mexico. Hughes popped up on telly, insisting he was the true victim, and suddenly I had an opinion." Sir Duncan flashed that wide smile again. "I wanted him dead."

Chapter Seven

"By all means, please, keep going." Kate smiled back. "I have so much on my plate these days, a confession would really lighten the load."

"Wanting him dead, however, is not the same as killing him. Especially when he made overtures to me specifically, inviting me to attend the gala as a guest of honor. Hughes felt he and I had a lot in common." Sir Duncan's eyes sparkled. "When he phoned me up to introduce himself, he told me we'd each been bystanders to tragedies, unfairly swept up in an overlarge net. Victims of circumstance, you see, pilloried by the court of public opinion."

"Did you consider his parallel accurate?" Usually Kate took at least cursory notes during these pre-interviews, texting bits to herself for inclusion in the formal report, lest she become overwhelmed by raw data and forget something crucial. With Sir Duncan, forgetting what he said would not be a problem. He was more likely to say something indelible, a stinging phrase or observation that would cost her sleep for years to come.

"Of course not, it's pure rubbish. Hughes and I are like

night and day. I have more in common with your average pre-adolescent ape, and all they care about is gobbling fruit, climbing trees, and masturbating."

"Oh, my." Blinking theatrically, Lady Isabel reentered the living room with a long tray in hand. "I have no idea how you arrived at that topic, but Dunc. Luv. Ease up on the aren't-I-shocking routine or Kate'll arrest you for sure. Irritation on the job can turn any bride into a bridezilla in nothing flat." Lady Isabel's big brown eyes widened. "Whoops. I probably wasn't meant to bring that up."

Kate was caught off guard. "Is my wedding a topic of casual conversation?"

Lady Isabel and Sir Duncan exchanged a glance. The silence stretched a bit too long before Sir Duncan spoke gently. "Oh, Kate. High society is destined to eat you alive, isn't it?"

Kate steeled herself not to react. Since accepting Hetheridge's proposal, she'd concentrated on the day-to-day with newfound ferocity, fighting to excel at the office, keep Henry on track in school, and keep Ritchie happy at home, all while paying as little attention to the event's minutiae as possible. More than once, she'd wished aloud for a civil ceremony, a tropical elopement, an exchange of rings on some lonely mountaintop in Tibet, for that matter, if it guaranteed peace, and fun, and two weeks with Hetheridge. But her future husband seemed to think a traditional ceremony was unavoidable, and Lady Margaret Knolls agreed.

Maybe tonight I'll put Tony's feet to the fire and find out why.

"As fascinating a topic as I find myself," Kate said, pushing a lock of hair behind her ear and giving Sir Duncan her cheeriest faux smile, "I consider you even more irresistible. Please tell me more about your relationship with Mr. Hughes."

"*Brava,*" Sir Duncan said as Lady Isabel placed the tray on the coffee table. "I'll be happy to bend your ear, but first I really must insist you try a nibble. Which would you prefer: walnut *gougères*, red pepper *rouille* on prawns, *dodine de foie gras de Canard aux trois poivres et sirop de tomates*, or *tagliatelle de céleri rave à la crème de truffe et parmesan?"*

Swallowing her frustration, Kate pointed at the only item on the tray she recognized, a jumbo prawn. "That. The red pepper thingy. My French is only fit for asking directions and talking about the weather, I'm afraid."

"Wrong answer. I've embarrassed you, or close enough. But you've a great many excruciating teas in your future, my dear, and lots of them will begin with just such a question. Try again."

Kate thought for a moment. "Right. Well. If it's all the same to you, guv, I'd like some pig snacks and a pint of Guinness."

"Much better. Now try the walnut gougères, they're the best of the lot." Spearing one with a tiny silver fork, Sir Duncan passed it over on a matching miniature plate.

"Here's another trick," Lady Isabel said, taking the chair opposite Kate and Sir Duncan. "Beam a great smile, bat your eyelashes, press your hand to your heart"—she demonstrated the gesture—"and say, 'Thanks ever so, but I'm watching my figure.' Then look the person who asked up and down in a way that communicates, 'And so should you.' Never fails."

The walnut gougère was wonderful, tempting Kate to eat a second one—would her wedding dress split its seams as she stomped down the aisle?—before getting back on task. "So after Mr. Hughes made his overture of friendship, how did you respond?"

"The only way possible. I asked him to show me the money. And how he and Peerless Petrol intended to spend it to undo the damage to the Gulf of Mexico. The sums he'd allocated would do for a start. But the plans were grossly inadequate, without practical safeguards to prevent a similar spill in the future. I told him I would match that sum, pound for pound, if he made me head of the board created to administer it."

"How much money are we talking about?"

"For me to match? Three billion."

Kate studied him, trying to decide if he were joking or

attempting to teach her some new lesson about high society. "Please don't be offended. I realize your inheritance was generous and you're quite comfortable, but—"

"That will never do," Sir Duncan cut across her. "All this middle-class waffling about money doesn't exist where you're headed. In fact, I daresay it doesn't exist where you've come from. I'm a rich man, I don't mind it said to my face. However, I'm not worth three billion pounds. But I could have raised that sum, I promise you. My connections are excellent. Scotland Yard might not trust me, but Greenpeace, Oceana, and the World Wildlife Federation do. If Hughes had been willing to give me control of the project, donations would have poured in, and I would have gone straight to work."

"I take it Hughes said no?"

"Of course he did, after listening to my pitch over drinks and pretending to think it over. From what I can tell, Peerless Petrol never meant to do more than the absolute minimum before shifting the ongoing cost to coastal communities and foreign governments. Whatever money they proposed publicly to spend on righting their wrongs, at least a third was earmarked to return through a back door. I'm not certain if the company was behind that scheme's built-in chicanery or if it was the brainchild of Hughes himself, but I can tell you this. Someone planned to pocket a billion pounds. Someone like me—an environmental czar, if you will—chairing the board would have made such a theft impossible."

"Seems like a lot for Hughes to confess over drinks," Kate said.

"Oh, he did nothing but lie and slag off on the press for quote unquote torturing him. The other details came to me through… other channels."

"You have friends inside Peerless Petrol?"

Sir Duncan shrugged.

"Disgruntled employees willing to grass on the boss?"

"More like eco-warriors embedded in the enemy ranks. Across the globe, we're losing the battle, Kate. Even when presented with incontrovertible evidence of the harm they've caused, people like Hughes think only of themselves. Of how to slip another billion into that Swiss bank account, in case the other billions get lonely. They live in splendor while the natural world is plundered to the point of no return."

Kate, who could still remember the icy linoleum floors and leaking roof of her mother's council flat, couldn't resist letting her gaze rove around the penthouse. It was more tasteful than Hughes's suite, without a doubt. But still opulent by almost any standard, unless you were a Vegas lion tamer/magician.

"I know what you're thinking." Sir Duncan didn't seem offended. "But money is power, Kate. In fact, the trappings of money are sometimes more influential than the cash itself, truth be told. Someday I'll chuck the dosh where it can do the most good and disappear into a jungle forever. But not yet."

"I hope you don't expect me to join you, and swing by a grapevine," Lady Isabel said. "Jane may have done it for Tarzan, but I've always suspected the epilogue to her story was death by malaria, if not baboons."

"Getting back to Mr. Hughes," Kate said. "After he rejected your proposal, how did the two of you get on? I understand you still attended the gala."

"Of course I did. I'm a celebrity to some, a figure of notoriety to others. I held up a gigantic sham check and let the press snap pictures. That was meant to be today's society page headline: 'Godington Gives Three Million from Personal Fortune to Gulf Relief.' But of course...." He shrugged.

Kate wished it were possible to pierce the man's assuredness, his magnificent calm, and catch even the tiniest glimmer of what lay beneath. If she didn't know Sir Duncan's history, if she hadn't heard him admit to the killings he'd been acquitted for, she would have asked a final question and hurried off to screen the hotel's other high-octane guests, convinced the baronet was an utter dead end. But in the context of who he was and what he'd done, how polished was too polished? What emotion should she look for?

Only Hetheridge had ever goaded Sir Duncan into

dropping the mask. And Hetheridge, unlike most of the Met, did not consider Sir Duncan a sociopath. Per the guv, another word applied to someone like Sir Duncan—a very old term, now somewhat out of style. Was it true? Was Sir Duncan evil?

"What time did you leave the gala, Sir Duncan?"

"Oh—elevenish. Half-eleven at the latest."

"Where did you go?"

"Home of a friend."

"Here in Hotel Nonpareil?"

"No."

"When did you return to the penthouse?"

"Around three or four a.m." Sir Duncan sounded amused. "Yes, I'm one of those men. Even after a lovely evening, I prefer to sleep alone in my own bed."

"May I take down the name of that friend?"

"I'd rather not."

Kate waited. Again, with anyone else, this line of questioning was going much too deep for a pre-interview. But for Sir Duncan....

"The lady in question is not precisely a free woman," Sir Duncan added. "If I fail in my discretion, Mr. Litigious Husband will take full advantage during the divorce."

"I see. Well. At this point, to pry more deeply is probably excessive. I'll return if more questions crop up. Thank you both for your time." Rising, Kate stuck out her hand. Lady Isabel stood up and clasped it warmly. Sir Duncan remained seated, eyes narrowed and mouth pulling up at one side, as if examining Kate on a microscopic level.

"I wish you joy on your wedding. Give Tony my best," Lady Isabel said.

"Oh, by all means, give Tony my best, too," Sir Duncan said. "It struck me after your team nabbed the ax murderer that I'd served as rather a red herring in his last case. I wonder if that annoyed him."

"Attending your Halloween party was an experience the chief will never forget," Kate said truthfully. Intent on leaving it at that, she turned to go. "I'll let myself out."

"Kate," Sir Duncan called. "One more thing. A bit of wisdom from one maverick to another."

"Yes."

"As far as marrying into the peerage. You'll never win them over. Never."

Kate forced a laugh. "Oh. Right. Thanks for that."

"I don't mean they'll never accept you. I mean if they do, it won't be because you worked to win them over. So never do that, Kate. Never work for it. Demand pig snacks and Guinness and laugh in their faces. It's the only chance you've got."

Chapter Eight

Interviewing Riley Castanet proved exactly as Detective Sergeant Paul Bhar expected. It was, by turns, excruciating, exasperating, encouraging (from the point of view of a policeman eager to close a case), and enervating (in the sense that the woman he was debriefing might prove to be absolutely innocent).

Taking no chances, he enlisted the presence of two witnesses, a female detective named DI Lindley and a male PC called Nwosu, the only idle non-white officer Bhar could unearth on short notice. Two minorities ought to make up for the lack of an equine presence.

"Are you going to record everything I say?" Riley asked, inspecting her chair thoroughly before deigning to sit upon it.

"Yes, of course. It wouldn't do for you to be misquoted," Bhar said.

"Good. More people should record what I say. Send it out as a podcast every daily and call it 'cosmic education.' I could even edit the best bits together and sell it as an internet course in wholeness. My own *Course in Miracles*, except unlike that particular author-twit, I'll be selling true enlightenment." Riley looked from DI Lindley to PC Nwosu. "Isn't one of you going to fetch me coffee? Wouldn't mind a pack of cigarettes, either. Menthol."

Bhar nodded at PC Nwosu, and then took his seat across from Riley. "I must admit, I thought tobacco was a no-go for most Americans. Especially those with your interests."

"What, you think because I'm a spiritual practitioner, I worry about eating organic celery and wearing Birkenstocks and shacking up in a commune with no running water?" Riley peered into the coffee cup Nwosu offered. "That's black. I need cream and two sugars." Tearing into the pack of cigarettes, she shook one out and held it up between index and forefinger. "Oh, there's nothing like the real thing. I've been on an e-cigarette for six months, so this is a relief. Don't make me dig in my purse. I'm bereaved, for God's sake. Somebody give me a light."

Bhar, who was never without a lighter—too many interviews contained a moment like this, and besides, he'd been known to smoke the odd fag when his mum wasn't looking—lit it for her. Riley took a long, satisfied drag, pronounced the doctored coffee Nwosu returned with as good, and gave everyone a smile as Bhar shut the door.

"Where do you want me to start? How I discovered my powers? Major predictions I've made over the years?"

"First things first." The large black tape recorder was due to be replaced, as soon as the wheels of bureaucracy turned, with a digital version. Switching it on, Bhar stated for the record his name and title, plus the names of the others in the room, as well as the date and time. "Now. Ms. Castanet has asked me to call her Riley, so I will address her in that fashion throughout this interview. Riley, earlier you told me you foresaw the death of Michael Martin Hughes. Please explain what you meant."

Riley heaved a sigh, as if describing her paranormal abilities to ordinary folks was a tedious duty. "My first encounter beyond the veil of ordinary mortal influence occurred at age seven...."

"Riley." Bhar touched her hand, praying his two Met

observers would be willing to swear in a court of law the gesture was altogether wholesome. "This interview needs to be focused like a laser on Mr. Hughes and his death. That's the best way for you to help him. Answer my questions as specifically as possible. When did you foresee his demise? Can you give me the precise date, or at least an estimate?"

Lips pursing in displeasure, Riley's face contracted like a fist. She took another sip of coffee. Two more puffs on the menthol cigarette. Then she spoke. "A couple of months ago, I flew to England to commune with the cosmic power center you call Stonehenge. Once upon a time, in the days of ley lines, Stonehenge was a hub of sacred feminine energy." Riley took another puff. "Now it's a tourist trap. Not that I blame anyone for cashing in. But as a spiritual practitioner, I should be encouraged to visit. Or at the very least, offered a discount."

Bhar, who happened to know Stonehenge's admittance fee amounted to only a few pounds, held his tongue.

"While I was meditating, a vision came upon me," Riley continued. "I saw a handsome man. Powerful. Misunderstood. Suffering a modern crucifixion, not with nails but words."

"You saw Mr. Hughes?"

"Of course. It's terrible, how the media and politicians have manipulated the facts for their own gain. Michael's company, Peerless Petrol, was at the mercy of contractors. They performed poorly: inadequate rig, shoddy cement, etc. But poor Michael shouldered the blame. The stockholders had demanded he cut costs to the bone. But when the oil rig failed, the very first question was, why oh why didn't he invest in gold-plated equipment? Let me tell you, if he'd done that and the drilling had gone perfectly, his head would still have been on a platter, for fleecing his stockholders." Riley blew out a plume of smoke. "It's not hard to work out. I don't know why people are so stupid. Michael was the head of a corporation. Corporations are meant to make money, just as scorpions are meant to sting. Why did the public turn on him after an accident, an honest accident, when they'd never complained before? It was a matter of public record that Peerless Petrol was drilling in the Gulf. Either people didn't care or they were all for it, as long as it reduced their family fuel bill without killing any seagulls. Or whatever else died out there that looks pitiful on camera when it's covered in crude oil."

Riley was warming to her subject, color heightening in her cheeks. "Go on," Bhar prompted her.

"Mind you, I'm not just pointing the finger at the UK. My country is no better. My own president said poor Michael should be sacked. Peerless's stock is as low as it's ever been. The fact is, Deepal, when I had my vision of Michael dying, I didn't consider it a portent of literal death. I assumed he'd lose his career, his entire life as he knew it, if I didn't step in." More smoke curled toward Bhar. "Who knows why I question my powers. They've never failed me before."

"So. After the vision," Bhar said. "How did you meet Mr. Hughes? Was there a mutual acquaintance?"

"Nope. No need when you have the universe on your side." Riley winked at him. "I happened to be in a funky little bar in Piccadilly called Catspaw. I ordered a dirty martini, got an olive between my teeth, turned around, and there he was—Michael Martin Hughes, fresh off the front page and the blogosphere, nursing a Jameson's and water like he didn't have a friend in the world. You think I'd let an opportunity like that pass?"

No, Bhar thought, scribbling in his notebook from habit, despite the tape recorder prominent on the table. *And I bet you made up that phony vision before you even shook hands.*

"I told him a little about myself, but I didn't have to say much." Smiling at Bhar, Riley held his gaze, batting her large green eyes. "We connected on the nonverbal plane right away, just like you and I did, Deepal. I didn't start by telling him who I was and what I'd foreseen. Just offered my sympathy. Told him how sorry I was about the political cartoons and all those statements out of context. He warmed up to me right away."

"I bet he did. Riley. I'm afraid I must ask. I understand Mr. Hughes was divorcing his wife, Thora. There are reports he had other, well, lady friends. Did those lady friends include you?"

Bhar expected another tantrum, a cigarette violently snuffed, a cupful of coffee splashed in his face. Instead, Riley preened, batting those eyes again as if finally receiving a long-awaited compliment.

"Gosh, Mr. Policeman. What do you think?"

"I think Mr. Hughes might have made a pass and gotten himself in trouble. Unless, of course, you were amenable." Bhar gave Riley his most winning smile.

"Damn right. And I was *amenable*, as you say, in that perfect British accent that drives all us American girls crazy."

"Was he already in the process of divorcing his wife?" Bhar strove to sound nonjudgmental, aware he might trigger another eruption. It had been at least a quarter hour since the last one, so surely the hot air was building up.

"Yes, Thora was served papers two years ago, but she's dragging it out. Told everyone she was still in love with him." Riley's laugh contained a vicious edge. "Let me tell you, if that was love, I don't want to see hate. Thora put Michael through hell, her and that son of his. Griffin. Griffin looks and behaves nothing like Michael. He's a carbon copy of Thora, which means neurotic, needy, and allergic to taking responsibility. I befriended him for awhile. Tried to help him self-actualize. It was a lost cause."

"I see. Given the nature of this investigation, I'm afraid it's routine to ask: did you ever hear Thora or Griffin speak to Mr. Hughes in a threatening manner?"

Another razor-sharp laugh. "Oh, Lord, yes. All the time. Thora was always screaming she ought to kill him. Griffin was always sending emails threatening to kill himself if Michael didn't hand over whatever he wanted. Money. A new car. Use of the summer house in Tuscany. You name it."

"Do you think Thora might have gone through with her threat?"

"No." Riley stabbed out her cigarette, replacing it instantly with a fresh one. Dutifully, Bhar lit it, and she continued. "Thora's all talk. I mean, if I were going to murder someone, I'd just do it, you know? No threats, no warnings, just boom!

Done. Oh, come on, don't widen your eyes like that." She blew smoke at DI Lindley's face. "If someone as spiritually evolved and respectful of all life as me has contemplated murder, I *know* a working stiff like you has."

"I've done it," Bhar said cheerfully. Then he remembered he was recording the session, and had just entered his declaration into evidence. Over the years, he'd threatened to kill DCI Vic Jackson several times, bragging that the crime would be perfect and the body never found. But this was the first time he'd virtually gone on record about it.

"So anyway, Thora's a non-starter," Riley went on, as if she'd assumed control of the interview. "Michael had tons of boardroom enemies and tennis court rivals and people in the press who would have liked to see him disappear. But I can't imagine any of those people would kill him. Not after seeing his body. It was hideous. Way past corporate revenge." Pausing as if reliving the scene, Riley shuddered. "No, if you want to make this case easier on yourself, go to the suspect who should be at the top of your list. Arianna Freemont."

Bhar jotted down the name. "Was she a friend? An employee?"

"Michael's head of PR. One of those cold British fishes with ice water in her veins and a refrigerator between her—oh, come on, lady, try to keep up!" Riley barked at DI Lindley. "I'm not insulting all English women. Just her. Go meet the ugly old popsicle and see if I'm not right. And mark my words." Riley turned back to Bhar. "Arianna will try and tell you she was Michael's fiancée, but don't you believe it. Michael and I were together. She was only his rebound fling after Thora. She just refused to accept it."

Bhar hoped his surge of interest didn't show in his face. "So. Mr. Hughes was divorcing Thora. He was engaged to his head of PR, yet also seeing you?"

"He was technically engaged to Arianna. She just hadn't given back the ring!" Groaning, Riley put down her cigarette and pinched the bridge of her nose. "Look. I'm beat. I really want to go home and cry, or get drunk, or both. Are we done here?"

"Yes, for now," Bhar said, resigned to Riley's sudden mood shifts. "Thank you for your cooperation. As a reminder—" He started to caution Riley not to attempt to leave the country, but she interrupted him once again.

"Deepal. Don't think I won't get to the bottom of this. I had that vision about Michael dying. Fate has drawn me into the center of this. I'm here because I'm meant to help you."

"Oh. Well. Thanks very much for that. I'm sure—"

"I mean, as soon as Michael settles down, as soon he accepts the transition and feels ready, I'll ask him."

Bhar felt like he'd lost the thread. "I'm sorry? You'll ask who what?"

"*Michael*," Riley said, pointing at a random spot on the ceiling. "I'll ask him who killed him. You'll arrest the bad guy. End of story."

***

The commute home made Bhar, who adored his Astra from a dating standpoint, think longingly of Kate with her Oyster card and her super-efficient Tube ride home. But if he ditched the Astra, what happened to all those cozy chats parked outside dance clubs and restaurants? Not to mention all those backseat makeout sessions. Yes, he was a little old for that sort of thing, but in the final analysis, he was a bloke who lived with his mum. The Met paid him well, but not nearly well enough to spend all his disposable cash on hotel rooms. In an era of joyless austerity, he needed that cash for trendy restaurants, bottles of champagne, and the occasional mini-break at a B & B. He wasn't the best looking chap on the planet, and when it came to romance, he certainly wasn't the luckiest, but Bhar knew how to maximize his appeal. The Astra added to that appeal, even if it burned hours of his life in traffic, forced him to pay London's congestion charge, and increased the size of his carbon footprint.

Of course, next to what Michael Martin Hughes and his company did to the environment, I look like a saint, Bhar thought, simultaneously thinking of the case and wondering if he should pop into Tesco for the usual—milk, eggs, bread. His mum did all the cooking, much of it traditional, but Bhar was expected to keep the pantry stocked. *I wonder if Riley was telling the truth about the degree of her relationship with Hughes. She did her best to paint both Thora and Arianna as crazy, but considering the source....*

His mobile chimed. The screen read KYLA SLOANE. Nowadays Bhar always checked before he answered, because he couldn't quite distinguish between Kyla's voice and that of her former best friend, Emmeline Wardle. And until one relationship kicked into overdrive and the other was kicked to the curb, well, he had to be sure he didn't overturn the proverbial apple cart.

"Paul. It's me. Hard day catching crooks?"

"No one can prove it wasn't. Actually, today was tough. Hear the news?"

"That oil guy who died under suspicious circumstances?"

"Exactly."

"During a posh to-do at Hotel Nonpareil?"

"Right." Bhar strove for a casual tone even as his naturally suspicious nature shifted into high gear.

Please don't ask, please don't know, please don't have occasion to know....

"I don't suppose Sir Duncan's still living there?"

"Yes. In the penthouse apartment."

"Oh." A moment's silence. "Does that mean he's a suspect?"

Bhar shut his eyes for so long, the Reliant Robin behind him honked, prompting him to accelerate through the intersection. "I can't talk about this, Kyla. You know that." He held himself back from adding, *You, more than anyone, know that.*

"Right. Sorry. Foot in mouth." Kyla tried to laugh, but the sound was much too forced. "Listen...."

"Hang on. Don't tell me you're getting cold feet about Saturday?" Bhar couldn't hide his disappointment. He'd bought tickets to an experimental dance troupe—just the sort of thing Kyla loved—and felt certain two hours of hell (for him) would be balanced by at least twenty minutes of heaven in the Astra's backseat.

"Of course not! Paranoid." This time her laugh was genuine. "I just... well. I hate to ring you up like this. And it's none of my business. But have you seen today's copy of the *Bright Star?*"

"Can't say I have. Why, did Daniel Craig punch out a paparazzi? Has one of the Kardashians given birth to a litter?"

"Oh. Yikes. I feel really awkward about this," Kyla said. "And my little sis is helping me make cookies and I need to get back. So, yeah. Check out the paper if you want to. If not, forget I said anything."

That cryptic phone call sealed Bhar's decision to navigate his neighborhood Tesco, open 24/7 and haunted by the hungry, the thirsty, and the inveterate timewasters. After choosing the usual milk, eggs, and bread—his mum didn't care if the label said "organic," but Bhar was convinced enough to usually spring for it—he found the red-topped *Bright Star* occupying pride of place on the newsstand. Despite efforts to curb the tabloid press after the *News of the World* phone hacking disgrace, *Bright Star* managed to deliver daily scandals, embarrassments, and celebrity tribulations without so much as a court-ordered apology. Either the tabloid was tightly edited, or it had enjoyed an amazing run of good luck.

The line was seven customers deep. Juggling his future purchases and the paper, Bhar managed to browse right to the middle, only to be stopped by the most unflattering full-color photo of DS Kate Wakefield he had ever seen. The headline screamed, THIS IS A BARONESS?

"Oh, no."

Chapter Nine

Detective Sergeant Kate Wakefield had worked for years to establish a home routine, which now unfolded like a play in which everyone knew their roles by heart. On arrival, she was greeted by Henry and the paid caregiver, Joslyn or Maggie or Sheeftah. Acknowledgement of the homework or test grade: Henry. Acknowledgement of any wrongdoing or broken items: Joslyn, Maggie, Sheeftah. Announcement of non-specific origin: Ritchie, who would draw attention to whatever was uppermost in his mind, be that a TV program, a Lego creation, ill-fitting underpants, or something he'd glimpsed out the window. No matter what it was, it was as important to Ritchie, Kate's mentally disabled elder brother, as recognition of homework was to Henry, her eight-year-old nephew.

After these niceties, Kate went to the cooker, praised whatever the caregiver was making for dinner (as Kate often told colleagues, she couldn't boil water without burning it), and retreated to her bedroom for five minutes of glorious peace. It took her less than two minutes to cast off her professional togs and change into "home clothes"—trackies, a T-shirt, and plush socks, her blonde hair pulled into a ponytail—and all the remaining time was hers alone. Three minutes before Ritchie started knocking or Henry started asking questions through the door or the caregiver announced the food was on the table. Three minutes of "Kate time" to check her phone, or flip through a magazine, or stare at the wall and think of nothing at all.

But the home routine was going away. And her south London flat was going away, due to be vacated in less than a month. Henry, unusually prescient for an eight-year-old, not to mention organized, had put the household on a moving schedule. And exceeding his timetable, had already transferred nearly everything he owned to his new bedroom in Hetheridge's London home, Wellegrave House.

"These sleepovers aren't enough for him. I think Henry's ready to move in, full stop," Kate told Hetheridge. She was already in bed; he was brushing his teeth in the master bedroom's *en suite* bath. "He's even tacked pictures on the walls. Superheroes. Some dinosaurs. A Jedi knight or two."

Smiling at her in the mirror, Hetheridge shifted from electric toothbrush to mouthwash. He always showered before bed, a habit Kate found remarkably civilized. If she ever had a daughter, she planned to advise that daughter to hold out for a man considerate enough to shower before the lights went out. Besides, she liked how he looked with his steel-gray hair combed back wet, a navy blue dressing gown tied round his waist.

"So. Moment of truth. If I said yes, could you handle it?" Kate asked, determined to push, though she wasn't quite sure if it were for Henry's peace of mind or her own. "An eight-year-old boy living here in the week or so before the wedding?"

"I don't see why not. Henry's not so difficult. Coming along with the fencing lessons, if a bit lazy about maintaining strict form. Doesn't break things or leave a mess. It's Ritchie I find rather more challenging. I hope that doesn't sound insensitive."

"Considering all the sensitivity training the Met has put

us through in the last few years, I don't blame you for being paranoid." Kate smiled at Hetheridge as he climbed into bed beside her. "But no, Ritchie takes some getting used to. The ceremony may unnerve him a bit. It's fifty-fifty on how he'll react to the honeymoon, much less the move. There could be some tantrums on the horizon. Thank you for understanding why I can't leave him behind. And if we're taking Ritchie on holiday, we really have to take Henry, too."

Hetheridge smiled. "Of course."

"And you know what? Ritchie likes you. He may never say it, but I can tell."

"Yesterday he asked me why I was so old."

Kate chuckled. "What did you tell him?"

"I said I had the misfortune to be born early." Hetheridge's delivery was deadpan, but his eyes twinkled. "It seemed to satisfy him. I thought he'd be more curious about the honeymoon details, or the wedding itself. In fact, I thought you'd be more curious about the wedding."

"Oh, Lord, no. I'm thrilled Lady Margaret has taken over. I don't want to go to cake tastings or flower shows or pick out music. I'd ruin the whole thing. What do the blokes say? Tell me what day and when to turn up. That's me all over."

"Kate." His sigh was affectionate. "It's your wedding. You can't ruin it."

"Of course I can. I don't know a prawn knife from a cake baster. The minute you and Lady Margaret put your heads together and told me you'd make all the arrangements, it was the biggest load off my mind. Just today, Sir Duncan proved to me I can't even be offered nibbles without making a spectacle of myself."

"Well, naturally, nothing I can say has any weight against the wisdom of Sir Duncan Godington. But let me repeat, in the strongest possible terms, Margaret and I didn't take over the wedding arrangements because we considered you incapable. It's just that… well." A touch of pink began creeping up his neck. "There are so many considerations that might not have occurred to you. You're in a rather atypical position, you see. So in the greater scheme of things... that is to say, with all things being equal...."

"Tony. You're dithering." Absurdly, Kate felt her original gratitude, which had been utterly sincere, transform into irritation. He and Lady Margaret must consider her the very model of graceless incompetence for Hetheridge to sound so defensive and look so guilty.

"Kate. Forgive me. I'm finding myself at a bit of a loss." He paused, transparently collecting his thoughts. "I know you wanted something simple. I did, too. But Royal Charter or no, the tabloids are as aggressive as ever. And when it comes to family, you might not be aware—"

Someone knocked at the bedroom room. It wasn't Ritchie's loud, arrhythmic "look at me!" knock, but the more furtive sound of someone who understood, at least in a vague sense, what he might be interrupting.

"Henry? What do you want?"

"Kate. Is this a bad time?"

Hetheridge coughed.

"You've picked better. Can it wait until morning?"

"I guess." Henry sounded doubtful. "It's just. Well. Mum's in the paper. And my grandmother. And you, too. Though you won't like the picture."

"Henry," Hetheridge called. "What sort of paper do you mean?"

"*Bright Star.* A boy at school was showing it around. I had to knock him down to make him stop. I wasn't going to tell you, but I don't think I can sleep until I do."

Rising, Hetheridge let Henry inside. "Bring it here. Spread it out on the bed so we can all see it."

The headline, THIS IS A BARONESS?, struck Kate first. Then she saw her picture, hugely enlarged. At that point, her recognition of human language failed, words devolving into mere squiggles as she gazed upon the horror.

The day it had been taken was obvious to Kate; that particular doorway and front step was someplace she'd never forget. The photo had been snapped during her first case as a member of Hetheridge's team. Her face was distorted with shock; she was mere seconds from vomiting. Already nauseous from what would turn out to be a miscarriage, Kate had heard gunfire inside the house. Believing Hetheridge dead, she'd collapsed as the press took pictures from every angle. Including this particular angle, which made her look not only ugly, but two stone heavier than she'd ever been in her life.

"That's my mum," Henry told Hetheridge, pointing to what appeared to be a very recent picture of Maura. She was tidied up, hair combed, makeup applied, but looking sad, as if the photographer had told her to think of a puppy shortage, or a ban on her favorite brand of crisps.

"And this is my grandmother," Henry continued. "I wouldn't have known it, of course, but that's what the story says. Assuming it's not wrong. They got lots of other stuff wrong."

"Oh my God." Kate said worse, a string of curses that tumbled out despite her efforts to curb all swearing around Henry. He was learning some beauts from her—handed down, in fact, from the very woman now pictured inside a council flat, looking old and sullen, as if the world had turned its back on her.

"I don't have enough to eat some days. My daughter Kate is going to be a lady, but she don't care about me no more," the white-haired, modestly dressed stranger was quoted beneath the picture. It seemed Kate's mum had readopted her legal name, Mrs. Louise Wakefield, and discarded her nickname, Lolo, which was known to everyone, including the coppers who regularly nicked her for petty theft and prostitution.

"Tony looks good," Henry said, as if that would help. The *Bright Star* had chosen to run Hetheridge's ten-year-old Scotland Yard portrait. Taken in full dress uniform, it featured an ill-conceived moustache he'd worn only briefly before shaving it off to unanimous applause.

"I look ridiculous." Hetheridge sighed. "And no matter

what I say or do, the papers will not stop running that picture."

"'Lord Anthony Hetheridge, never married, has no children, no pets, and not even an interesting vice, says a Scotland Yard insider. Still, he's too good for Kate, who's an utter slag,'" Henry read aloud. "See why I knocked that boy over? I had to!"

"Give me that." Picking up the tabloid, Kate forced herself to read it even as she struggled to regulate her breathing. The story was written in typical *Bright Star* style, simple declarative sentences with a limited vocabulary, nothing to intimidate the loyal readership.

Scotland Yard's in for a big wedding, and the mystery is, who is Kate Wakefield? And has the prospect of marrying up gone to her head?

As Sherlock Holmes once said, "the game's afoot," and big, buxom Kate knows a thing or two about being on the game. Her mum was jailed for prostitution, back in the day, and Kate herself banged up a few ladies of the night during her time on the beat. But Kate's a detective sergeant now, with an eye on moving up.

"She strolled into the Yard like she bought the place," said a source from within the Met that is close to Bright Star. *"Cheap and tatty as you please. Not much on the job but plenty of other assets. Tony never knew what hit him."*

"Tony" refers to Lord Anthony Hetheridge, ninth Baron Wellegrave, or as he's known around the Yard, Chief Superintendent Hetheridge. Called lonely and excessively private, Lord Hetheridge was quickly drawn in by the siren call of Kate, thirty years younger.

"Twenty-nine," Kate muttered. Why did it always go back to age?

Upon marriage, commoner Kate will be elevated to Baroness Hetheridge and entitled to a share of Lord Hetheridge's personal fortune, estimated at close to ten million pounds.

"Ten million?" Kate shrieked at Hetheridge.

"I do believe I told you."

"I do believe I'd remember!" Steeling herself for the worst, Kate returned to the article. As she suspected, it wasn't long in coming.

But some say cold, ambitious Kate has already forgotten where she came from. "I've spent the last few years in care due to my health," says older sis, Maura Wakefield. "I'm lucky to get a visit twice a year, or even a Christmas prezzie. Kate only cares about her career."

"I haven't heard from Kate in ages," says Mrs. Louise Wakefield, a pensioner who lives alone. "I wasn't the best mum, but I wasn't the worst, neither. And she was no angel growing up. You think she's at least be curious about her old mum, but I reckon she's moving in higher circles these days."

What a sad state of affairs! Looks aren't everything, but it seems in future baroness Kate Wakefield's case, ugly is as ugly does.

In a red box at the conclusion of the article, *Bright Star's* agony aunt, Cosmic Connie, weighed in with her own "therapeutic advice":

Sometimes young career women rush to leave their families behind in a vain attempt to better themselves. But the chickens always come home to roost. Kate needs to reconnect with her flesh and blood, in case she finds Lord Hetheridge's family isn't exactly waiting with open arms.

"Mum should have said you were taking care of me," Henry offered as Kate lowered the newspaper, struggling to hold back another torrent of profanity. "Hey! Maybe she said so, but the reporter didn't write it down! And my grandmother... you didn't know where she lived, did you?"

"Of course not," Kate snapped. Straightening her shoulders, she took a deep breath, passing the tabloid to Hetheridge and giving Henry a long, tight hug. "I wasn't even sure my mum was still alive, Henry, not till this moment, I swear it. I'm so sorry you had to read that. If your school calls because you knocked that boy down, I'll take care of it. But next time, don't bother fighting. Just walk away."

"Maybe the next article will be nicer."

Henry sounded so earnest, Kate's vision blurred. It was all she could do to get him out of the room and off to bed. When she closed the door and turned back to Hetheridge, her hands were trembling and her voice shook. "This is bad, Tony."

"It will pass. There's always some pop star misbehaving or some news of the royals, thank God. We'll never be under that sort of microscope, I promise. It was probably a slow news day for the paper."

"You don't get it. I knew you were comfortable, I knew you had some money...." Kate stopped, remembering Sir Duncan's rebuke from earlier. "Hell, I knew you were rich, at least for my world, but I never dreamed you were worth so much. Ten million pounds? I can't even imagine it. And now that Maura knows—now that Mum knows—you'll never have any peace. Maura will threaten to take Henry back, just for spite, even though she doesn't want him. They'll be pestering you for 'loans' morning, noon, and night. I knew this was a mistake." Angrily Kate pulled at the antique engagement ring on her left hand. "I knew I'd have to give this back!"

"Kate," Hetheridge thundered. "If you give me back that ring, I swear by God, I'll—"

She stopped, shocked out of her tears by the aristocratic whip crack of his voice. "You'll what?"

Hetheridge winced. "I'll... ask you politely to put it back on?"

Kate stared. Then, in spite of herself, she started to laugh. He laughed, too, and she didn't shake him off when he slid his arms around her.

"Tony, you don't understand these people," she whispered, pressing her face against the warmth of his neck. "You have no idea what they're like. I'm one of them, and sometimes even I can't believe what they are. Grasping, conniving, bone idle... every nasty joke about the dole ever made, every working class stereotype ever invented—"

"Kate! That's quite enough. They're your family. You didn't choose them, and you needn't be ashamed of them. Or yourself."

"You do realize they'll probably crash the wedding?" Kate added, fighting to keep her voice low lest Henry overhear. "Maura's been moved to a halfway house. That means she can get a day pass from her carers. She'll be at the wedding with bells on, embarrassing Henry to death. And Mum? She'll have her hand out. I'll bet my mobile's already crammed with messages, demanding dates and details. What am I supposed to tell them? If I lie, they'll just go on the internet and snoop until they find out...."

"Kate. Look at me."

Kate forced herself to obey, expecting to see guilt again, the same guilt she'd glimpsed when the discussion of wedding plans had put him at a loss. To her surprise, he looked far happier than he had any right to be, given the harassment his future now contained. Happier—and relieved.

"The wedding shall be lovely. You'll be pleased, I promise. In the meantime, if you find yourself confronted by your estranged family, tell them the truth. As you pointed out, there's no real way to conceal the basic details, not in the computer age. Otherwise, put the ceremony out of your mind. Let me and Margaret shoulder the burden."

Sighing, Kate let herself relax back into Hetheridge's embrace. "Honestly, Tony. I wasn't trying to put you on a guilt trip earlier. I'm overjoyed I'm not involved."

"Yes. Well. Perfect. I just don't want you to feel cheated if things are different than you envisioned. If there are, er. A few surprises."

"Surprises? You mean like armed guards?"

He kissed her. Not a consoling kiss, but a serious one, its invitation unmistakable. "Trust me," he said.

And Kate, despite lifelong misgivings on the topic, realized suddenly that she did.

Chapter Ten

As usual, Bhar was the last driver on his street to arrive home, meaning he was forced to park around the corner and walk a short distance. As he passed a neighbor's boxwood shrubbery, he heard what sounded like something large rustling on the other side. His response was automatic: shouting incoherently, he jumped aside, turning his ankle on the curb and falling into the street. From a lighted doorway came a whoop of laughter. And from behind the boxwood, a high, aggressive yapping.

"Hey, sorry about that, mate," the man called, still laughing. "You need a hand up? Mrs. Peacock got herself a Pomeranian is all. Ain't that perfect? Always thought she looked like one and now she has a mini-me."

"I'm fine," Bhar called, wincing as the effort to rise jarred his shoulder. Thank goodness Kate hadn't been around to see, or he'd never hear the end of it. True, he'd been thinking of the legendary Grim, remembering the black shape he'd glimpsed that morning and fearing it might leap out. He'd never liked large dogs much, especially not when they were off the lead and prowling about in the wee hours. But he'd also been remembering a certain knife, ice cold against his throat, then red hot inside his shoulder. Would the pain and fear always return when he was startled or alone? Surely any detective worth his salt—any *man* worth his salt—ought to be capable of putting the past behind him.

Except I've bungled it on the job twice now. First, I torpedoed Sir Duncan's trial. I don't care what the guv says, I know I did, and he knows it, too. Second, I let an ordinary bloke with no knowledge of hand-to-hand get the drop on me. Both times, I got caught up in the moment, forgot my training, and let something bad happen. Next time, will it get me killed? Or Kate? Or the guv?

Brushing himself off, Bhar waved at his across-the-street neighbor, and even made an effort to smile at the loathsome little Pomeranian, still yapping in frustration at the boxwood-iron fence barrier between them. The Grim, surely, was over-imaginative nonsense—he'd seen that particular Harry Potter movie too many times—but blokes with knives did pop out of the darkness sometimes, as anyone who'd ever watched the ten o'clock news knew. If he felt endangered, he needed to call upon his training and take control of the situation, not shriek like a howler monkey and fall on his backside.

I can let Kate give me a refresher in hand-to-hand. I can keep my gob shut during the Hughes case. And if Sir Duncan is guilty, if there's so much as a shred of evidence against him, I can redeem myself by putting him away forever, Bhar told himself as he walked up the steps to no. 18 Rushmore Road, the house he shared with his mother, Sharada. A single lamp burned in the parlor; otherwise, the house was dark. And coming home to a dark house was something Bhar, though in his mid-thirties, was still struggling to get used to.

It wasn't that he didn't support his mum's career as a romance novelist. Once he'd gotten over the "ick factor," the realization that his mother was, indeed, penning love stories of a highly detailed nature and strangers were, in fact, enjoying them, Bhar had begun taking pride in the notion his mum earned money doing something she loved. After his father's desertion and withdrawal of financial support—apparently it took everything Mr. Bhar earned to keep his mistress in the style to which she was accustomed—Bhar had feared he might never be able to move out. If he married, it had been assumed he would bring his bride home, to fight for a share in his mother's household as best she could. But the success of Sharada's romances, including *The Lordly Detective*, very loosely based on Hetheridge, *By His Hand Uplifted* (in which pseudo-Hetheridge married an obvious facsimile of Kate), and now *A Mystery Made in Heaven*, meant that Bhar could move out whenever he wanted.

And for the first time, he found himself wondering if he was ready to go.

As for Sharada, she'd ditched those internet author cronies who'd often left her in tears, not to mention angrily unfriending people *en masse*, and started her own group for new and aspiring romance authors. It met three times a week, sometimes in a coffee shop, sometimes in an Anglican church hall, inexplicably located miles away. Three times a week had sounded excessive to Bhar, but Sharada assured him it was necessary.

"These days it isn't enough to write the books. You have to hire an editor. A good editor, not some university twit," Sharada had informed her son. "You need a nice cover, and you need to market the book on the internet without losing your mind. Or bankrupting yourself on scams. Trust me, Deepal, we could meet every night and have things to talk about. Three nights is the minimum."

Sharada had seemed unusually intense, and Bhar, accustomed to letting his mum have her way whenever possible, hadn't dared argue, despite his concern about what he'd eat for dinner those nights. So much take-out was expensive, and he hated tinned soup or frozen blocks of what, judging from the ingredient label, seemed more "food-like" than food. Once, he turned ambitious and bought the materials for his mum's special stew, or what he could locate of such materials after a grueling day at the Yard. Instead of red potatoes, he'd gone with sweet; instead of cream of coconut, he'd tried condensed milk; purely by mistake, he'd grabbed candied ginger instead of grated. The result had been a disaster best never discussed, except as a warning to the untutored or the arrogant.

I wonder why Mum doesn't cook my dinner in advance before she leaves, he thought. *She seems so distracted. We were supposed to get a new cooker for the kitchen, but instead she bought two brand new dresses and all that skin cream.*

Staring into the refrigerator as if he could will hot, home-cooked Indian food to appear, a new possibility crossed his mind. *Is this what happens to women that makes them crazy? The change of life?*

He tried to reckon his mum's age, which was difficult since she refused to reveal her year of birth. Then he briefly considered Googling the usual range for menopause, before deciding the topic was too unsettling to pursue. There were certain things he didn't want his mum looking into, mostly pertaining to his sex life, and when it came to the natural rhythms of her hormones, ovulation, and so forth… no. Just— no.

His mobile chimed. Thinking it was Kyla calling back to ask his reaction to the tabloid, Bhar nearly answered with, "Kyla." Fortunately, he remembered to check the screen before he spoke, and saw the caller was E. WARDLE.

"Hey." He did his best to sound casual. Emmeline, blonde, blue-eyed and rather intimidatingly pretty, was the type who hated obvious effort from males. In fact, she liked to take the lead. In contrast, her former friend Kyla, a delicate brunette, always seemed diffident, waiting for Bhar to make any move of a passionate nature. On balance, Bhar preferred Emmeline's decisive streak. In fact, he sometimes thought it was her best quality.

"Paul. What are you up to?"

"Starving. Wondering if I should bother finding some dinner, or go to bed hungry and hope for a big brekkie in the morning."

"Oh, boo-hoo. You should be glad your mum's doing

the book club, or whatever it is. I'm dying to get out from under mum and dad's thumb. It's like a prison camp in here." Her voice took on that teasing edge that always made him grin. "You up for some fun?"

"What kind of fun?"

She gave a huff of displeasure. "You know, there's playing it cool and there's coming off like a tosser. You're verging more on tosser at present."

"Sorry. Just—" He actually started to say, 'thinking about the Hughes case,' and cursed himself inwardly. Mr. Gobshite, about to strike again, spilling details to people who had no right to know, all to make himself seem more interesting. "Just worried about my mum. These days, she's letting everything slide. I don't think she's vacuumed in at least a week. I can see lint on the parlor carpet. That's never happened before. What's your opinion? About the thing that comes along and makes women crazy?"

"You mean men?" Emmeline laughed.

"No, this is my mum I'm talking about. I meant the change of life. Or, you know, one of those diseases where you need pills to keep your brain focused."

"Well, seeing as I've never met your mom, since apparently I've yet to pass that exalted level of security screening," Emmeline said with a hint of displeasure, "I guess I'd have to go with, figure it out yourself. Now. I've already had dinner. Want to take me out for drinks or not?"

"Perfect. I'll pop round in half an hour?"

"Fine. I'll try not to hold my breath." Emmeline disconnected.

***

After the previous morning's emergency visit to Muswell Hill, Bhar practically burst into song to discover Mrs. Snell back at her post. Not to mention a complete breakfast spread, including porridge, poached eggs, fried kidneys, bacon, black pudding, and beans on toast. It had been a musical morning.

He'd spent his shower whistling, hummed along with satellite radio on the way to Scotland Yard, and started whistling again the moment that deliriously decadent scent registered. As expected, Emmeline hadn't allowed him time to gobble down a late dinner at a gastro-pub. She'd insisted on hitting a nightclub straightaway. But as Bhar hoped, their night out ended on the best possible note, thanks to the Astra. So he arrived in Hetheridge's office still starving, yet not inconvenienced in the least.

"Oh, Lord. What do you have to be so happy about?" Kate asked. "Did Mummy swear off the book club?"

"It's a writer's club. And no. She has my full support. Good morning, Mrs. Snell," Bhar called. "Thank you, my lady, for this wonderful repast." Bowing deeply from the waist, he ignored her look of withering disapproval and began loading his plate.

"Oh, no." Kate, face as yet devoid of makeup and hair messier than usual, massaged her temples with both hands. "Which one was it? Frick or Frack?"

"I don't know what you mean. I hope"—Bhar popped a piece of bacon in this mouth and spoke around it—"you don't expect me to kiss and tell."

"No, you have way too much class for that," Kate said dryly, allowing him time to chew and swallow. "All right. I'm betting Frack. Little Miss Kyla, led astray but technically innocent."

"Oh. Jealous much? Did someone take their eyes off the bride for two minutes? Kyla doesn't deserve your snark. She's very sweet."

"I knew it."

"But you're wrong," Bhar grinned, putting his plate on Hetheridge's desk and shaking a white linen napkin into his lap. Kate, apparently still dieting for her final wedding gown fitting, was having nothing but dry toast and coffee. Cruelly, Bhar sliced his black pudding in front of her, eating a huge piece before continuing. "It was Emmeline. There's a very strong attraction between us, thank you very much, and I'm only human."

Kate shrugged. "Good for you. One thing about Emmeline, you always know where you stand with her. Personally, I'm glad you gave Kyla the boot."

"The boot?" Bhar scoffed. "What are you on about? We're all adults, the three of us, and no one's said the word 'exclusive.' I'm taking Kyla out on the town this Saturday. Who knows what might happen? Monday morning, I may come in singing opera."

"Oh, Paul. Come on." Kate covered her mouth to stifle her amusement.

"Meaning?"

"Meaning you're not man enough for two women."

"What's that?" As usual, Hetheridge entered already at full steam, since he typically arrived at the office long before Kate or Bhar. Even when Kate and the boys spent the night at Wellegrave House, she stayed behind to coax Ritchie out of bed, pack Henry's lunch, check over his homework, and see him off to school. Hetheridge, by contrast, never deviated from his routine unless genuinely ill, which happened to him about as often as it did to Mrs. Snell.

"I'm sorry, guv, but Kate reckons you're not man enough for two women," Bhar said.

"Is that so?" Hetheridge waited until his administrative assistant stalked out with a sniff of disgust, then gave Bhar a wink. "That's where you're wrong. Now. Paul. Kate. As much as I enjoy this sort of banter—which is to say, in limited quantity—I'd like us to share impressions of the Hughes case, informally, before we submit our reports to the Incident Room."

Sinking into his well-worn leather office chair the way other men might ease into a hot bath, Hetheridge pushed back, balancing on two legs as he regarded his subordinates. Bhar had seen the guv do this many, many times, and yet he never stopped hoping, deep in the boyish recesses of his heart, that Hetheridge might one day lose his balance and topple over. As far as he knew, it had never happened. But surely Bhar couldn't be the only one at the Yard secretly awaiting a tell-tale crash.

"Yesterday," Hetheridge continued, "I toured Hughes's accommodations, which certainly supported his vilification in the press as a modern-day Marie Antoinette. I saw his corpse, as did Paul. Although we await the formal report, murder is the only credible assumption, and strychnine is almost certainly the method. It appears Mr. Hughes let someone into his suite, then drank poisoned whiskey. That makes the likelihood of a stranger virtually nil. As there is a CCTV camera pointed at Suite 800, one might hope for a break in that direction, but the feed was misdirected. And after a tedious exchange with the head of security, Mr. Junkett, I have little confidence the correct footage will be retrievable."

Swiveling his computer monitor so Bhar and Kate could see while continuing their breakfast, Hetheridge said, "Here's Junkett's file from his time with the Met. Twice reprimanded; once for mishandling evidence, once for insubordination. Passed over for promotion. There was a letter attached, but since redacted. He left the force to pursue a career in the private sector, briefly ran his own security firm, and then signed on with Hotel Nonpareil."

"No smoking gun?" Kate asked.

"Afraid not. I've emailed his final commanding officer and hope to speak with her soon. In the meantime, I found Junkett's manner sometimes cloying, sometimes brittle. He overreached his authority at the crime scene, as I have noted in my report, and may have compromised the entire investigation. To discover the crucial CCTV footage has also been diverted—missing or destroyed, more likely—troubles me."

"Meaning?" Bhar popped the last bit of black pudding in his mouth.

"Meaning we have no reason to bring Mr. Junkett back at this moment, or to formally name him a person of interest. Still, I've asked a very distinguished profiler to review his record and tell me if Junkett is likely to commit a crime, or help cover one up, purely for the thrill of being included in the investigation. The loss of that camera footage is unforgivable."

"True. But not necessarily his fault, at least through malicious intent," Kate said. "He's a bit of a moron. I could see a hacker running circles around him, someone in IT who Junkett got high and mighty with. Besides, there's bound to be hours and hours of footage from other hotel cameras. The first thing is to review the gala itself," she said brightly. "Discover who Mr. Hughes left with."

"I say. What an idea." Hetheridge's tone was light.

"Tony."

"Kate."

"Don't make fun of me. You know my brain doesn't fully engage until I get my makeup on. Who'd you assign to review the film?"

"DI Kelly, not five minutes before I entered this room. It's quite a task. There are four cameras in the ballroom. The gala lasted over five hours, and no one is sure when, precisely, Mr. Hughes said goodnight or who remained behind. DI Kelly will watch the footage raw, then enhanced if necessary, and ring us up the instant she can identify who Hughes left with. Of course, he may have exited the gala alone, in which case there are scores of other CCTV cameras to review. Several PCs shall be assigned the task this afternoon. The usual thing, to be thorough, of course. But if the gala's four cameras offer us nothing helpful, DI Kelly will be asked to go over the secondary camera footage as well."

Hetheridge leaned forward, putting his chair back on all four legs. "Now, as to the crime scene itself, there wasn't much to see, apart from the kitchen. Though the SOCOs swabbed and photographed every inch, so there's no harm in praying Forensics solves the case for us, just as they do on Sky TV." Hetheridge smiled. "After poisoning Hughes' drink, it appears the killer settled himself, or herself, on a barstool to watch the extraordinarily grotesque manner of Mr. Hughes's passing at close range."

Bhar groaned. "Three words: Sir. Duncan. Godington. He's an environmentalist, a psychopath, and a sadist. That amounts to motive and method. Plus he lives at Hotel Nonpareil. Giving him opportunity."

"Not so fast," Kate said. "Don't you remember—"

She stopped as if she'd blurted out something awful. Bhar went cold, guessing her point before she said it.

"Er, sorry. I mean to say, I remember it well. Going to visit Tessa," Kate said. Bhar found her effort to speak coolly, in a professional manner that implied nothing, particularly excruciating. "When we told her about the ax murders, the first thing Tessa asked about the victims was, 'What did they do to him?' She seemed confused by the idea Sir Duncan was accused of committing an impersonal crime."

"Yes." Bhar tried not to sound hostile, but it was impossible. How could Kate have imagined, even for one thoughtless moment, he didn't recall every word Tessa had said? He'd loved her once. And still dreamed about her sometimes, as she'd been before the murder, before the descent into madness.

"She also said Sir Duncan learned something in Borneo. A ritual about bathing in the blood of his enemies," Kate went on. "Tessa said when he commits a crime, there's always blood. This method—rat poison—goes against everything we know about Sir Duncan."

"Maybe he decided to change things up," Bhar said. "Maybe he thought about it for two minutes and figured, right, I'll pick a new method and those imbeciles at Scotland Yard will never look my way!"

"I talked to him yesterday. Lady Isabel was there as well. Sir Duncan's difficult to read, but I didn't get the impression—"

"Oh, please, Kate, he's a master manipulator," Bhar cut across her, pulse singing in his ears. "What, did he charm you again? Waltz you around the penthouse? Promise to speak up for you at parties and make sure all the best people invite you to their fêtes?"

"You little—"

"And here, once again," Hetheridge said in a tone that

brought Bhar up short. "We slide from useful debate into utter nonsense. Which I could better tolerate if the entire world were not watching this murder investigation, eager for results. What's worse, we're under strict scrutiny, not only from Assistant Commissioner Deaver and above, but from Downing Street. The first memo I opened this morning suggested, given my advanced age and upcoming nuptials, I might be too 'distracted' to handle an investigation of this size without significant help. Meaning, it should be passed on to someone younger."

"Are you kidding?" Bhar and Kate swapped glances. "They actually said you were too old to handle the case?"

"They implied it, actually." Hetheridge smiled. "Specifically, the memo said I seemed tired. Nowadays, 'tired' is a euphemism for old. But it named my upcoming wedding as a specific concern. Especially in light of this."

Minimizing Junkett's Met record, Hetheridge navigated to *Bright Star's* homepage. Like the printed tabloid, it was garish and easy to read, with big color photos, enormous headlines, and stories of just a few paragraphs. Bhar expected him to click on **THIS IS A BARONESS?** but instead, Hetheridge selected, **PAGING SHERLOCK HOLMES!**

Yesterday, Bright Star *was the first to inform readers about Scotland Yard's big wedding between Lord Anthony Hetheridge, sixty, and commoner Kate Wakefield, thirty-one. Naturally,* Bright Star *wishes them all the best. But insiders at the Yard confide that since Hetheridge popped the question to blonde bombshell Kate, his reputation as a detective has gone off a cliff. With an elderly bridegroom heading up the case, will Michael Martin Hughes's killer ever be found?*

"It all started when he got Kate assigned to his team," said a Met source close to Bright Star. *"He stopped caring about the job. No more perfect record! He was even thrown off a case for threatening a witness."*

"Oh, my God," Kate said. "That source is Vic Jackson. It's got to be."

"Notice they don't say the witness was your ex." Bhar sighed. "Or you'd just found out she'd hidden your daughter for twenty years."

"Keep reading," Hetheridge said.

Bright Star *has learned that the Chelsea ax murders, covered extensively in this paper, might have gone unprosecuted, thanks to Lord Hetheridge's negligence and poor judgment.*

"With Hetheridge, it's all about who kisses arse," the police source revealed. "He was told to keep Detective Sergeant Deepal Bhar away from anything to do with Sir Duncan Godington. But that would have meant replacing a crony with a competent officer, and Hetheridge wouldn't do that. He was too busy taking Kate to society balls and putting a big diamond ring on her finger. Compensating for something, I reckon."

"It was one ball! And we were working a murder case! As for 'compensating' … I'm gonna punch Vic's lights out." Kate sounded like she meant it.

"Never mind that." Hetheridge tapped the next paragraph. "This is what troubles me. Because—forgive me, Paul—it's true. And though past is past, this is the worst possible time for such an episode to be revived in the press."

Bhar fought hard to show no emotion. What followed was a breathless recap of Sir Duncan's triple murder trial. As always, Bhar was painted as the goat who escaped his rightful punishment, back on the Hughes case to derail it, too.

"I hate to speak ill of a colleague," the source informed **Bright Star,** *"but Bhar's one of those bunglers kept on in the name of diversity. No white bloke with his record would have lasted this long. I hope the powers that be will wake up and reassign the Hughes case before it's too late. Otherwise, a killer might remain at large because Lord Hetheridge cares more about his future trophy wife than his job."*

"Don't marinate in it," Hetheridge said, closing the webpage when Bhar and Kate continued to stare. "I've been attacked in the press before. Alas—this is the first time the top brass has seemed to listen. Odd, since the case is only twenty-four hours old. I told Mrs. Snell I'd made enemies over the years, and they'd be coming for my head. I just thought they'd wait until after the wedding."

"I have an answer. Take me off the case," Bhar blurted.

"Me, too." Kate lifted her chin. "They can't talk about you this way. It isn't fair!"

"No, it's not. But that doesn't mean I should jettison my team, or let some scandal rag effect my professional judgment. We have nothing to apologize for. Not on the Comfrey case, the double ax murder, or the Hughes case." Hetheridge's gaze was serious, but his voice was reassuringly calm. "All I ask is that you work with all possible haste, yet all possible care. As for me? As the Americans say, this is not my first rodeo. Have faith I shall ride it out. Now. Paul. Speaking of Americans, I'd very much like to hear your considered opinion of Riley Castanet."

Chapter Eleven

"My considered opinion? Here goes. She's a nutter."
Kate sniggered. She liked Bhar no matter what, even when he became oversensitive on two topics that never failed to push his buttons, Sir Duncan Godington and his ex-girlfriend, Tessa. Laughing at the right moment was an easy way to let him know everything was okay, without delving into a discussion about emotions, something neither of them was particularly good at.

"Did Riley really say she was a horse in people-skin?"

"A horse having a human experience? Hah! That's the least of what she said." Pushing his plate away, Bhar threw his napkin on top of it. "Of course, being mental doesn't preclude her from being a person of interest. She claims to have been in the midst of a torrid love affair with Hughes. According to her, they met in a bar. He said he was divorcing his wife, Thora, whom Riley described as an absolute nightmare."

"What a shock," Kate said.

"I know. Anyway, sometime during that first meeting, Riley told Hughes she'd foreseen his death. Meaning he needed her professional services as a seer to avoid his fate."

"She told you that?"

"Proudly."

Kate gave a low whistle.

"In fact, I've captured it all on tape for your listening pleasure." Bhar grinned. "Riley claimed she saw Hughes crucified by the press, like a modern-day Jesus. *But* she interpreted his death in her vision as figurative, not literal. Then she followed up with some nonsense about wondering why she ever doubted her infallible powers. Even offered to interview Hughes from the Great Beyond, once he gets all comfy, so she can ask him whodunit, and close the case herself."

"Jeez, Paul, you get all the good ones," Kate moaned. "I had to eat Digestives from Junkett's grubby paw and listen to Sir Duncan speak French to me. He claimed he was describing nibbles, but it could have been half a dozen dirty come-ons, for all I knew."

"Speaking of come-ons, Riley claimed she and Hughes were an item," Bhar said. "Only problem is, Arianna Freemont is down as his official fiancée. Even Riley admitted Arianna has a ring on her finger, though she claims Hughes broke it off and Arianna was simply in denial."

Kate snorted. "What do you want to bet Riley was the one in denial?"

"It's possible one woman was misinformed. It's also possible Hughes was lying to them both. Either way, a love triangle is promising indeed," Hetheridge said thoughtfully. "Kate, I'd like you to interview Arianna Freemont. Try to get a sense of her as one 'engaged lady' to another. Perhaps wear— you know."

Withdrawing the magnificent engagement ring from her purse, Kate slid it onto her finger, turning her hand back and forth to make the gems flash. Something about the proprietary gleam in Hetheridge's eyes pleased her no end.

"Paul, I'd like you to investigate Thora and Griffin Hughes," Hetheridge continued. "No matter how eager he might have been to finalize the divorce, the fact is, Hughes died whilst still married to Thora. It will take a few days for us to become privy to the details of his will, but in the meantime, I'd like impressions. Not to mention Thora and Griffin's version of how each spent the last night of Hughes's life."

"Sure, we can go that route." Bhar shot a mischievous look at Kate. "Or I can just ring up Riley and see if she's grilled Hughes's ghost yet."

"I'm actually quite looking forward to a transcript of that conversation." Hetheridge rose. "Paul, would you mind giving me a moment alone with Kate?"

"Oh, I see what's going on." Bhar waggled his eyebrows. "Want me to lure Mrs. Snell away from her desk with smoldering looks and sweet words? Give her a shot at her own personal slumdog millionaire?"

"That won't be necessary."

"Shall I shut the door behind me? Hang a sock on it?"

"Good-bye."

Chuckling, Bhar pulled the door closed. Kate walked around the desk, smiling as Hetheridge took her hands. Neither felt free to behave this way at the Yard if someone was watching, even if that someone was Bhar.

"I should have asked you this last night, but we had too many other concerns," Hetheridge said. "And I see no reason to get Paul's blood up when he's already so keen at a second chance to convict Sir Duncan. But what's your true impression there? Are we wasting our time again?"

To Kate's surprise, she started to answer in the affirmative. But why? Hadn't Sir Duncan casually, in that endlessly provocative manner of his, admitted to wanting Hughes dead? Was the baronet so charming, so unexpectedly supportive in his own arch way, she sought to eliminate him purely because of emotion? And not just any emotion, but one uncomfortably akin to admiration?

"He's Sir Duncan. I think we have to include him as a person of interest until forensic evidence or old-fashioned detective work eliminates him. With him, going on gut instinct is too dangerous."

"Noted. But what is your gut instinct?"

Kate tightened her grip on Hetheridge's hands. "I almost... well, like him. And that bothers me a lot."

"I can't say I approve, I either." Hetheridge's smile disappeared. "What was that about him plying you with what could have been French come-ons?"

"Oh, he was trying to make a point. That when I'm Lady Hetheridge, even a simple offer of nibbles will be a test of good breeding, or the lack thereof. That the upper class will smile in my face while doing their level best to slag me off."

"I hope you told him you were forged in the Met's fire, thank you very much, and can navigate complex hierarchies with your eyes closed. As for the possibility he threw in a few inappropriate suggestions...." Hetheridge shook his head. "I can't help thinking he's genuinely attracted to you, Kate. And if he is, I'll be forced to call him out."

Startled, Kate let out a nervous laugh. Judging from what could only be called an un-Hetheridge-like scowl, mirth was the wrong response.

"You think I won't?"

"I think you'll knock his bleedin' block off," she said, slipping momentarily into the dialect of her childhood. "Mind you, he might break into your house and carve you up for Christmas lunch, like he apparently did with dear old dad. He's a dangerous man."

"Of course. But you'll find any lawman on the job as long as I've been is dangerous in his own right. And unlike Paul, should I ever decide to commit the perfect murder, I'll never be tempted to brag about it."

Kate kissed him, taking her time, grateful the office door was shut. "That, I believe."

***

Getting in to see Arianna Freemont took all of Kate's power as a Detective Sergeant, plus a lengthy discussion of her credentials with Arianna's bodyguard, an ex-Ukrainian soldier called Mykhailo, plus a phone call from Hetheridge, who resorted to what Kate privately called "the full baron" to get his point across.

"You will be respectful?" Mykhailo asked Kate as he punched in the security code that would allow her access into Arianna's Shepherd's Bush home.

"Of course."

"See that you are." Mykhailo, tall and bony with a shaved head and a face as rocky as the Carpathians, pushed open the door for Kate and held it. "Ms. Freemont is a good woman. Whatever the police intend for her, she doesn't deserve it."

Arianna Freemont's home looked like something out of a magazine ten to fifteen years past: a "gracious home," as American TV programs called such living spaces, that twentyish Kate had envied right down to her marrow. Instead of wallpaper, there was paint, a cross between oatmeal and honey, the perfect welcoming color for a living room. Indeed, the term "parlor" seemed altogether wrong for this space, given its wall-mounted telly, beige Berber carpet, and lack of ostentatious bookshelves or knickknacks. None of the clutter Kate accepted as part of her own unglamorous life—Ritchie's Legos, Henry's action figures, discarded carpet slippers, empty juice boxes or piles of soiled clothes—intruded here. The room even smelled perfect, not cloying as if doused with air freshener but delicately fragrant, authentic. The mass of yellow and orange chrysanthemums, situated in the middle of the coffee table in a polished silver bowl, were not mere silk.

"Before we start, I want you to know I consider this an unforgivable intrusion," Arianna Freemont told Kate by way of introduction. A petite woman, no more than five feet tall in low heels, Arianna was pretty in a cool, unencouraging way, like a blind date who'd resolved to be polite but nothing more. Her thick dark hair had the look of a curly mop chemically straightened into submission; her makeup was tasteful, highlighting her features without attempting to enhance them. Arianna's blouse was ivory silk; her skirt, which fell just below her knee according to the standard of mature professional women throughout the western world, was navy blue linen. On the third finger of her left hand, a diamond solitaire winked at Kate. Two carats set in platinum, if Kate was any judge.

"Well, then, before we start, I'd like to apologize for the necessity of this interview." Kate didn't mind beginning with an apology. In fact, she often did, whether the subject seemed genuinely bereaved or not. "My name's Detective Sergeant Kate Wakefield. I'm with Scotland Yard." Despite the fact her credentials had been verified thrice over, Kate flashed her warrant card from long habit. "I'm charged with uncovering what happened to Michael Martin Hughes. The circumstances in which he died. And if there was foul play, which appears to be the case, I need to know why anyone might wish him harm."

Arianna's face remained expressionless, but her voice was edged with anger. "Watch television, Sergeant Wakefield? Read newspapers?"

"Both, from time to time. Mr. Hughes wasn't popular after the oil spill in the Gulf. But unpopularity doesn't always result in murder. Look at Bernie Madoff. O.J. Simpson. The Octomom. Most people get away with unpopularity. Even the rotten tomatoes thrown at them are figurative."

"True. Please. Sit down." Arianna remained stiffly at attention, as if this was the military and she was being subjected to some unspoken inspection. "May I offer you tea?"

Ordinarily, Kate would have said yes, just to grease the social wheels. But in this case, she felt the opposite response was called for. That Arianna was in pain, real pain, and the mention of tea was a dodge, her attempt to flee the scene and compose herself before something was inadvertently revealed.

"No, thank you." Kate eased down onto the sofa, upholstered in warm brown herringbone fabric and perfectly stuffed, not too firm and not too soft. What sort of planning went into a piece of furniture like this? What sort of testing was required to arrive at the perfect marriage of pliability and strength?

Whatever it takes, it's made by people without a Ritchie or Henry in their lives, and selected by the child-free, Kate thought. *Wouldn't last six months in my flat before it collapsed in the middle and wound up on the curb for the binmen to carry off. Oh, Tony. I hope you aren't too attached to your heirloom furniture.*

Arianna seated herself on the wingback opposite Kate. That is to say, Arianna perched at the cushion's edge, knees and ankles firmly pressed together, back ramrod-stiff. Her expression was correct, not hostile but almost blank. It rang a distant bell in Kate's memory.

"Since I didn't say so explicitly, please accept my condolences on the loss of Mr. Hughes. Investigations always entail what may feel like prying or outright snooping, yet the accumulation of details, many quite personal, often result in a conviction. And thus, closure for the victims' families," Kate said, using a speech she had lifted word for word from Hetheridge. "I understand you worked for Peerless Petrol's PR department?"

"I am head of PR." Arianna's voice was carefully measured, nearly as blank as her face.

"I also understand you were engaged to Mr. Hughes?"

"Yes."

"If I may share a personal detail, I'm also recently engaged." The revelation sounded clunky. All her life, Kate had found it more difficult to chat with females than males; "girl talk" was excruciating for her. Nevertheless, Kate forged on, deliberately flashing her ring as she pulled out her smartphone to take notes. "I can't imagine how hard it must be for you, to have lost Mr. Hughes when your wedding was... how far off?"

"We'd set no date."

Kate forced a smile. This was worse than her usual attempts at female bonding. This was like interviewing a robot.

"I suppose it might have been incorrect to announce one, since your fiancé was finalizing his divorce to Thora Hughes."

Arianna just stared back at her.

"Now I'm going to ask some basic questions. Please don't be offended if some are of a personal nature." Kate was so unnerved by Arianna's impenetrable blankness, she hit the wrong button on her smartphone. Backtracking to locate her email program, she asked, "How and when did you meet Mr. Hughes?"

"At work. He hired me almost two years ago."

Look up examples of PP ad campaigns. How does a woman so stiff and emotionless greenlight successful adverts? Kate sent herself.

"Was there an immediate attraction?"

"No."

Kate beamed that false smile again. "Any particular reason?"

"I was hired at Peerless to do a job. Not find a husband."

Kate decided to say nothing and see what happened. After almost thirty excruciating seconds, Arianna volunteered a second reason.

"Besides, Michael was married."

"How long ago did circumstances change?"

Arianna shifted the tiniest bit. "Last Christmas. He split from Thora and moved into the family's London townhouse. Soon after, he asked me out, and our relationship grew from that point."

"When did he ask you to marry him?"

"On Valentine's Day."

"That was, er, remarkably fast." Kate struggled to achieve half the blandness Arianna projected so effortlessly. "Were you impatient for Mr. Hughes to divorce Thora?"

A flash of reaction in Arianna's large brown eyes, swiftly concealed. When she replied, her tone was as controlled as ever. "No."

"Did you feel there was any danger of a reconciliation between Mr. Hughes and his wife?"

"I wouldn't call it danger."

"Meaning?"

"Meaning Michael was a free man. He could stay with me, or he could return to Thora. I preferred the former, yet I wouldn't call the latter a 'danger.'"

That bell rang in Kate's head again, louder this time. In childhood, a few of Kate's classmates had sat rigidly like Arianna, simultaneously on guard yet expressionless, aware that drawing attention from the wrong authority figure might be catastrophic. Danger, for children from a certain kind of home, didn't mean a lost boyfriend or social humiliation. It meant blood, broken bones, and grotesque violations many adults preferred never to see.

"I assume you know Riley Castanet?"

"Of course."

"She told my colleague she was Mr. Hughes's personal assistant."

"No."

"What was she, then?" Kate asked.

"She did his horoscopes. Dream analysis. Something called Reiki therapy, which I know nothing about. It was all meant to help Michael cope with the stress of the oil spill."

"Ms. Freemont, Ms. Castanet has asserted she was engaged to Mr. Hughes. That he had broken off his attachment to you and planned to announce his upcoming marriage to her around the time of his death."

"No." Arianna's expression didn't waver, nor was there a note of surprise in her voice.

She knows something about Riley. She was braced for the question, Kate sent to herself.

"Can you speculate as to why Ms. Castanet would tell the police such blatant lies?"

"She's a liar. Some people are." Arianna's gaze traveled to the impeccable Berber carpet.

Kate put her phone aside. Sometimes the only way to reach another person was to gamble. After all she'd overcome in her life, why was she still so afraid of other women, their coolness, their frequent cliquishness? Most people found

Ritchie intimidating, yet she had broken through to him many times, usually by throwing caution to the wind.

"Ms. Freemont, I'm going to be upfront with you. The way Mr. Hughes died, not only the poison itself but certain other details, suggests the killer enjoyed his or her actions. That can mean simple, garden-variety sadism. It can also indicate a thirst for personal revenge. All of my questions go toward one point. Did someone you know want to harm him? Can something you witnessed lead me to his killer?"

Many interviewees would have balked right away. Wincing or tearing up, they would have complained Kate had no right to share such distressing details, to drive home the agonizing manner of Hughes's death. Pink lips pressed together stoically, Arianna only nodded.

"Do you think Riley Castanet had any legitimate reason to believe Mr. Hughes cared for her?" Kate persisted. "That he might marry her?"

"They had an affair. Slept together once or twice," Arianna said.

"This was while he was still married to Thora, and engaged to you?"

"Yes."

"How did you find out?"

"Michael told me. We didn't share everything. I don't care what anyone says, I don't believe two adults ever do. But he told me what I needed to know, and I did the same. His dalliance with Riley was a non-issue to me. Michael strayed. All men do, whether they admit it or not. That's just a fact of life. But I suppose Riley might have become fixated as a result."

"I see." Kate, who did not believe for a moment that all men cheated—or that any trait under the sun was universal—refrained from saying so. "How did she behave toward you?"

"Like a disturbed person. I never knew if it was because she's a spiritual practitioner, or simply because she's an American."

Kate bit back a laugh. "Did she ever seem to turn on Mr. Hughes? Threaten him?"

"No."

"There's a story that she foresaw his death. Did he confide as much to you?"

"No."

"Very well." Kate picked up her phone again, feeling more confident. Arianna's tone and answers had scarcely changed, but Kate thought she detected a faint warmth in the other woman's eyes. "What's your impression of Thora Hughes?"

Arianna considered the question for much longer than should have been necessary. "She was too much in privilege, for too long. As wonderful as it sounds, I think growing up with everything you want, not to mention everything you need, doesn't prepare you for the real world. Thora's family is the most supportive clan you can imagine. They've fought from time to time, but when push comes to shove, they'd literally die for one another. When Thora married Michael, she expected the same level of devotion. When they grew apart and he filed for divorce, it seemed to cripple her. Talking to Thora is like talking to the walking wounded."

And so is talking to you, Kate thought. *The scar we consider invisible is the first thing others notice about us.*

"Ms. Freemont, do you think Thora would have harmed Mr. Hughes? Or hired someone to harm him?"

"Thora? Kill Michael herself? Never. Would she hire someone?" Arianna thought for a moment. "Only in fantasies. Physical pain and death aren't real to someone like her. Seeing the fantasy through to the end would be trial enough. Now, Griffin…."

Kate looked up. "Hughes's son? What about him?"

Arianna's gaze retreated to the carpet. "I don't know. I have no children. Until Michael proposed, I expected to live out my life alone. And yet… I wonder about Griffin."

"Why?"

"Because Michael gave up on him a long time ago. Don't get me wrong. Michael never lifted a hand against his son. Barely raised his voice. But the lack of love was obvious, even to me, Sergeant Wakefield." Arianna gave a little laugh. "And heaven knows I'm no expert on love. But when a young man has too much coddling from his mother, not to mention her family, and open contempt from his father, it makes me think of tornadoes. Do you know about tornados?"

Kate waited.

"They result when hot, wet weather collides with a cold, dry front," Arianna said. "Then they spin round, destroying everything in their path. That's Griffin. If he didn't kill his father, I'd like to know who did."

Chapter Twelve

Thora and Griffin Hughes lived in Belgravia, a London neighborhood Detective Sergeant Paul Bhar had become very familiar with during his time on Hetheridge's team. Designed in the 1820s and originally called Belgrave Square, the original plan had featured several terraced houses, some detached mansions, and a central green intended only for residents. But time had marched on, the proud imperialism of the Victorian Era replaced with the grim necessities of the Second World War. When KEEP CALM AND CARRY ON was a government imperative, not an internet meme, British tanks had parked in Belgravia; in the present day, numerous foreign embassies called the area home. Nevertheless, certain genteel English families still resided in converted Victorian homes, including the estranged wife and son of Michael Martin Hughes.

As a uniformed maid opened the door, a middle-aged woman with bobbed white hair appeared behind the servant, dismissing her with a nod.

"Oh, you must be Sergeant Bhar! So glad you've come to help. It's a sad time for our family, very sad indeed, but we have every confidence in Scotland Yard. No doubt you'll get to the bottom of poor Michael's death in a jiffy!"

"Er, absolutely," Bhar muttered, forcing himself to return the woman's smile, as wide and white as a toothpaste advert. He was accustomed to being met on doorsteps with clenched teeth and preemptive threats, not a blanket statement of confidence in the Metropolitan Police Service. "And you are...?"

"Bonnie Venicombe. Thora's mum." The woman shook Bhar's outstretched hand by taking it in both of hers. The practiced meet-and-greet gesture, along with the memorable surname, told him at once who she was.

"Venicombe. Your husband's in the government, isn't he? Some sort of minister?"

"Yes. Alastair's the Secretary of State for Environment, Food, and Rural Affairs," Bonnie agreed. "A bit of a scrape for him, you know, the environmental grand poohbah being father-in-law to Michael. But family comes first, and Alastair stood by him. What's politics without the occasional drubbing? Do come in."

Bhar followed Bonnie into a cramped, dark hall that led directly into a small, equally dim parlor. Most Victorian properties had been converted by the 1960s, but this house seemed preserved to an unusual degree. The burgundy wallpaper was patterned with white cabbage roses. An electric fire rested on the hearth, but it looked at least fifty years old, and the ceramic tiles around the mantle harkened straight back to Charles Dickens. Something about the room's chaise lounge, covered in plastic to protect what had to be vintage velvet cushions, and the faded India rug with its numerous tobacco burns, finished the connection in Bhar's mind between "Alastair Venicombe" and parliament.

"Oh," he said aloud, only to be met with Bonnie's wide, questioning look. Once again, his mouth had boldly gone where the rest of him, upon reflection, preferred not to tread.

"Sorry." He gave her the innocent smile he usually reserved for his mum. "I just realized your husband, er. Well. Lost a general election about ten years back. Time flies, eh?"

"Yes, it does. And I fear the campaign proved a slightly disappointing experience for him," Bonnie said, taking the art of British understatement to new heights. "Look, here's a framed photo of Alastair with Mrs. Margaret Thatcher. Don't they look lovely together? The baroness was a true lady. Never a hair out of place, I can tell you. Oh, how I envied that iron coiffure."

Bhar nodded politely, wondering how a man like Venicombe, who once famously opined that "So long as the sun revolves around the earth, I shall continue to speak out against moral decay," had managed to reinvent himself as a minister for, among other things, the environment. During his ill-fated campaign for the nation's highest elected office, Venicombe had made little headway, except to provide fodder for sketch comedy and standup comedians. His slogan, "The Benefits Culture Benefits None of Us," had proven to be only that, a slogan, with no real plan behind it for specific reforms or alternatives. During the campaign, Bhar had written Venicombe off as a relic of an earlier era, when puffing cigars in the right company and slapping the proper backs invariably led to high office. Unfortunately for Venicombe, who, with his comb-over, stooped shoulders, and bright red cheeks, certainly looked the part of a PM, those physical characteristics weren't enough to reassure voters who'd heard him speak on, as it turned out, anything.

Giving the portrait of her husband beside Margaret Thatcher a final beam of pride, Bonnie said, "I expect you'll be wanting Thora now. Shall I bring down Griffin as well, or will you talk to them separately?"

"Separately, please."

"Very well. Sergeant Bhar, I know you have a job to do. And I have no doubt you'll perform it with the utmost discretion and delicacy. But may I ask a personal favor?"

He nodded, unwilling to answer in the affirmative, for fear Bonnie might try and hold him to it. Either the woman was naturally affectionate and encouraging, or during the course of her husband's political career, she'd become adept at setting out honey to catch flies.

"Be gentle with Griffin. He's having a hard time coming to terms with it."

"I'll do my best. How old is he?" Bhar withdrew his notebook. In the course of an ordinary investigation, the Met's researchers filled in the gaps, emailing him long biographical statements composed from the public record. This included, at the very least, date of birth, educational details, and any prominent connections, like a grandfather who'd humiliated himself on the national political stage. But with a plethora of hotel guests and gala attendees to sort through, the researchers were running far behind, and Bhar had yet to receive any information on Thora or Griffin.

Yet Downing Street has the nerve to lean on the guv for near-instantaneous results? All on the strength of a tabloid rag?

"Griffin's nineteen," Bonnie answered. "But young for his age, and fragile. He wasn't ready to lose his father." Placing one hand on Bhar's shoulder and the other on his upper arm, she leaned so close, he felt her breath on his earlobe. "Griffin was quite ill as a child, and it set him back. We don't like to draw attention to it."

"I see. Thanks for letting me know." Bhar extricated himself as politely as possible. Despite Bonnie's unusual cordiality, he found himself eager to escape her presence. Aggressive friendliness worried him more than outright hostility. "May I sit down?" he asked, realizing the sofa and both chairs looked as old as the chaise lounge, and both were covered with the same zippered plastic.

"Anywhere you like. I'll fetch Thora, and ring for tea."

***

There were Vikings somewhere in Thora Hughes's family tree; her first name, which Bhar recognized as a female variant of the Norse thunder god, had been well-chosen. Over five foot ten, with a strong brow, deep-set eyes, and high cheekbones, Thora was pale, with hazel eyes and long hair the color of straw. A smattering of faint freckles covered her nose, throat, and arms. Though she must have been forty, she looked ten years younger, especially in a shapeless floral maxidress, her features distorted from weeping.

"Mrs. Hughes, I'm so sorry to disturb you at this time," Bhar said, rising as she entered the parlor.

"I don't suppose you've come to tell me who murdered my husband?"

"No, I'm afraid not. This is just a preliminary interview as the investigation gets underway. I apologize if the questions seem intrusive, but—"

"There are cameras all over that hotel," Thora snapped, digging in the pocket of her dress for a wadded up tissue. "There are security officers. I should know, they treated me and Griffin like criminals! Michael's suite had cameras and a panic button. Poor Griffin went there to talk to him, and Michael wouldn't even open the door. He threatened to use that panic button on his own son! How did the killer break in, murder Michael and slip away?"

"I'm afraid I can't share every detail of the case," Bhar said. "Please, won't you sit down? Your mother promised to bring tea."

"I don't want tea." Thora sounded like a petulant schoolgirl. "I want Michael back. I want our life together back. This is so unfair."

"Of course it is." Bhar sat down again, wincing as the plastic squeaked beneath him. "Mrs. Hughes, we're working to create an accurate picture of your husband's final hours. That means we need to know who was close to him. I understand the two of you were married for about twenty years?"

"Yes."

"Griffin is your only child?"

Thora nodded, dabbing at her eyes with the tissue.

"I'm afraid there's a story that you and Mr. Hughes were separated. That he'd served you with divorce papers."

"Oh, yes, but these things happen, Sergeant Bhar," Bonnie declared, sweeping into the parlor with a large silver tray in her hands. "Even in the best of families, they happen. It doesn't mean reconciliation wasn't imminent. Alastair had a private chat with Michael not a month ago, and let me tell you, certain issues are best dealt with man to man. Everyone makes mistakes, especially powerful men under stress. Sometimes in the course of a marriage, a separation becomes necessary. Alastair and I married young, and we had our trials, too. But that doesn't mean divorce is inevitable. Ring up Michael's solicitor if you need confirmation the divorce was on hold."

"Oh, mum, he isn't going to do that." Sniffing, Thora mopped her nose with the tissue's fragile remains. She seemed to be in a state of ongoing misery, neither openly sobbing nor quite composed. "The details of our marriage don't matter to the police."

"Of course they do. Everything matters. That's how investigations work." Shooting a glance at Bhar, Bonnie shook her head slightly and mouthed something like, 'Poor dear,' as she placed the tray on the coffee table. "Now, then, Missy, all your favorite things. Don't embarrass me in front of this smart young detective by turning up your nose. Tea, Sergeant Bhar?"

"Yes, please."

"Milk and sugar?"

"Just milk." Accepting an elegantly patterned bone-china tea cup, Bhar held it up for examination. "Violets and heather—my mum would fall in love with this service. Is it antique?"

"Of course." Bonnie smiled. "Only the best for my Thora and the gentleman from Scotland Yard."

"I'd rather have Horlicks." Thora stared resentfully at the tray.

"Horlicks is for bedtime, dearest. How else will you sleep?"

"There is such a thing as Ambien, Mum."

Bonnie laughed as if that were the wittiest remark in the world. "Cook was busy with a special project, so I didn't trouble her for fancy sandwiches. Still, there are ladyfingers, custard tarts, and shortbread. Sergeant Bhar?"

"Shortbread," he said, watching Thora. Her pale face had grown redder, hands shaking as if she verged on explosion.

"And you, dear?" Bonnie asked Thora.

"I've already told you. I want Michael back. Can you give him to me, Mum? Can you?"

"No, sweetheart, but here's what I can do. Pass me that sodden tissue. Yes, I insist. Take these." Pulling fresh tissues from her pocket, Bonnie passed them to her daughter, closing her fist around the horrid original. "Now! Isn't that better!"

Thora sniffed and dabbed her nose, although Bhar had begun to suspect the redness was from constant touching, not constant crying. "I want to talk to the policeman alone."

"Of course. Anything to help you, dear. Of course." Beaming from Thora to Bhar and back again, Bonnie backed slowly out of the parlor, closing the door behind her.

Grateful for the teacup and shortbread, both of which gave him something to do with his hands, Bhar sought to resuscitate the interview. "Perhaps it would be easier if we take a few steps back. Can you tell me, Mrs. Hughes, how you met your husband?"

Thora rolled her eyes.

"Fair enough. I can see how that might seem frivolous," Bhar said. "Let's skip to the days or weeks before his death. Certain witnesses have claimed that this was a contentious time for you and your husband. According to statements recorded before witnesses, Mr. Hughes didn't want you or Griffin to attend Peerless Petrol's gala at Hotel Nonpareil. I was told he rowed with the hotel's chief of security, Bob Junkett, when you and your son booked a room on site. Is this true?"

Thora reached for Bhar's leather notebook, which he'd placed on the coffee table. When he made a startled noise, she shook her head rapidly. Flipping the pad to a fresh page, she used his pen to scrawl a sentence, passing the notebook back to him.

My mother is listening at the door.

Bhar stared. "Why?" he mouthed.

Thora gestured for him to return the notebook, taking far longer to write the reply, as if the act were physically difficult.

Because she wants me to say Griffin can't be guilty.

Bhar took a moment to absorb the statement. That morning he'd spent most of his commute ensconced in a delicious fantasy where Sir Duncan was convicted and he, Detective Sergeant Deepal Bhar, was lauded for single-handedly putting a serial killer away for life. Now, hearing something utterly unexpected, he pushed aside his private desires and focused on his job.

Did he do it? Bhar wrote back, returning the notebook to Thora.

"I hope not," Thora whispered, leaning across the silver tea service and speaking so quietly, Bhar was certain no one lurking outside the parlor could hear. "But Griffin doesn't confide in me. He tells Mum, or he tells no one. Can't you arrest me? Take me someplace private where we can talk?"

"I won't arrest you." Bhar was startled by the suggestion. "Are you sure you can't leave the house for awhile? Your mum seems obliging enough."

"She's a straitjacket," Thora whispered back. "Cut me loose or send me back to the padded room."

Chapter Thirteen

Tony!" Lady Margaret Hughes beamed as her Jamaican-born housekeeper, Kalisa, escorted him into her parlor, which her favorite nephew, an interior designer, had recently redone. This time, the theme was retro, harkening back to the late 1960s: pendant lampshades that seemed formed out of stiff macramé, orange shag carpet, chrome fixtures, and vinyl-upholstered furniture. Even the 70-inch flat screen TV had been wall-mounted within a frame that resembled a wood-paneled console, complete with huge speakers and a three-channel dial.

"I've gone back in time," Lady Margaret added, laughing. "Oh, my dear Tony. Such a face. You don't approve."

"I don't approve," Kalisa said. "This isn't interior design. This is taking the mickey."

"Yes, thank you, Kalisa, I noted your reaction when the carpet was fitted." Lady Margaret's gray hair looked freshly shorn, standing out on her skull in what Englishmen called a number six and Americans called a buzz cut. Her clothes were softer, a long taupe tunic with matching leggings and slippers.

Though something of an expert in the world of fashion, Lady Margaret never wore anything that wasn't loose, wrinkle-free, and comfortable.

"I happen to think burnt supernova is a perfectly lovely color," Lady Margaret continued. "None of the neighbors have it, and isn't that half the point?"

"None of the neighbors want it," Kalisa said. "Lord Hetheridge isn't the only one who curled a lip. Ms. Vivian told me—"

"Never mind what she said. If Ms. Vivian told you once, she told me ten times, I assure you," Lady Margaret interrupted Kalisa. "It's nearly three o'clock, Tony. What would you like? Tea, or something stronger?"

Hetheridge, who'd missed lunch due to a lengthy conversation with Bob Junkett's former supervisor, didn't think alcohol was a wise choice. "Tea, please. With sandwiches, if you can manage, Kalisa."

"I can manage." The housekeeper shrugged. "But after you're married, I hope you turn up properly fed."

"I could hire better help," Lady Margaret stage-whispered as Kalisa departed for the kitchen. "But I despair of finding better commentary."

"You won't hear me complain. I keep a notebook of Harvey's pithy observations," Hetheridge said. "Someday I'll publish them to international acclaim. But tell me. How are you?"

"You mean with regards to the wedding? I have it very much in hand." Grinning wickedly, Lady Margaret settled herself on a wingback chair upholstered in bright orange vinyl with faux-wood accents. "Do you know, I actually had lunch with Victoria Beckham?"

"Indeed. Did you call her a stick insect to her face?"

"Certainly not. She's come a long way from shrieking onstage in her knickers. Quite the businessperson, these days. Kate Middleton considered Victoria's wedding gown designs, which is no small recommendation. I thought your Kate should appear interested as well." Lady Margaret, always frank, didn't mince around the obvious segue. "Kalisa showed me that libelous article about Kate in *Bright Star*. I spoke to an old friend. Next week they'll run a puff piece, three pages long and in full color, speculating on the wedding and every glorious high society detail. They'll be sending a photographer to take appropriate pictures of Kate, to erase the memory of that ghastly one."

"That's a start. Thank you."

"To do any less would be inconsistent with my role as Goddess of Everything. What about you, Tony? Care to become the subject of an admiring career retrospective? All your past triumphs, offered up for public adoration?"

"Certainly not."

"Too proud?"

"Perhaps. If nothing but a planted article in a tabloid can save my career, I don't want it anymore."

"Perhaps not." Lady Margaret sighed. "Tell me, how did Kate handle the accusations from those dreadful relatives of hers?"

"She was beside herself." Ordinarily Hetheridge would not have shared Kate's private response with anyone, but he'd trusted Lady Margaret for decades. "Nearly pitched the ring in my face."

Lady Margaret chuckled. "Say it, Tony."

"You were right."

"Don't I know it." She lifted her chin. "The ceremony will go off exactly as planned, I promise. And if Kate in any way dislikes the result... well. You can blame me. From the safe distance of your honeymoon, of course."

"Of course." He smiled. "Mind you, I wasn't actually inquiring after the wedding plans. Just about you. On a personal level."

Lady Margaret's eyes reduced to mere slits. "Why?"

"No reason. I simply heard—never mind. I don't know what I heard." He quailed under Lady Margaret's sharp sapphire gaze.

"I am accustomed to you coming to me for society gossip. Not attempting to produce it for my dubious pleasure. Have things changed? Has my universe turned upside down?"

"Not at all."

"I'd prefer it if you wanted help with that petrol CEO's murder. I enjoy thinking of myself as Scotland Yard's unpaid, unsung, secret weapon."

"Well, as a matter of fact…."

"Perfect. May I also assume your paramount question is in regard to your daughter, Jules?"

Hetheridge sighed. "We may as well go there first. Hotel Nonpareil had so many guests that evening. Thankfully, Jules wasn't invited to Peerless Petrol's gala. Nor did she crash it, according to current data, which is far from complete. But yes, I saw my daughter's name on the hotel guest list, and it worried me. My team is very busy, so I decided to handle the initial concern myself."

"Not surprising. Though some might call it a conflict of interest."

"Only if her presence proves significant."

"Ah, but will you be trusted to decide what is coincidental and what is not?" Lady Margaret winked. "I suppose that's between you and your superiors. By the way, I hear the girl has traded 'Jules Comfrey' for 'Jules Hetheridge.'"

"Given the circumstances, especially regarding her mother, one can hardly blame her. She asked me beforehand, for whatever that's worth. Sent an email asking my permission. Which I gave, freely."

"Oh, an email. The epitome of class."

"Her generation is different."

"Perhaps, but her general sort is perfectly familiar to me, now or forty years back. Tony, I do hope you and Kate intend to have a child as soon as possible. Otherwise, given the changes to certain laws of succession, I fear an opportunistic creature like Jules may hire a smart young lawyer to challenge all comers for the barony. Including the son or daughter you and Kate may yet produce."

Hetheridge shrugged.

"That's not an answer."

"As a man who never expected to *produce* children, as you put it, and who was inured to the prospect of Roddy inheriting the title, I must admit I've lived my life without giving the issue much thought. I suppose I'll need to bring it up to Kate. Since she's almost certain to outlive me, I'd like her to have a cordial relationship with my heir, whomever that person proves to be." He smiled as Kalisa returned bearing a perfectly hideous vintage tea service: a brown thermos-shaped pot surrounded by squatty little cups and saucers bearing a pseudo-space age pattern.

"The tea of the future. But served in the actual future. Which makes this a tea of speculation that fell wide of the mark, thank you, Jesus." Kalisa poured Hetheridge a cup. "Lord Hetheridge, I have a theory. The artist who created this set? A charlatan. The punter who bought it the first time round? Colorblind. But the person who bought it the second time around, in hopes of making a fashion statement? There's a word for that one. Right on the tip of my tongue...."

"Petit fours. Just the thing." Hetheridge selected two pastel-colored cakes. "I adore these. My compliments, Kalisa."

"Marks & Spenser will be glad to hear it. I'll ring them up with the good news." Shaking her head, Kalisa departed.

"As regards the look of this service," Lady Margaret said, adding lemon to her tea. "I fear Kalisa is right, though it would never do to acknowledge such a victory. I begin to doubt my nephew. In the early days, I let him turn my home into a showplace because I thought he had real talent. Now I suspect he's phoning it in or deliberately choosing the ugliest themes he can, to test me for dementia."

Hetheridge laughed. "You? Senile?"

"Sometimes I wonder." Lady Margaret's eyes met his. "Tell me. Do you feel mad, changing your life so radically? Marrying Kate and telling the world to go hell, no matter how you've dashed its expectations?"

"I feel alive," Hetheridge said honestly. "I wish... well. I wish every dear friend of mine would take the same chance, if it meant feeling the same way."

"Hm." She sipped at her tea. "You're utterly transparent."

"Would you prefer I conceal my thoughts?"

Lady Margaret gave one of her harsh laughs. "No. And for the record, the gossip you've heard is quite true. Vivian has left her husband. Told her children about herself. 'Come out,' as they say, with all fanfare. Now it's up to me. Join her in the harsh light of public scrutiny, or risk losing her after more than thirty-two years together."

"Oh?" Hetheridge kept his voice light. "I'd only heard Vivian was conspiring with Kalisa to get your house redecorated, posthaste."

"I wish. Maybe I don't want to come out." Lady Margaret contemplated her tea cup. "Maybe I like my privacy. Maybe I prefer to remain a terrifying old woman with no skeletons in her closet, brokering the secrets of others. It used to be, all this public spewing of one's inner life was nothing but behaving badly. You kept quiet, kept your chin up, and kept on."

Hetheridge polished off a petit four before replying. "Bugger."

"Oh, how elegant." Lady Margaret laughed. "Do you mean to say, cowardice doesn't become me? Now that Vivian's made her choice—now that her husband can finally marry his mistress and Vivian's children, each well past the age of eighteen, can wish her well—I ought to swallow my fears and go along?"

"I meant what I said. Bugger. Now. Forgive me for steering the conversation back to my daughter," Hetheridge said, well aware his old friend desired nothing more than a change of subject. "But communication between the two of us is strained at best. Jules blames me for arresting her former lover, Kevin, who has since moved on to greener pastures. She also blames me for being an absentee father, despite the fact we learned of one another's existence barely three months ago. In short, she blames me. But Hotel Nonpareil's records show that, upon check-in, Jules asked for two electronic room keys. The second one, given to heaven knows who, was used to enter her room eight times in the last ten days. My first question: why has Jules taken up residence at a hotel, when she has more than sufficient income to rent a flat? My second question: whom did she entertain in her room?"

"Oh, Tony, you do sound like an old-fashioned father. I'm surprised you haven't pored over the hotel's CCTV footage."

"I have subordinates doing it now. In the meantime, I'd appreciate greater insight from you, Margaret, if you possess it."

"I do." Selecting a white petit four with a red rose on top, she took a dainty bite, scowled, and set it aside. "Promise not to panic?"

"No." The tea and cakes settled in Hetheridge's stomach like a lead balloon. He barely knew Jules, and liked her no more than she liked him. Yet his physical response was no less automatic than it was startling.

"Well. Here goes, old sport, so brace yourself. It appears Jules has taken up with Lady Isabel Bartlow. Not to mention her infamous brother, Sir Duncan Godington."

It took Hetheridge a moment to push the word out. "What?"

"I don't know who arranged the introduction, or why. But you know Sir Duncan. He always has a coterie of young friends, willing and eager to do his bidding. Word is, Jules is the latest hanger-on."

For the first time in longer than Hetheridge could remember, he was angry at Lady Margaret. "And it only occurred to you to tell me this *now?*"

"I heard just two days ago. I was trying to decide if calling to inform you would be an intrusion or a kindness, given how little you and Jules-formerly-Comfrey-now-Hetheridge have had to do with one another up until this moment. And suddenly Michael Martin Hughes was dead, everyone in Hotel Nonpareil was being questioned, and there was no point in striking because the iron, as they say, was no longer hot."

Hetheridge pondered the idea until he was fully under control. He forced himself to take a sip of tea before saying, "I fear Sir Duncan has taken an interest in Kate. Now this, the notion he's also befriended Jules...."

Lady Margaret said nothing, but her gaze over the teacup told Hetheridge she comprehended him perfectly.

"I don't tend toward paranoia. Or needless pessimism. But Sir Duncan's friendliness toward Kate and this apparent interest in Jules, when taken together, point to one thing."

"But Tony. Why would he fixate on you? You had little to do with his first trial. As a matter of fact, it was the foolishness of a certain overconfident young man under your protection who sealed Sir Duncan's freedom."

"Perhaps it's what I represent? I'm about the age of his father. Or I would be, if Sir Duncan hadn't hacked him up with a machete." Replacing his cup in the saucer, Hetheridge rose. "Please thank Kalisa again for me. I'm off to interview Jules."

Chapter Fourteen

"Chief Inspector Hetheridge, how wonderful to see you again." Hotel Nonpareil's manager, Leo Makepeace, stumbled over the phrase like a condemned man blowing his final words in a rush to get to the noose. "I don't suppose you h-h-have any findings to report?"

"No findings as yet." Hetheridge gazed benevolently at Makepeace, careful not to smile. A smile might spook him. "Tell me, have you remembered anything which might be of significance? Come across any information, perhaps seemingly benign, which now strikes you as worth mentioning?"

Makepeace's watery eyes shone. He wanted to say something; he was visibly gathering the courage to speak.

"Anything you say will be held in strictest confidence," Hetheridge added. "Unless and until an arrest is made, of course. In which case you would have the full weight of the Met on your side. We could speak in your office."

Nodding, Makepeace fumbled in his jacket. His key ring was suspended on an oversized string and bead talisman Hetheridge recognized, after a brief consideration, as a dreamcatcher.

"I've seen those." He followed the truth with a plausible lie. "In fact, I've seen Riley Castanet with a dreamcatcher."

"She's wonderful." Makepeace's enthusiasm sounded sincere. "I never spoke to her till yesterday, and it's like she's already taken me under her wing. Last night, she did a past life session with me. Turns out I used to be a bank robber. In the American West. With guns and a mask and a fast horse. Can you believe that?"

Another lie was unavoidable. "Of course. We all have a little larceny in our souls."

"Yes, sir, indeed we do." Straightening his shoulders and lifting his chin, Makepeace seemed cheered by Hetheridge's declaration. "Come in. Forgive the mess. Riley said my clutter is rather like the protective coloration of an insect clinging to a tree."

"No predator is likely to pick you out in all this." Hetheridge looked around the office. Makepeace's books were haphazardly shelved. His desk was stacked with files, folders, overflowing binders, and reams of loose papers. Some were typed, some were handwritten, and others appeared photocopied. Half buried in the midst of all this was a computer. Judging from the paper tsunami around it, the PC's digital storage capabilities must have been largely untapped.

"Please, sit down. May I offer you some tea?"

"No, thank you. I'm due upstairs in just five minutes. Now, Mr. Makepeace. What would you like to tell me?"

"Well. I'm sure it's nothing. And I'd hate to bother you with nonsense. I can't imagine how much time and energy, to say nothing of money, the Met must lavish on silly remarks and observations that ultimately lead nowhere. I wouldn't want—"

"Mr. Makepeace. I assure you. Whatever you wish to say, I want to hear."

"Well." Makepeace sat down at his desk, half-obscured behind his towering piles. "I know the head of security, Mr. Junkett, confessed a certain problem to you. A CCTV camera with a misdirected feed. A feed directed, not to Mr. Hughes' suite, but to the, er, Gorilla Kingdom of the London Zoo."

Hetheridge nodded.

"It just so happens, the hotel employed an IT expert called Steve Zhao. Seemingly nice young man. Always wore trainers and jeans, even to our fancy dress Christmas party. I didn't hold it against him," Makepeace added, with a twist of the mouth suggesting he did. "Anyway, Steve and Bob Junkett didn't get on. Bob cautioned Steve just three days ago for tardiness, and Steve resigned on the spot. I believe his resignation letter, if you can call it that, may be germane to the case. Here!" Digging into one of his many piles, Makepeace seized a handwritten note, placing it triumphantly before Hetheridge.

"I can't be certain," Hetheridge said after a moment's perusal. "But this appears to be someone's takeaway lunch order."

"What?" Flustered, Makepeace patted himself down until he located a pair of reading glasses. Peering through them, he read what he'd handed Hetheridge and moaned. "Sorry. That's Steve's handwriting, though. Big and overbearing, like he deserves twice the paper of a normal man." Two more forays into the piles on his desk, which Makepeace seemed to understand the way a rabbit knows its warren, finally produced the correct piece of paper, written in the same sprawling hand.

BOB,

YOU CAN'T SACK ME, I QUIT. THE LOVELY LADIES OF GORILLA KINGDOM ARE LOOKING FOR A STUD LIKE YOU. HOW ABOUT SOME VIDEO DATING WITH YOUR OWN KIND?

SZ

Hetheridge used his mobile to snap a picture. "This note isn't dated. When did you receive it?"

"The day Steve quit. Three days ago, just hours before Peerless Petrol had its gala."

"Did you make note of his resignation through the usual channels? A log entry? An email? Something dated?"

Makepeace wrung his hands. "I'm sure I must have."

"Were there any witnesses to Mr. Zhao's resignation?"

"Of course. Me. And Bob Junkett. Shall I call Bob in to corroborate?"

Hetheridge glanced at his Rolex. "No. Thank you, I must be going. May I take custody of this letter, Mr. Makepeace? I'd like to enter it into evidence."

"Of course."

Removing a small evidence bag from his inner coat pocket, Hetheridge tucked the handwritten note inside. He didn't know if it was authentic or not. Nor did he know if Junkett had played some role in the note's discovery, which absolved him of a devastating security failure, placing it at the feet of a disgruntled ex-employee. But Hetheridge *did* know that after Makepeace watched him take charge of Steve Zhao's resignation letter, the little man seemed calmer and happier than he'd been since the murder. And that, in itself, signified something.

***

"Oh. Hello. Come in." Jules opened the door of Hotel Nonpareil's suite 508, stepping back to permit Hetheridge entry. "This must be weird for you."

It was, but he shook his head automatically, offering a bland smile. He'd been reared never to draw attention to socially awkward moments, especially not when playing host. But if his ex-lover, Madge Comfrey, had imparted such social rules to her only daughter, Jules seemed not to have learned. Or perhaps the world had changed so much, at least among twentysomethings, that the done thing nowadays was to fearlessly acknowledge discomfort head-on.

"Sit down. Do you want a drink?" Jules giggled. She had recently turned twenty-one, but looked no more than seventeen, whip-slim with blonde hair, recently shorn in a pixie, and ice blue eyes. It was the only physical characteristic they shared. "Am I allowed to offer you a drink while you're on duty?"

"I can't think of anything I'd like more. I don't suppose you have whiskey?"

"No. I have lager. Cider. And vodka."

"Vodka. Neat, please."

"Coming right up." Jules's top, a pink kurta with silver threadwork, and her skirt, long and ruffled, reminded Hetheridge of Riley Castanet. When he'd met Jules, she'd favored skinny jeans, Converse trainers, and baby T-shirts that clung to her angular frame. Now she seemed to affect more of a hippie look, complete with bare feet and woven bracelets around each ankle.

"If you don't mind my asking," Hetheridge said, seating himself on the leather sofa as Jules went to the drinks trolley, "what's the attraction of living at Hotel Nonpareil instead of taking a flat of your own?"

"Great furniture. Concierge. Valet. Room service. A nice bar if I feel stir crazy. Oh, and maid service every day." Jules poured him a double. "I'll get my own place eventually, after I've had time to really look. There's a housing shortage in London, you know."

"I had no idea every strata of society was affected." Hetheridge tried not to sound too arch.

"The best flats go only to the rich," Jules said, pouring one finger over ice and drowning the mixture in tonic. "And by certain people's standards, you and I aren't rich. Barely comfortable, as a matter of fact."

"Would 'certain people' include Lady Isabel Bartlow? Or Sir Duncan Godington?"

He expected Jules to splutter, but she grinned. "Is that why you're here? So I can give Scotland Yard the lowdown on Sir Duncan's movements?"

"If you have something to tell me, please continue." It was exhausting, trying to decide what look or tone was appropriate with this girl. He'd never held her in his arms as an infant, never witnessed her childhood milestones, never dealt with episodes of teenage rebellion. Of course, it was quite unlikely her father of record, Malcolm Comfrey, had been any

better, not through ignorance but by choice. Leaving Jules
both contemptuous of fatherly overtures and transparently
desperate to receive them.

"I barely know Sir Duncan." Jules dropped on the sofa's
opposite end, a pile of throw pillows rising between them.
"I've been around him once or twice, but we've hardly spoken.
I think he's shy of gawkers. People who just want to know him
because he might be a murderer."

Shy? Sir Duncan?

There was nothing polite he could say to that, so
Hetheridge tasted his drink. "Thank you for this."

"Vodka, neat. Not even I could botch that up." Jules set
her glass on the table. "Are you excited about the wedding?"

"Yes, of course."

"What's it like, getting married for the first time at—
what? Sixty-five?"

"Sixty," Hetheridge corrected, stung.

"Fair enough. What's it like?"

"Well. It's wonderful. Yes. Perfectly wonderful. And
you? How is it for you, now, living on your own, after—erm.
All that happened?"

"Well. It's wonderful." Jules flashed a smile that didn't
touch her eyes.

Hetheridge had another sip of his drink. Jules tasted her
vodka and tonic. The mantle clock ticked loudly, an absurdly
intrusive noise from such a dainty timepiece.

"You think I'm worthless," Jules said suddenly. Though
her face had gone white, her voice was calm. "You think I'm
the worst daughter a man could possibly have. And you and
that police lady will never dare have a baby for fear it will turn
out as useless as me!"

"Jules—"

"I mean, really, what did you expect? Someone
beautiful? Adored? Perfect? Or at least someone who never
admits she's none of the above? Someone who swallows all the
injustice and pretends to be a good sport while other people
get *everything?*" Reaching under one of the pillows separating

them, Jules withdrew an iPad. Opening its cover, she signed in with record speed, using her internet browser to pull up a saved page. "Look at this question to an agony aunt. You could have written it about me!"

Hetheridge accepted the tablet. The question, condensed into typical tabloid style, headed up a lengthy column of complaints and quasi-therapeutic answers.

What's wrong with young people today? All the navel-gazing and soul-searching and bleating about being loved? As if any generation that came before was ever so self-obsessed? My daughter is the worst. When I was her age, I held down a job, ran a household, and started saving toward my old age. She reads self-help books, sees therapists, gets her colon cleansed and her aura adjusted. She tells me it's my responsibility to love her unconditionally, or she'll never properly get on with her life. Who taught the younger generation such a load of rubbish?

"Jules. I can assure you—"

"No! Don't try and soothe me with lies! I've had plenty of that, especially from Mum and Kevin! I *do* soul-search! I *do* want to be loved! I mean, I'm sure, once upon a time, people grew up thinking they deserved nothing. That they had no right to expect anything, and lived and died grateful for the privilege of breathing. But times have changed! I've seen *Grey's Anatomy*, for God's sake. I've read *Twilight*. I know there are women my age who experience real emotion. Real happiness. And I want to join them!"

"If *Grey's Anatomy* and *Twilight* have caused such generational unrest, their creators have much to answer for." Though he kept his tone deadpan, he dared offer Jules a smile.

Despite the tears standing in her eyes, she laughed. "You don't even know what *Twilight* is."

"I do. It's the story of how a boy wizard defeats Darth Vader."

Jules blinked once, firmly, and all danger was past.

"Or it's a love triangle. Vampire, werewolf, human," Hetheridge continued.

"How do you know that?"

"I wish I could say it's because I'll soon be stepfather to a quite bookish young man. Alas. The truth is, one of my detectives read the entire series and bent my ear, despite objections."

"Really? Which one? Paul or Kate?"

"The truth must go with me to the grave. To protect the guilty." Hetheridge touched her shoulder. Jules gave him a startled glance. Pulling his hand away, he nevertheless continued. "The reason that ridiculous question upsets you isn't because I could have written it about you. It's because you could have written it about yourself."

"Oh? You're saying you like who I am? You're proud of who I am? After all that with—" She swallowed hard. "With my family? With Kevin? You looked at him like he was scum. And if I loved him, that makes me scum, too."

"Jules." Hetheridge put all his authority into her name, determined to get through to her, or know the reason why not. "Do you like who I am? Are you proud of who I am?"

"I—I don't know you. Not yet."

"Well said. I don't know you, either. It's true we met under dreadful circumstances. I daresay you weren't at your best. I can promise you, I wasn't. But we can't go back."

Jules seemed to digest this. "It's just… when I read this question…." She pointed at the iPad.

Hetheridge tapped one control, then another, erasing the page from her browser's favorites. "Whatever I feel for another human being, however paltry or unimpressive, I can promise you this. The depth of my sentiment will amount to far more than a few lines in some agony aunt's weekly column."

"You mean it?"

"Completely."

Jules fiddled with her drink. It seemed to interest her only as a prop, not a social lubricant. "I don't want much from you. Not your money. Not to live with you in Wellegrave House. I know you're getting married, and she has a nephew and a brother and an uncle...."

"Just a nephew and a brother."

"Okay. I only mean, I know you'll be busy, and I promise, I don't expect much."

Hetheridge sighed.

"I don't!" Jules insisted, eyes wide.

"I'm afraid I feel quite differently. I expect you to come see me. Spend time with me. Let me get to know you. I expect a commitment from you, Jules. Your promise you'll give us a real chance before you write me off as not worth the effort."

"Oh." Jules looked away. After what seemed like a long time, she swiped at her eyes and dared look back at him. "What if it goes wrong? If you write me off in the end?"

"The only way out is through. It won't be easy. But I want to try."

Someone rapped at the front door, three times in succession, then jabbed the doorbell.

"Lost my key card!" the man called. "Jules! Open up!"

Jules leapt to her feet. "Coming!" Shooting a grin at Hetheridge, she dashed toward the front door. "I want you to meet someone. I hoped the planets would line up, and they did!"

Jules switched off the alarm and drew back the bolt. Into the suite bounded a youngish man, perhaps twenty-five, perhaps thirty-five, with no lines on his handsome face. Around five foot two, he wore distressed denim jeans, red Converse one-stars, a Manchester United jersey, and an iPod around his neck, one earbud hanging free. His black hair was long in the back and shaved on the sides, giving him a vaguely punk appearance without the usual piercings or tattoos. Except for the six studs in his left earlobe, and the cheeky grin on his face.

"Steve—this is my real dad. Anthony Hetheridge. He works for Scotland Yard, and he's here to investigate the murder. You know, the oil guy. That's what my dad does, solves crimes." Beaming, Jules threw an arm around the young man, pulling him close. "Dad, this is Steve Zhao. He used to work for the hotel. Now he's a free agent and an amazing hacker."

"Thanks for grassing on me to Scotland Yard," Steve protested, sounding pleased nevertheless.

"I take it back," Jules said obediently. "Steve's not a hacker. He's an IT rebel. And I'm crazy about him." The smile she turned on Hetheridge was wide and trusting. "There! I said it. Steve's the reason I checked into Hotel Nonpareil."

Chapter Fifteen

I don't understand!" Bonnie Venicombe rushed toward the front door, intent on preventing Bhar from leaving with Thora and Griffin. "Why not conduct the interview here? Sergeant, I don't wish to sound unkind, but taking my daughter and grandson away from their home for questioning strikes me as highly irregular. Even antagonistic. And it troubles me, because you seemed so professional at first. I would hate to ring up your superiors and tell them I've lost all confidence."

There it is, Bhar thought. *Threat number one. Familiar ground at last.*

"Mrs. Venicombe. This really isn't unusual, I promise. And I'm not interrogating Mrs. Hughes or Griffin. I'm only interviewing them in hopes of better identifying who might have harmed Mr. Hughes. Sometimes a completely neutral environment yields the best results."

"Fine." Bonnie's once-warm voice turned quite cool. "Thora, dear, you should ring the family barrister straightaway. And Griffin, you're scarcely of age. Don't say a word without counsel present. Shall I call for you both?"

Thora regarded her mother with narrow eyes and tight lips—Viking stoicism, if Bhar had ever seen it. Griffin, equally pale, blond and firm of mouth, was heavily muscled all over, as if he spent all his free time pumping iron. Judging by the flash in his eyes, the observation he was 'scarcely past a minor' didn't sit too well.

"I can handle talking to a policeman without you holding my hand, Bonnie," Griffin called. "So can Thora."

Griffin's on first name terms with both mum and grandmother, Bhar thought. It was unusual enough for him to make a mental note. One never knew what incidental detail might later prove significant.

Having offered to buy them lunch, Bhar's next order of business was to find a welcoming establishment, not too empty, not too overcrowded. After loading Thora and Griffin Hughes into his Astra, Bhar didn't have to drive far to locate a Caffé Concerto in Piccadilly that met their expectations.

"I want risotto," Griffin told the waiter. "Make sure it's fresh."

"Irish coffee for me," Thora said.

"As a starter?" The waiter blinked.

"As an afternoon pick-me-up. Make it two. With biscotti." Bhar passed over their menus, flashing a smile at Thora. It was a strange choice, true, but the bereaved often made strange choices. Of course, the same could be said for the guilty. Either way, Bhar was ready for caffeine with a kick.

"Now. Let's start from the usual jumping-off point," Bhar told Thora and Griffin as the waiter departed. "Were either of you privy to any threats to Mr. Hughes's life? The existence of someone who wished him ill?"

"Of course. Environmentalists hated Michael after the drilling rig made a mistake, as if Michael planned it himself," Thora said. "People like Sir Duncan Godington wanted Michael nailed to the cross. Sir Duncan's a madman, everyone knows it. Poor Michael. He must have been utterly desperate for public support to approach a man like that for help."

"I can name someone else who hated Dad. Arianna Freemont. His head of public relations," Griffin announced.

"I'm aware environmentalists called for your father to fall on his sword, at least symbolically," Bhar told Griffin. "But what hostility did you notice on Ms. Freemont's part? From what I gather, she was your father's—erm. Well, the person he intended to marry, after he divorced your mother."

"Divorce was never by any means certain." Thora sat up straighter in her chair. "Arianna was just another gold digger, like Riley Castanet."

"No. Dad loved Riley. And she loved him." Griffin sounded obstinate.

"Two Irish coffees," the waiter announced, placing cups in front of Bhar and Thora before turning to Griffin. "And water for you, sir?"

"Of course." He rolled his eyes as if it was the stupidest possible question.

"Oh. How silly of me. I'm sorry." Something in the waiter's wide smile and upright carriage made Bhar suspect Griffin's risotto would arrive with a large quantity of spittle mixed in.

"I'm telling you, Dad fell in love with Riley," Griffin said. "Sorry, Thora. That's just how things go. It doesn't mean something's intrinsically wrong with you. You can still dust yourself off and hook up with someone new."

If I said that to my mum? Dead, Bhar scribbled in his notebook.

"Griffin." Eyes narrowing, Thora's voice took on the husky tone of female command. "Reality check. You were never one of Michael's confidants. He had no time for you, not since... you know. All your information comes from Riley, who never cared a fig for you, just her own agenda. Pumping you for details about our family so she could feed them back to Michael in those ridiculous séances!"

"I feel sorry for you," Griffin said.

"Not as sorry as you may feel before this nightmare's over."

"And I'm, well, terribly sorry to be sitting here intruding," Bhar said, hoping to redirect the ugliness toward something relevant. "Thora, I take it you believe Riley is a fraud?"

"Obviously."

"And Arianna was only interested in your husband's money? Why do you say that?"

"Look her up," Thora snapped. "Do five minutes' research. Really, I thought detectives did that sort of thing routinely, even when the crime wasn't murder."

"We do, I promise. But there's pressure to make an arrest as quickly as possible—"

"That'll be Bonnie. Rack and thumbscrews have got nothing on her," Griffin said.

"So, tell me, Thora." Bhar cleared his throat. "What in Arianna's background do you consider relevant?"

"She's from Liverpool. Spent a few years in care after the Toxteth and Brixton riots," Thora said. "Was adopted by a rich uncle, but they fell out. He wound up dead before the will was changed, and she inherited."

Bhar scribbled that down. "I'll look into it, but I assume she wasn't charged?"

"She was." Thora's deep-set eyes gleamed. "But she was a juvenile, and eventually the case was thrown out. On some sort of technicality, I think. This much is certain: she spent the old man's legacy on a first class education. Then she climbed the ladder until she got all the way to Peerless Petrol, surrounded by dozens of rich men. And apparently only the best would do, even if he already had a wife."

"Oh, sure, Dad was the best." Griffin chuckled, glancing around the restaurant as if everyone should be equally amused.

The reference to "Dad" rather than "Michael" captured Bhar's attention, and reminded him of an earlier remark.

"Thora mentioned there was some estrangement between you and Mr. Hughes," Bhar said. "That he had no time for you after... what was it?"

"I went to rehab when I was thirteen. Yes!" Griffin flashed a grin. "I'm the only human being on the planet who went to rehab at thirteen. Dad started spending long nights at the office, Thora started therapy, and the rest is history. I destroyed their marriage," he continued. "Made it happen, and made it go up in smoke. I have amazing powers. All I need to do now is father some babies and kill a few timewasters. Then I'll be God Almighty, eh?"

"You made it happen?" Bhar repeated, momentarily confused, and then could have kicked himself for giving Griffin the opening.

"Sure did. This one never had family planning in school." He pointed derisively at Thora. "Or if she did, I reckon she slept through it, because I was born five months after the wedding. Dad never wanted me. I was like the boot round his car tire."

"Oh, really? Tell Sergeant Bhar about your childhood. When you were diagnosed with leukemia and no one thought you would live to see seven years old!" Thora was shouting. The waiter, approaching with Griffin's risotto, halted a few paces from the table. Patrons across the dining room stared. "Boot round his tire, eh? Who put his career on hold to sit up with you in hospital? Who passed up a promotion to spend extra time with you? You survived because we loved you, Griffin. There's no child in the world with more tangible proof of devotion than you!"

"Loved. Past tense, did you catch that?" Griffin told Bhar. His voice was calm; only the rising color in his cheeks betrayed his emotions. "Okay, here goes. See these?" Pushing up his shirt sleeves, he showed Bhar a long vertical scar on each wrist. "Dad hated me because I got into booze and coke. I felt like I was nothing, so I tried to kill myself. Doctors told him it was a cry for help, but that just made him hate me more. I didn't want to go to the hotel or crash the gala, but Thora made me. She told me to go to his suite and beg his forgiveness. Which I did, at first. When he wouldn't listen, I said I'd kill him. Just to get his attention."

"How did he react?"

"Threw me out. Threatened to hit the panic button and get me arrested. But the point is, I didn't kill him. I just said I would!" Clenching his fists, Griffin looked ready to pummel something—the table, Thora, or himself.

"Terribly sorry," the waiter mumbled, taking this moment to slide the risotto in front of Griffin. "Will there be anything else?"

Griffin panted, visibly controlling himself. With a shaking finger, he pushed the plate aside. "Take it away. I don't want it."

***

"Sorry it took me so long," Bhar called, shrugging out of his coat and handing it to Harvey. "Cheers."

"My pleasure. And you're not significantly late, sir. Lord Hetheridge has been on a conference call for the better part of an hour. With Downing Street," Harvey added softly. Hetheridge's manservant, a frustrated actor who had given up the stage for a life in service, often reminded Bhar of a bit player in a Julian Fellowes costume drama. Harvey never gossiped about his employer's habits or moods, but he did seem to take a keen interest in police work, occasionally passing details to Bhar, who looked cleverer to Hetheridge as a result.

"Before Downing Street called, Lord Hetheridge had a personal visit from Dr. Garrett," Harvey continued. "Apparently, the early forensic report has been rushed into existence. One hopes nothing was overlooked."

"One hopes," Bhar agreed, astonished at the speed with which departmental wheels were turning. He'd never seen anything like it. "Where's Kate?"

"Also engaged with her phone."

The lack of detail told Bhar the call was either something innocuous or more trouble for Kate, perhaps from her relatives. Now that her mother and sister knew about the wedding, had the harassment begun?

"Since milord requested a spur-of-the-moment meeting, I thought tea might do," Harvey said, positively glowing with false modesty. "If you'll come through?"

"Tea" consisted of more than mere tea, although there was plenty of that. Something strong, probably Earl Grey, in Hetheridge's elegant Japanese tea pot. And something gentler in the heirloom silver pot that had been handed down to him, along with virtually the entire contents of Wellegrave House. In addition, there were biscuits, tarts, and the sort of crustless finger sandwiches that looked bland but were, on Harvey's watch, filled with devilled ham, egg salad, or salmon and capers. In short, Harvey's spur-of-the-moment tea suited Bhar perfectly. He'd just polished off two sandwiches when Kate blew in with what appeared to be a new smart phone in hand.

"Upgrade, eh?"

"Forced upgrade. My mobile died. I can't tell you how many pictures and files I lost. Now I have to wait for this buggery piece of crap to activate. I've been waiting two hours already!"

Smiling serenely, Bhar removed his leatherbound notebook from his inner coat pocket and placed it between them. "I never need an upgrade."

Kate glared at him.

"I never find myself in a holding pattern, waiting on technology."

Kate pressed her lips together.

"I never lose important case notes because of an overdependence on—"

Snatching up the notebook, Kate unlatched the dining room's double-paned, unscreened window, chucking the beloved notebook into Hetheridge's back garden. "Well. Now you have."

"You're mad. Barking mad!"

By the time Bhar trooped outside, fought his way through a row of dormant rose bushes, retrieved his notebook—thankfully the ground was much too cold to be muddy—and returned to the dining room, Kate was nibbling on a sandwich and viewing a website on her new mobile.

"Activation finished. I'm back in business."

"Wonderful. Aren't you supposed to be slimming? Or are you trying to live up to that picture in the *Bright Star?*"

He expected a roar of fury, but she shrugged. "That picture's the least of my problems. At this point, I'm living for the honeymoon. I plan on spending every minute stretched out beneath an umbrella, drink in my hand. Well, not every minute. But close enough. What?"

"Nothing." Bhar resumed his place at the table, hoping his face didn't give away his thoughts.

"You gave me the strangest look. Why?"

"I just, er, hadn't heard about the honeymoon plans. The guv and Lady Margaret are playing it pretty close to the vest."

"It can't be outside of the EU. I'll bet there would have been all sorts of paperwork for Henry and Ritchie to travel someplace like Hawaii or Belize. That means a beach somewhere more local. Probably the south of France. I checked with Mrs. Snell. It's Tony's favorite holiday spot. He thinks he's pulled the wool over my eyes." Kate tapped her forehead, echoing one of Hetheridge's familiar gestures. "*Detective.*"

Bhar poured himself another cup of tea.

"So you might as well grass. I know you're the best man."

"What?"

"You. Tony's best man. You have to be."

"I'm not." Bhar cast an eye toward the dining room's sliding doors, wondering how much longer it would take Hetheridge to appear.

Kate peered at him. "Wow. Either you became a better liar overnight, which I won't rule out, or you're telling the truth. I guess Harvey was grandfathered in. You're not miffed, are you?"

Bhar pretended to study the biscuits. "Under the circumstances, of course not."

"What circumstances?"

"Er. A family thing. My mum's family gets together once a year. This year it just happened to fall on your wedding day. I won't be able to attend."

"Paul! You can't give my wedding a miss!"

"Look. Kate. Nobody's happier for you and the guv than me. You know that. It's just one day. It's not like I won't be there in spirit."

"Spirit? What a load of wank! I expect you to stand there and suffer just as much as I do! My phone didn't go kaput on its own," Kate confessed. "I threw it against the wall when my mum called. She's back in my life, and I'll never wrestle that genie back in the bottle. Tony and Lady Margaret don't trust me to handle so much as a cake tasting! And now you can't even be bothered to turn up?"

"Bridezilla," a deep voice said.

Bhar hoped his sigh of relief didn't sound too obviously heartfelt. "Hello, Ritchie."

Ritchie, who didn't always "do" greetings, remained focused on his sister. "Henry calls you bridezilla. Bridezilla," he repeated happily.

"Stinker." Kate poked him in the chest. "Ready for our airplane trip?"

Ritchie poked her back. "Not going."

"Yes, you are. And you're coming to live here. Henry's settling in early. You can't let Henry outdo you."

"Not living here."

"You are. I'll marry Tony. You'll sit through the ceremony *quietly*. We'll all have a wonderful holiday and come back to live here together."

"Bridezilla."

"Stinker."

Hetheridge entered through the sliding doors Ritchie had left ajar. "Oh, hello, Ritchie."

"Not living here," Ritchie told Hetheridge.

"Yes, well, Kate may have something to say about that," Hetheridge said. "In the meantime, will you go back to your Legos? Let us do a spot of police work?"

"Not living here," Ritchie repeated twice before finally leaving.

"He just likes the phrase," Kate said, closing the door behind him. "Your telly is bigger than mine. That will be the deciding factor in Ritchie making the transition without a huge tantrum, I promise. But Tony—Paul says he isn't coming to the wedding."

Hetheridge looked as pained as Bhar felt. "Kate. You know as far as I'm concerned, marriage cannot come soon enough. But at this point, the merest thought of the ceremony gives me a headache. Can we focus on something more pleasant? Like murder?"

Chapter Sixteen

K ate took a deep breath. Slow, calming breaths were supposed to lower the blood pressure, eliminate body toxins, and promote relaxation. Or so said the website she'd consulted as soon as her new mobile came to life. At this point, Kate was willing to try almost anything.

"Murder sounds great."

"Excellent. Off you go." Hetheridge poured himself a cup of tea.

"I spoke to Arianna Freemont," Kate began. "She's a very controlled person. I had the impression she doesn't trust easily. Perhaps not at all."

"Did she strike you as genuinely bereaved?"

"Impossible to tell. Prickly, without a doubt, like she was combing everything I said for hidden insults. Then again, she's a public relations executive. Maybe for her, every statement has a second meaning or agenda."

"I heard she had a tough childhood," Bhar said. "Thora Hughes knew all about her. Called her a gold digger."

"Well, judging from what the statement reader sent me from the Incident Room, Arianna Freemont put herself through university and has supported herself ever since. With a big boost from her uncle, who died under mysterious circumstances and left her everything at age seventeen."

"Thora implied it was murder. Said Arianna was sprung on a technicality."

"Only if you call lack of compelling evidence a technicality," Kate said, opening the document on her phone and re-reading a part of it before paraphrasing aloud: "Bert Freemont, aged sixty-two, died in his home in Liverpool. He was dead for three days before his landlord discovered the body. Soon after, witnesses reported to police that Arianna and Bert often fought. On what the forensic surgeon determined the night of his death, Arianna moved out with nothing but her purse and the clothes on her back. They tracked her down in East London, where she'd taken a bedsit in Seven Dials, to tell her she'd inherited almost a million pounds."

"Her uncle was a millionaire, but the landlord found him?" Bhar asked.

"Yep. Owned three tobacco shops. Total miser, apparently. Racked up lots of complaints with customers and neighbors."

"What triggered Arianna's arrest?"

"The witness reports. Her demeanor, which was called excessively cold. Her lack of an alibi. Plus the fact her uncle was poisoned with drain cleaner. Someone held him down, probably while he was passed out drunk, and poured the chemical down his throat. Arianna, who worked part time as a cleaner in addition to her schoolwork, seemed the most likely suspect."

"I wonder why he bothered to give her a home, if he was such a bastard," Bhar said.

Kate narrowed her eyes at him.

"Oh, that's right, I saw her picture. If she was as pretty then as she is now...."

"Half the time, pretty has nothing to do with it. She was younger, smaller, and dependent on him. For a predator, that's the unholy trinity."

"Good point. Did Arianna accuse him of molestation?"

"Only after he was dead," Kate said. "Anyway, after three months in remand, the case was thrown out by the judge and Arianna went off to school."

"I received the same information," Hetheridge said. "And it just so happens, despite the fact Ms. Freemont was not convicted, her genetic profile resides in the NDNAD."

Kate wasn't surprised. In the last few years, the entity officially called the United Kingdom National Criminal Intelligence DNA Database, had been the subject of controversy and debate. Not because the UK stored the blood and genetic material of convicted criminals, but because, since 2003, it had stored DNA samples of all individuals placed under arrest, retaining them whether or not those individuals were ultimately judged innocent. Critics of the NDNAD argued that an arrest for, say, public drunkenness did not give the state the right to capture and maintain genetic material indefinitely. Proponents insisted the database had already been invaluable in solving hundreds of crimes. But the notion of storing the DNA of the innocent was popular with few.

"Final thoughts on Ms. Freemont?" Hetheridge prompted Kate.

"I don't know if she's grieving for Hughes or not. I have no idea if she's capable of murder. I *did* look at some of her ad campaigns for Peerless Petrol, and they're excellent," Kate said. "Surprisingly warm and emotional, coming from someone so tightly wound. In the course of the interview, she made an accusation. Seems to think Griffin Hughes killed his father."

"After meeting Griffin, I understand her suspicions," Bhar said. "The research team sent me a dossier after I met him, which was about an hour too late, but I read it in traffic. He was very ill as a child, but went into remission. Apparently he took a hard corner around puberty. Started experimenting with every drug he could find. Was packed off to rehab, came home, tried to kill himself. According to my notes,"—he opened the notebook, paging back to his interview with Riley—"Riley claims Griffin habitually called his dad, asking for money and favors. Sometimes he threatened to kill himself. I guess at some point, the threat lost traction, even after one genuine attempt. Griffin was arrested twice last year, both times for petty theft. Let off with a caution the first time. Convicted and paid a fine the second time."

"Adding to NDNAD's database. Which supposedly expands by over twenty-five thousand samples a month," Hetheridge said.

"Hello, crime-free society," Bhar said.

"Goodbye, civil liberties," Kate said.

"I place my own reaction somewhere in the middle." Hetheridge sipped his tea. "I'm old enough to remember when we lacked such technology, and a great many serious crimes went unsolved. Or worse, were pinned on the wrong person. But I'm also old enough to have witnessed how quickly use degenerates into abuse. Focusing on the matter at hand, however—it appears Arianna Freemont may have a history of violence. Or Griffin Hughes's self-harm may have expanded to include his father. If only that CCTV camera had yielded something other than mating habits at the Gorilla Kingdom."

"Bob Junkett should be nailed to the wall," Kate said.

"At first I said the same, but now I see the blame can't be laid at his feet. Not directly, at least," Hetheridge said. "Last week, Junkett attempted to sack the hotel's IT manager, Steve Zhao. Mr. Zhao's letter of resignation made reference to gorillas. And although he denies it, I'm confident he engineered the camera's misdirection."

"But why *that* camera, out of dozens?" Bhar asked. "The one pointing at a murder victim's door?"

"I don't know."

"As a method of framing Junkett, or even making him look complicit in the murder, it's a failure. Junkett's a moron. He couldn't pull off a techie feat like that with a gun to his head," Kate said. "But how about this? Suppose—Tony. What is it? What's wrong?" Instinctively, she touched Hetheridge's hand.

"Am I so obvious?" He smiled. "Well. I'd be lying if I didn't admit I hoped it was a wild coincidence, given Mr. Zhao's personal connections. He's dating my daughter, Jules."

"No way!" Kate regretted her tone the second she heard it. "I mean, er, wow. Small world. What are the odds?"

"Less astronomical than you might think." Hetheridge sounded unruffled, but she recognized the concern in his eyes. "Jules took up residence at Hotel Nonpareil two months ago. During that time, according to Lady Margaret, Jules formed a friendship with two other residents, Lady Isabel Bartlow and Sir Duncan Godington. When I asked Jules today, she insisted 'friendship' is too strong a term, and they're merely acquaintances."

"So maybe Lady Margaret's wrong," Kate said.

"Lady Margaret's never wrong." Bhar sounded morose. "Believe me, no one's ever wanted her to be wrong more than me."

"This time, you may wish differently." Hetheridge lifted his chin, and Kate knew whatever he felt, those emotions would not be aired at this table. "Think about it, Paul. Sir Duncan has a long history of using starstruck admirers to accomplish his ends. We know the triple murder was aided and abetted by some of those hangers-on, even if we failed to make our case in Crown court. Suppose he took Jules under his wing. Told her a certain CCTV camera presented a problem only her boyfriend could neutralize. If Jules agreed to help, either naïvely or with true complicity, there it is. A circumstantial link between Sir Duncan and the murder, if we can compel Jules and Mr. Zhao to confess."

Kate looked at Bhar. He, too, seemed at a loss about how to respond. Finally, he reached for a biscuit. Hetheridge did, too. In solidarity, Kate did the same, picking a chocolate one crammed with calories.

"Slimming be damned."

Bhar chuckled weakly. So did Hetheridge, although his biscuit ended up on his saucer, untouched.

"With regards to Mr. Zhao." Hetheridge cleared his throat. "I informed the Incident Room that we require all public details of his life. Until the dossier arrives, I can offer nothing of his character beyond an impression, and here it is. Highly intelligent. Dropped out of University because acumen in his field is more valuable than a degree. A bit of a chip on his shoulder when it comes to authority figures. Naturally, that includes the police and puffed-up, self important types like Bob Junkett. Enjoys taking the piss—"

"Be fair, guv. That's the national pastime," Bhar said. "Any bloke Jules dates will be guilty of the same."

"True. One final observation: Mr. Zhao is a bit of a braggart," Hetheridge said. "I think it cost him a great deal, being asked if he engineered Junkett's Gorilla Kingdom humiliation and finding himself forced to deny it. I saw it in his eyes, the desire to flash a cheeky grin and dare me to do something about it."

Kate exchanged another glance with Bhar. No doubt Hetheridge, who prided himself on his self-control, was unaware that a note of paternal menace had crept into his tone.

"As a result, I've asked the PCeU to look into Mr. Zhao's online activities. I suspect somewhere, in a chat room or on a message board, he's boasted about diverting that camera. If so, the admission will come to light."

Kate ducked her head to hide a smile. Something about the way her future husband sicced the Met's Police Central e-crime Unit on Steve Zhao pleased her very much. Some might argue she was responding to the caveman in Hetheridge, but Kate didn't think so. He always fell back on his cerebrum, a trait she found infinitely sexier than a club over the head.

"Speaking of Junkett and all that camera footage. Any final verdict, guv?" Bhar asked.

"The team is working shifts around the clock. I've been assured we'll have a full report within forty-eight hours, including snippets of any relevant footage."

"Will that be fast enough for Downing Street?" Pushing back his straight-backed dining chair, Bhar balanced on two legs in a fashion similar to Hetheridge's contemplative office posture. "I can't say I like Thora for the murder. She's needy. Convinced Hughes wasn't about to divorce her, and blaming Arianna and Riley instead of her husband. But it's clear Thora's mum, Bonnie Venicombe, still has ties to power, even if her hubs made a fool of himself on the national stage. Bonnie's the one leaning on the Met for a quick arrest, guv."

"I know. I dated Bonnie, when she was separated from Alastair."

Bhar's chair overbalanced, sending him into the wall. Hurrying to his side, Kate helped him up, setting the dining chair to rights while fighting to contain her amusement.

"Sir?" Harvey entered so quickly, Kate was startled. Either he was remarkably quick on his feet, or he'd been very close to the sliding doors when Bhar fell.

"All is well," Hetheridge announced without turning. He, too, was grinning at Bhar, obviously savoring the younger man's fall, though he said not a word.

"Kate?" Henry appeared. Like Harvey, he'd responded to the crash with suspicious speed. Surely they hadn't both been lurking just outside the doors?

"We're fine! Still at work in here. A little privacy, please," Kate called.

Harvey kept his dignity, but Henry looked crestfallen. Still, the doors closed, and the trio found themselves alone again.

"You dated Bonnie Venicombe?" Bhar asked as he returned to his chair. He seemed more shaken by the news than the fall. "Smiles a lot? White-haired? Offers Horlicks?"

"Yes, I dated her. Meaning I squired her about, nothing more," Hetheridge said. "Your generation takes 'dating' to imply a great many things. Mine does not. I socialized with Bonnie Venicombe, whom I assure you was very good company. Her husband had taken a mistress, so she felt free to acquire friends of her own. Bonnie was quite vivacious, at least off the record, with a wicked sense of humor and a taste for younger men. Alas, her tendency toward opposing personas, public and private, disconcerted me. And I was too old for her, being roughly her own age. So we parted. But the moment I realized she was connected to the Hughes murder, I feared at least some pressure would come from that direction. Since she and her husband reconciled, she puts family before all."

"Thora says Bonnie thinks Griffin killed his father. Full stop," Bhar said.

"I doubt it. If she did, Bonnie would want the investigation slowed. Expanded. Tampered with, if at all possible," Hetheridge said. "You said it yourself, Griffin's emotionally vulnerable. More likely, Bonnie wants her grandson cleared with all haste, to prevent another meltdown."

"Too bad. I haven't seen anything to exclude Griffin," Bhar said.

"No, indeed." Hetheridge sighed. "I've been friends with Peter Garrett, the divisional surgeon, for a dog's age. He's three years shy of retirement. But yesterday he was threatened—obliquely, of course—with enforced retirement, not to mention a reduction of benefits, if his office didn't turn over the Hughes forensics in record time. Therefore, we have a report already. Much of it is incomplete, mind you, until we visit the interviewees and receive permission, or denial, for genetic material to attempt matches."

Kate sat up straight. "What do we have?"

Hetheridge withdrew his mobile. Unhurried, he located the correct file. Then, withdrawing a pair of half-glasses from his breast pocket, he put them on and read aloud:

"'Genetic material found at the Hughes murder scene includes the following individuals, identified by SRTs, also called DNA microsatellites or short tandem repeats. Eleven remain unidentified. Doubtless, at least four belong to the hotel's maid service. But numbered among the positively identified are the following people: Arianna Freemont. Robert "Bob" Junkett. Leonard "Leo" Makepeace. Griffin Hughes. And Sir Duncan Godington.'"

***

"Sometimes I hate the 'no police work in bed' rule," Kate said. Already in her nightshirt, a soft, well-worn T-shirt from her early days in the Met, she was removing her makeup in the *en suite* bath.

"I don't know why. You initiated it." Half-glasses perched near the end of his nose, Hetheridge was reading something on his ereader. Probably a biography of a dead white bloke Kate had never heard of.

"I don't find it suspicious that Arianna was inside Hughes's suite," Kate said. "She was his fiancée of record. I'm more interested in knowing if Riley was there."

"If she was, her DNA numbers among the as yet undetermined, since she was never detained or arrested in the UK." Hetheridge's gaze remained on his ereader.

"Griffin admitted to going inside at least once," Kate continued. "But why was Bob Junkett inside Hughes's suite? That's a little odd, don't you think?"

"Perhaps Junkett was there to discuss Thora and Griffin's residence in Hotel Nonpareil? As I recall, Hughes complained, and Junkett defended himself on the grounds no one told him the CEO of Peerless Petrol's wife and son were unwelcome."

"Are you making excuses for Junkett?"

Taking off his glasses, Hetheridge put the ereader aside. "No. But that's precisely the sort of accusation that led to a 'no police work in bed' rule. The occasional break is necessary to see things clearly."

"True. You worked fourteen hours today." Kate loaded her electric toothbrush with Colgate.

"It's not unusual."

"You need sleep."

"Sleep when I'm dead."

"I just can't help wondering why poor little Leo Makepeace entered the suite," Kate said. "Maybe to welcome Hughes?"

"Maybe to offer him strychnine?"

Snorting, Kate turned on the toothbrush. When she was finished, she joined Hetheridge in bed. "Leo Makepeace is no murderer."

"According to Riley Castanet, he was an American bank robber in a past life. Black mask, fast horse, and all."

"From what I hear, Riley works a horse into every séance. Because she's a reincarnated Appaloosa called God knows what." Curling up beside Hetheridge, Kate closed her eyes. "Do you like Griffin Hughes for the killer?"

"No."

"According to Paul, Griffin had a terrible relationship with his father."

"Yes, well, Griffin wouldn't be the first innocent man to say the same. I fall under that category. Father despised me. And truth be told, the sentiment was mutual."

Kate kissed Hetheridge's ear. The ripple of reaction in his flesh was proof of her power, as tangible as anything else he said or did. "What about Sir Duncan?"

"You already know what I think. Privately, between the two of us."

"Say it." Kate bit his earlobe.

"Guilty till proven innocent."

"Oh, admit it. You just loathe how cordial he is to me."

"And Jules. Don't forget about Jules."

"Maybe Sir Duncan doesn't mean any particular compliment he pays to me or her. Maybe he just wants to unsettle you," Kate chuckled. The soft T-shirt was history; Hetheridge's arms already encircled her.

"Why do you come to bed dressed at all?"

"Same reason Sir Duncan does what he does." Kate kissed Hetheridge's mouth. "To keep you from turning complacent."

Chapter Seventeen

K ate turned up a half-hour late the next morning, but it made no difference. The day consisted mostly of fact-checking, meetings to guarantee all relevant information was shared, and a guided tour through HOLMES's findings, which were inconclusive. Quite often, the Home Office Large and Major Enquiry System (given its laborious name to create a snappy acronym that conjured deerstalker hats and oversized magnifying glasses) was invaluable, helping the Met identify criminal patterns. HOLMES was especially beneficial when the crimes were separated by time or space. But in the case of Michael Martin Hughes, HOLMES turned up only two matches, one moderate, the other weak.

"Arianna Freemont. Her uncle died by poisoning, presumably when he threatened to disinherit her. Now her fiancé is dead by poisoning," DCI Vic Jackson announced weightily, as if he'd uncovered all this himself. The conference rooms were booked, so the habitually unkempt detective chief, whose suit jacket always seemed dusted with dandruff or crumbs, had decided to hold court in the computer room. This meant Kate, Bhar, and twelve other officers were clustered around a computer, looking at the HOLMES report and wishing Jackson would stop talking.

"After finding out Hughes cheated on her with the fortune teller, I think Arianna fell back on her old tricks," DCI Jackson continued.

"If she did, she made friends in hotel security or IT first." Kate, who despised DCI Jackson as she despised few others, strove to keep her tone professional. "Which is interesting, because as Hughes's fiancée, she's one of the few people who could justify entering his suite at any hour of the day or night."

"Oh, let me guess. Freemont's a man-hating feminist nutcracker like you, so you're hot to defend her?" Jackson elbowed his current favorite brown-noser, a DC who never failed to chuckle at Jackson's so-called-witticisms.

"You sound worried, Vic." Bhar grinned. "Don't be. Got to have nuts to fear a nutcracker."

"That explains how you and *milord* prosper around Kate, then." Vic paused extravagantly, giving his crony plenty of time to appreciate the insult. "Come on, Paulie, we see right through you. Stuck on HOLMES's second match, eh? You're like a bird who's been dumped. Refusing to move on while you moon over the bloke who got away."

Jackson referred, of course, to Sir Duncan Godington, whom HOLMES had offered because of the baronet's proximity to the crime scene, as well as his environmentalist sympathies.

"Sir Duncan's under scrutiny," Bhar said with what Kate considered admirable calm. "But it's worth noting that Arianna Freemont isn't the only suspect with knowledge or experience about poisons. As a former police officer, Bob Junkett would have received training on how strychnine works and where to obtain it. Plus, his genetic signature was found in Hughes's suite."

"Take note: I have no patience for stunt detective work," Jackson told his crony, as if no one else gathered around the HOLMES report could hear or understand. "Real life murder investigations are nothing like cheap mystery novels. The character with the fewest spoken lines and thinnest connection to the case might be guilty in *CSI: Dibley*, but not in reality, boys. Logic!"

Warming to his lecture, DCI Jackson adopted a stentorian tone, unaware of shifting and murmurs near the computer room's door. "Never be afraid to perceive patterns, even well in advance of hard evidence! Twenty quid says Lord Senile turns up convinced Hughes's poor doormat of a wife must have done it, since we don't have a scrap of fiber or DNA to implicate her."

"Senile, I may be. Deaf, I am not," Hetheridge said by way of introduction. Suddenly all the officers, with the exception of DCI Jackson, Kate, and Bhar, seemed to find themselves called away on pressing business. In fifteen seconds, the room was otherwise empty.

"Vic, may I see you in my office, please?"

"Of course." Cheeks reddening, DCI Jackson followed Hetheridge out. Bhar started chuckling while the man was still in earshot, but Kate, determined to be professional, kept a straight face for another five seconds. Then came the laughter and the high fives.

***

"Put us in the picture, guv. Did you threaten to haul Jackson before AC Deaver?" Bhar sounded hopeful.

It was half-five, and the trio had reassembled just before that long-awaited briefing regarding Hotel Nonpareil's hundreds of hours of CCTV footage. Judging by the meeting's scale and distinguished attendees, Bhar expected it to prove useful. A classroom had been engaged to accommodate not only Hetheridge's team but the case's temporary staff, which numbered in the double digits. When Downing Street required quick results, the Met strove to obey.

"The assistant commissioner?" Hetheridge frowned. "Why on earth would I do that?"

"Vic called you senile behind your back."

"Yes, well, you should hear some of the things I've called him to his face. Albeit behind closed doors." Hetheridge shrugged. "He's not that much younger than I. We came up in more or less the same era, adhering to roughly the same creed: never involve a superior officer unless it's truly a matter of life and death. No. The fact is, I've been asked to make greater use of Vic in this investigation."

"Oh, no" Bhar said.

"Because of the tabloid story?"

"No doubt. At any rate, I called DCI Jackson into my office to request he look into a tip I received this afternoon implicating the hotel manager, Leo Makepeace."

"The little nervous guy?" Kate sounded incredulous.

"Talk about *CSI: Dibley*,"Bhar said.

"According to the person who called the Met's crime stopper hotline, Mr. Makepeace has been living beyond his means. Swapped his Ford Anglia for a BMW. Bought a small house in the Cotswolds. Turned in his resignation, effective next week, citing a desire for early retirement." Hetheridge smiled. "Our favorite seer, Riley Castanet, told Leo Makepeace he was a Wild West bank robber in a past life. Perhaps she saw him more clearly than we did, if he's cooked Hotel Nonpareil's books."

"That's interesting." Bhar recalled when Makepeace offered his office for Riley's pre-interview, the manager had perspired so copiously, he'd rendered his door keys almost too slick for use. "I suppose anyone might decide to embezzle, if temptation or need became pressing enough. But you can't tell me Leo Makepeace handed Hughes a poisoned drink. Much less pulled up a barstool and watched him convulse, foam, and die in agony."

"Perhaps not." Hetheridge sounded neutral. Unlike DCI Jackson, he tried to prejudge as little as humanly possible, and encouraged his team to do the same. "But the tipster claims to have seen Makepeace spending an inordinate amount of time around Hughes during the gala. If this evening's CCTV camera analysis corroborates that testimony, the case may take an unexpected turn."

***

The officer in charge of the CCTV footage presentation, PC Gulls, was perhaps five foot one with strawberry blonde curls and a round, enthusiastic face. Plump rather than fat and childlike rather than actually underage, she put Bhar in mind of a puppy. One that had attained human form and speech without losing any of its other essential qualities.

"Hell-ooo, Scotland Yard," PC Gulls called into her microphone, voice echoing absurdly around the classroom. It was as if a warm-up comedian had wandered into the presentation and decided to do what D-list entertainers did best.

There was no reply, apart from audible seat-shifting and the occasional cough.

"I'm so excited to address you all," PC Gulls continued, undaunted. "Working on this project for Chief Superintendent Hetheridge and his team has been the high point of my life!"

"Oh, no," Bhar muttered to Kate.

"She's an embarrassment," Kate whispered back.

"If enthusiasm is a crime, neither of you will ever face conviction," Hetheridge said repressively. "Listen, please."

"I am going on *no sleep*," PC Gulls confided to the classroom at large, the way someone else might announce a long-awaited holiday at Disneyland. "But it's all been worth it! Let's start with Peerless Petrol's gala. The murder victim, Michael Martin Hughes, entered the ballroom forty minutes before the doors opened."

On the classroom's wide projector screen, footage appeared of Hughes. Handsome in evening dress, he strolled around the empty ballroom examining flower arrangements and sampling the punch. A lovely, if rather cold, woman followed, nodding and smiling mechanically each time Hughes made an inaudible comment.

"Mind you, there's no audio track," PC Gulls added. "But you knew that! I'm a dozy donkey. That lady by Mr. Hughes's side is Arianna Freemont. They spent most of the evening together." Pressing a button on her laptop, PC Gulls moved the presentation forward to the next point. "Now. Here's a montage of notable guests arriving. Among the first, of course, are the hotel's paid employees. Leo Makepeace arrives at 7:59. Bob Junkett at 8:02." PC Gulls pressed another button. "Riley Castanet at 8:31. Thora Hughes at 9:02. Griffin Hughes, right behind her, also at 9:02."

Bhar waved a hand, but he was forced to stand up in order to capture PC Gulls's attention. "What about Sir Duncan Godington?"

Somebody groaned. Bhar ignored it.

"Oh, sure. Silly me." Looking overjoyed to comply, PC Gulls queued up the correct bit of footage. "He arrived in the company of his sister, Lady Isabel Bartlow, at 9:24. They posed for snaps with a sham check representing Sir Duncan's contribution to Gulf disaster relief. Danced one dance. Ignored the nibbles. Consumed no alcohol. And exited together at 10:03, never to return."

"How 'bout a smoking gun?" someone near the front row barked. "You ever gonna get to one of those, sweetheart?"

Another uniformed PC would have shrunk at such contempt, particularly from a plainclothes male detective playing to the crowd. Not PC Gulls. If anything, she stood a half-inch taller, beaming and full of pride.

"What a good question," she enthused, clapping like a Sunday school teacher presented with pages of macaroni art. "However, based on CCTV footage alone, I believe I can exclude at least three people. Watch this." She tapped her laptop's keyboard. "See that man sitting near the bar at 12:07? That's Bob Junkett. Second man to arrive. Last to leave at 2:32. See the cleaners sweeping up behind him? They had to tell him to go. Time of death hasn't been fixed yet, but—"

"It has. Your pardon, PC Gulls," Hetheridge called. Unlike Bhar, he didn't have to stand; his voice carried effortlessly to every corner of the classroom, which was instantly silenced. "This case has advanced almost too quickly to facilitate proper sharing of information, but I spoke with Divisional Surgeon Garrett last night. Barring new developments, Mr. Hughes's time of death is now fixed at 1:46 am."

"Thank you, chief. That means Bob Junkett is eliminated, at least from doing the deed himself." The way PC Gulls swelled with happiness, not to mention her breathless pronunciation of the phrase "doing the deed," touched off another wave of laughter, but friendlier this time. It was too soon for her to win them over—Bhar knew of no tougher crowd in the world—but Hetheridge's support at that key moment had not gone unnoticed among the room's veteran officers.

"What is it about you and hopeless cases?" Bhar whispered to Hetheridge.

Hetheridge looked Bhar up and down before answering. "A question I've pondered for a very long time."

"Moving on," PC Gulls said, queuing up a new montage of footage. "Here's Thora Hughes. We have quite a long montage, some of which looks exciting. She arrives without an invitation at 9:02, goes straight to the bar, and gets a martini. She follows Mr. Hughes and Ms. Freemont around the room for the better part of an hour. Pretty stalkerish, I'll grant you. At 10:11 she finally approaches her estranged husband in the middle of a dance, and this is one time when audio would go down a treat, eh? But never fear! We enhanced the footage, slowed it down, and got a linguistics bloke to caption it. Here goes."

The footage seemed to zoom in, courtesy of the enhancement. Hughes looked embarrassed; Arianna looked merely cool. Thora, martini in hand, was pointing a finger at Hughes and speaking rapid-fire. This, however, had been slowed to permit lip-reading, with white captions along the bottom of the screen.

THORA: He hasn't been the same since he found out! You have to talk to him!

HUGHES: You're being melodramatic. This isn't the place.

THORA: He'll kill himself!

HUGHES: You know what the doctor said. There's a difference between suicidal intention and a pathological need for attention.

THORA: [inarticulate cry]

FREEMONT: Perhaps we should get some air.

HUGHES: Thora always does this to me, this is my hell. I'm used to it. The Gulf is nothing compared to what her and Griffin have put me through.

THORA: You can't mean that!

For the first time, PC Gulls's enthusiasm seemed dimmed. "I know. It's sad. But look! Bob Junkett's marching Thora out. Goodbye. And she doesn't just leave the gala, she leaves the hotel!"

More footage followed, much of it taken from outdoor cameras and consequently so grainy, the assembly could only take PC Gulls's word for its significance. "Here she is, driving away. Stopping at a traffic light. Disembarking at her home and not leaving until news of her husband's death the next day. That clears her, in my book. Now here's my final bit of good news. Arianna Freemont."

PC Gulls hit the button. Arianna, looking as calm and fresh at 12:42 as she had upon arrival, stood next to Hughes, deep in what appeared to be whispered conversation with another man. Their faces were turned from the camera, making lip-reading impossible.

"I don't know if she's bored and walks away to make a point," PC Gulls said. "Or if she and Hughes agreed ahead of time to part at a certain hour. There's no evidence, in the footage leading up to this, of anything amiss between them. Even after Thora Hughes's confrontation, Ms. Freemont seems perfectly serene. But look, off she goes, while Hughes keeps right on talking to Leo Makepeace, the hotel manager. And watch this. Hotel cameras follow her to the fifth floor. She goes to her room, engages the security devices, and doesn't emerge until the next day. Another elimination."

"Unless there's a conspiracy!" someone called.

"Well. Of course." PC Gulls grinned as if nothing thrilled her more than wide-ranging murder plots. "But this is—well, you know. The money shot." Giggling, she queued up footage of Hughes exiting the ballroom with Leo Makepeace in tow, heading for the elevator. "It's 12:57. Hughes disappears into a bunch of Gorilla Kingdom footage. And Leo Makepeace? He leaves the gala at 1:01, only to mysteriously reappear on the first floor at 2:02. Enters his office for a short time, goes home, but returns at 5:45 the next morning. Almost as if he expected bad news for Hotel Nonpareil and wanted to be there to handle it personally."

Bhar elbowed Hetheridge. "I don't care how much circumstantial evidence piles up. You can't tell me that little milquetoast is a murderer."

"How extraordinary. I would have taken a bet you didn't know the term 'milquetoast,'" Hetheridge replied. "More fool me."

"PC Gulls!" Kate stood up and waved.

"Yes! Sergeant Wakefield. Congrats on your upcoming wedding!"

Lots of noise followed that remark, not all of it friendly. PC Gulls didn't seem to notice, and Bhar was pleased when Kate affected the same indifference.

"Do you have footage of Griffin Hughes leaving the gala?"

"I do. He exited around midnight," PC Gulls said. "But since his suite was on the eighth floor, he disappeared into the same void as his father, I'm afraid. And definitely didn't leave Hotel Nonpareil that night."

"What about Riley Castanet?"

"Remember what I said about stalkerish?" PC Gulls beamed. "I have untold footage of Ms. Castanet watching Hughes and Freemont. Whenever they're dancing, Ms. Castanet is nearby. Practically doing the tango, even if she has to grab a waiter for a partner. Whenever they get in line for drinks, she's there, laughing and boogying and doing everything possible to draw attention to herself. But she never directly causes a scene. And when Hughes and Makepeace leave, she leaves, too, not five minutes later."

"Where does she go?" Kate asked.

"I have footage showing her returning to her room. On the eighth floor." PC Gulls shrugged. "Which puts us back at Gorilla Kingdom."

"Got any good footage of apes humping?" somebody shouted.

"I do, but it'll cost you," PC Gulls shouted back.

Bhar couldn't contain himself. "What about Sir Duncan Godington? You said he left around ten o'clock. Does the CCTV footage give him an alibi or not?"

For the first time, PC Gulls looked unhappy. "Wonderful question. So glad you asked. But as a matter of fact, that's where things get strange. Let me find the correct montage."

As it began to play, she said, "This is Sir Duncan leaving the gala at 10:03. He and Lady Isabel return to the penthouse. And here, at 10:55, is a moment when the cameras near the penthouse just—stop. For exactly twenty-two seconds, they transmit nothing but static. Fifty-one seconds later, the same thing happens on Hotel Nonpareil's first floor. Again, twenty-one seconds later, in the parking garage."

"Flash technology? Bright light from a torch or mobile scrambling the cameras?" Bhar whispered to Kate.

"Sure sounds like it. Though I can't think of a time it's ever actually worked in practice, rather than theory."

"... never happened," PC Gulls continued.

"Sorry!" Bhar called. "Say again?"

"All this might lead to the impression Sir Duncan or Lady Isabel—or, let's be thorough, both of them together— left the penthouse, took the elevator to the parking garage, and consequently left Hotel Nonpareil. But neither of their vehicles exited the garage. Nor was either person photographed on the street," PC Gulls said. "Moreover, as far as any footage of either or both returning to the penthouse? Sorry, never happened."

"Do you have other anomalies? Other times the hotel's CCTV cameras seem to fail?" Bhar asked.

"I do," PC Gull said. "At 12:42, in the parking garage. And at 2:03, outside the penthouse."

Bhar looked at Hetheridge, then Kate. He didn't want to speak up, but he had to, no matter how much unfriendly ribbing it cost him later.

"So you're saying someone in the penthouse traveled down to the garage. Someone who, according to all prior footage, had to be Sir Duncan or Lady Isabel. And that person came upstairs after Hughes left the gala, yet returned to the penthouse only after Hughes died?"

"Yes." PC Gulls looked slightly deflated. "But that's all I'm saying. There's no hard evidence to support any further conclusion."

Chapter Eighteen

Ritchie was having trouble adjusting to the reality of Henry's early move to Wellegrave House, so after the CCTV footage conference, Kate went home to console her brother. Kissing her goodbye, Hetheridge exited Scotland Yard onto Broadway, where Harvey waited inside the idling Bentley. As Hetheridge climbed into the limousine's capacious rear, he was startled to find Henry inside, a book about dinosaurs open on his lap.

"I say. Why aren't you at the house?"

Henry blinked owlishly. "It's half-seven."

Hetheridge nodded, uncertain what working late, something he'd done at least three times a week for the last thirty-odd years, had to do with anything.

"Harvey had to leave home to pick you up."

Hetheridge waited.

"There are no other servants. I'm eight years old. I'm not meant to stay home alone."

"Oh. Well. Of course not." Hetheridge cleared his throat. "Is that, er, homework?"

"They don't give me homework about dinosaurs."

"Do they not? A pity, that."

They sat in silence as Harvey pulled away from the curb. Feeling Henry's eyes upon him, Hetheridge was tempted to pull out his mobile and pretend to work. He liked the boy, but up until now, their interactions had been scheduled. This was the first time Hetheridge had left the Yard bone-tired, ready for a late dinner and nightcap, only to find himself the object of juvenile interrogation.

"I like my new room," Henry offered suddenly. "But Kate says Ritchie had a huge meltdown when I didn't come home."

"Yes. Odd. He didn't seem troubled before."

"He never does, until something actually changes. Wait till we all move in." Henry peered at Hetheridge as if sizing him up. "Are you still trying to catch the murderer?"

"Yes."

"Did you get a look at the dead body?"

"Hughes's body, you mean? I did."

"Was it cool?"

"No."

"I wonder how Dylan looked," Henry said, meaning Kate's former lover, who'd left a hole in the boy's life with his sudden disappearance. "When he was dead, I mean. I know you went with Kate to identify the body, but she won't tell me about it. It's not fair. I knew Dylan as well as she did."

"Perhaps she wants to spare you. Many people are barely recognizable in death. Better to remember them as they were."

Henry was silent until the next traffic light. "You won't die, will you?"

"Not on purpose."

"I know what happened to Paul. He got stabbed. Could you get stabbed?"

"I suppose. We don't get to choose these things."

"You could have picked a safer job."

Hetheridge laughed. "Yes, I could have. But in that case, I wouldn't have met Kate, and I wouldn't have met you. We just have to pick a direction and hope for the best."

"I'm glad you met us," Henry said. Squirming, he pushed his glasses up his nose and bent over the book, as if wholly reabsorbed. Hetheridge, equally uncomfortable with such declarations, was relieved. He had just settled back on the seat and closed his eyes for a power nap when his mobile rang. It was the Met, an extension he didn't recognize.

"Hetheridge."

"Hello, Chief Superintendent. This is PC York with the PCeU. We have preliminary findings regarding your inquiry into one Ming Xu Zhao, AKA Steve Zhao."

"Continue."

"Mr. Zhao is difficult to pin down. His personal emails go through proxies. He appears to have created an FTP server on his home computer to conceal his IP address. For Facebook and Twitter, he seems to utilize a password generator that—"

"Forgive me," Hetheridge broke in. "I take this to mean you can't eavesdrop on Mr. Zhao's personal emails? Or his social networking?"

"Yes, sir. Exactly, sir," said PC York, whose squeaky voice made him sound as if he were twelve years old. "So we had to fall back on the next best thing. We found a less gifted friend discussing Mr. Zhao in a hacker forum, and followed that IP address back to Hotel Nonpareil. We'll send you the complete details tomorrow, but it seems like a promising lead. Mr. Zhao's friend is still employed at Hotel Nonpareil. His name is Dirk Oakenwood."

"Come again?"

"Dirk. Oakenwood. I know, it sounds like a dwarf from the *Lord of the Rings*. Or a porn star. Or some combination of both. Anyway, sir, Mr. Oakenwood made the following statements in a chat room called Whackhack: 'Stevie Zhao is God.' 'SZ makes the cameras his bitches.' 'Never laughed so hard when BJ saw the live ape feed.' It all sounds relevant, eh, sir?"

"Highly relevant. Thank you very much." As Hetheridge rang off, he wondered how a good father, as opposed to a good policeman, would treat the revelation. Calling Jules to warn her was out of the question. Not only was such an action out of bounds, as far as professional ethics, it would be profoundly foolish, given their tenuous father-daughter relationship. If told, Jules would surely pass the news to Steve Zhao, who might try to flee. And if Zhao had tampered with hotel cameras at Sir Duncan's behest, and could be convinced to turn Queen's Evidence, the baronet might find himself put away at long last.

"Who was that?" Henry asked.

"Impertinent question."

"I'm just trying to learn." Henry heaved a great sigh. "I can't help you with the case if I don't hear the details."

"Does Kate give you the details?"

"No."

"Then why should I?"

Henry looked aghast. "But we can talk to each other. Man to man."

"Oh. Of course. Well. Do you know anything about email proxies?"

"Proxies are like middlemen. So you can make your emails untraceable."

"What about an FTP server?"

"Your computer has a permanent address called an IP. Anything you do on the internet can be traced back to it. Unless you go through something like an FTP server. Then what you do on your computer, if traced, points to other addresses, making it impossible to prove you did anything bad." Henry grinned. "Basic hacker trick."

"I begin to think these man to man discussions could prove useful," Hetheridge said. "Tell me—" His mobile chimed again.

"Is that Tony? Tony Hetheridge?"

"It is." Flummoxed by the plummy female voice, Hetheridge feared his nephew Roderick's wife had called his mobile number, perhaps to plead that the wedding be called off. "To whom do I have the honor of—"

"Bonnie! Bonnie Venicombe! I know you haven't forgotten old Bonnie Blue." That nickname had arisen from her habit of swearing a blue streak at the slightest provocation. One of many personality traits that had been forced underground after she and Alastair reconciled, and he ran for general election.

"Of course I haven't forgotten." Easy manners came naturally to Hetheridge; it took more effort for him to be rude, or merely standoffish, than to respond with the correct measure of warmth. "How are you, Bonnie? Ghastly business about your son-in-law. I do hope you're holding up."

"Striving on, old boots! Striving on," Bonnie said, sounding for all the world like a woman on vacation, shouting down a phone line from some tropical paradise. "I'm afraid I've called to ask a personal favor."

"Bonnie." Hetheridge let the pause draw out. "You understand my position at Scotland Yard. It's unlikely I can grant any favors. I might even be obliged to make your request public."

"Tony." She sounded shocked. "You'd never do that."

"I'm afraid I would. Tread with care, Bonnie."

"Very well. I don't care if this runs on the *Guardian's* front page tomorrow. I want you to eliminate Griffin Hughes as a suspect. I give you my word the boy is innocent. And I happen to know you don't have a shred of evidence against him, because that would be impossible."

"Bonnie. We know Michael Martin Hughes didn't want Thora or Griffin anywhere near him. We know Griffin threatened to kill him. We have DNA evidence that Griffin was inside the suite at least once—"

"Of course he was! They were father and son! Griffin has a sad history. He tried to kill himself, and he'll do it again if pushed to the limits." Bonnie paused, and Hetheridge realized she fighting to control herself. "What does it matter if he prevailed upon Michael to let him in the suite for a few minutes before the gala? A little bird told me Michael died *after* one in the morning, and if so—"

"Who have you been talking to?"

"Just a friend. I still have a few in high places, you know. And if Michael died after one a.m., Griffin couldn't have been with him when the murder happened."

"Why?"

"Because he was with me."

Hetheridge was so startled, it took him a moment to reply. "Bonnie, Griffin is your grandson. What—what precisely do you mean?"

She laughed. What followed was a flood of coarse language, a throwback to the old Bonnie Blue. "I didn't mean he was *with* me. Heavens, are you still stung because I threw you over for a younger man? As if you haven't found a pretty young thing of your own these days." Another laugh. "No, I mean I met Griffin at Hotel Nonpareil. I arrived after he left the gala—the hotel's security cameras should prove I'm telling the truth. Thora was so angry with Michael, she stormed off to be alone. But Griffin called me to the suite and spent half the night unburdening himself to me. It's only natural." Bonnie paused. "I am his mother, after all."

Hetheridge struggled to let that sink in. "Explain."

"Oh, heavens, I thought you were a detective. It's simple. I met Michael some years ago, when he was handsome and wet behind the ears and looking for some fun. It went a little too far, and after I reconciled with Alastair, I found myself with child. By that time, Michael was dating Thora, and we were all looking for a solution. So I went to the country and had Griffin in a private clinic. I turned him over to Thora and Michael once they were wed. The transaction would have remained hush-hush, of course, but for Griffin's childhood leukemia. Then, in the interests of genetic profiling, the doctors had to know everything, and inevitably Griffin heard."

She sighed. "To say the truth rocked his world, his sense of self, is not to say enough, I fear."

"I imagine it did," Hetheridge said, thinking of Jules. "Bonnie. It's not that I doubt you. Indeed, I feel strongly you're telling the truth. But if you want me to exonerate Griffin, I'll need more than your testimony. Michael Martin Hughes was murdered, and my primary responsibility is to him."

"I don't understand. What more can I offer, beyond my testimony?"

"Something objective. Did Griffin call anyone that night? Text anyone? Use his computer?"

"As a matter of fact, we were on the laptop half the night," Bonnie said. "Griffin loves to Skype. He can't just text anyone, he has to see their face as they talk."

"I see. One moment." Covering the mouthpiece of his mobile, Hetheridge turned to Henry, who'd blatantly followed the conversation as best he could. "If someone Skypes for several hours, is that traceable?"

"A normal person with a normal IP address? You bet," Henry said.

Hetheridge put the phone back to his ear. "Bonnie. I can't promise anything. But there's a very good chance Griffin will be excluded as a person of interest sometime tomorrow."

***

"Almost there," Harvey said over his shoulder. Despite the late hour, London traffic had been slower than usual. Fender benders, road closures, and an unusually high number of cyclists were to blame. "Must be a bloody bike festival. But our turn's in sight, Lord Hetheridge. And Master Henry."

Master Henry, the boy mouthed silently to Hetheridge, beside himself with pleasure.

Just as Harvey pulled into Wellegrave House's drive, Hetheridge's mobile rang for the third time. Hoping it was

Kate with some good news about Ritchie, Hetheridge found himself looking at a less welcome name: VICTOR JACKSON.

"Vic. It's Tony. What's up?"

"The little weasel's lost his marbles."

"Ah. Mr. Makepeace, I assume?"

"Yep. He's dirty. Whoever called the tip line had him pegged. Dumb bugger barely covered his tracks. He wouldn't have lasted six months in the Cotswolds before the Yard came calling."

"And I assume he's aware of the probe."

"Yes."

"What's his status?"

"Locked in his office, sobbing and demanding to speak to Riley Castanet."

"Really? Or what?"

"He says he has a shooter, and he'll blow his brains out if his demands aren't met." DCI Jackson sighed. "You know he's a liar. At most he might have a replica gun, but I doubt it. I've half a mind to call for special response. Stand back and watch while they blow his office to smithereens. But I figured you'd want me to call you first. This is your specialty, isn't it? Finding the rich and their hangers-on *in extremis* and feeling their pain?"

"Something like that. Don't call special response. Just the usual backup. I'll be there inside half an hour."

When Hetheridge disconnected, he found both Harvey and Henry regarding him with exaggerated interest. "I need to go to Hotel Nonpareil," he said. "If you'll let me out here, Harvey, I'll walk to the garage, engage the Lexus and drive myself."

"It would be quicker to turn around, sir," Harvey said.

Hetheridge sighed. Suppose Makepeace, against all odds, actually had a gun? How would Kate like it if her future husband's first night of babysitting consisted of keeping an eight-year-old out late on a school night and exposing him to potential harm?

"Here's something even quicker." Hetheridge dialed Bhar's mobile, telling Henry, "One of the perks of command."

"Pulling rank?" the boy asked eagerly.

"Delegating."

Chapter Nineteen

Perfect, Bhar thought when the call came through. *Absolutely perfect.*

"I do hope I'm not putting too much strain on your romantic life," Hetheridge said. Generally there was zero tolerance for such concerns during a high-profile murder case, but given his own upcoming wedding, the guv had noticeably mellowed. Not that he would hesitate to ruin Bhar's late dinner with Kyla Sloane. But he'd learned to apologize for the inconvenience, rather than simply issue orders from on high.

"Well, I did have a date, but since I've already called once to push the time back, I don't suppose phoning her up to cancel will come as a huge shock."

"Blonde or brunette?"

"Brunette."

"I'm surprised your mum will stand for you dating two young women, neither of whom has been brought round for inspection."

"What she doesn't kn—bloody hell!" Bhar stamped the brake, almost hooking the Astra into the curb to avoid a collision. The drivers behind him honked, pedestrians fell over themselves, and the big black dog he'd nearly hit disappeared toward a public green. Bhar saw a shaggy coat, no collar, no lead, and yellow eyes. Then it was gone.

"Paul," Hetheridge was saying in his ear. "Are you all right?"

"Fine. Fine. I really need to pull over when I answer the phone. Something always happens."

"Taxi?"

"Nope. Just the Grim, or the Black Shuck, or whatever you want to call it. Again." As the pedestrians moved on, and angry drivers behind him climbed the curb to get around the Astra, Bhar continued to idle, waiting to see if the dog would stop or double back. Although Central London was remarkably well-lit after dark, Bhar saw nothing. The animal had vanished.

"I've refrained from saying anything until now," Hetheridge continued. "But you returned to work rather quickly after your surgery. Most officers injured in the line of duty take more time. Perhaps you should—"

"I'm not hallucinating and I'm not having a nervous breakdown," Bhar insisted, hoping it was true. "I'm in tip-top condition, hot on the trail, ready to rumble, and every other cliché. I mean, you're the one who's entered the final countdown, guv," he added, rejoining the flow of traffic. "Cold feet yet?"

"Of course not. Impatient, if you want the truth."

"You're not alone. Mum's dying for details about the honeymoon. Maybe that's why she's been so distracted lately. Over the moon for you and Kate, swept up in a vicarious romance."

"Give your mum my best."

Bhar chuckled. "Careful. Married or no, she might write another sexy book about you," he said and rang off.

***

"Vic! What's the word?" Bhar called to DCI Jackson. Hotel Nonpareil's valet stand was blocked by police cars; a gauntlet of uniforms had required Bhar to hand over his warrant card four times to get from point A to point B. The hotel's lobby had been evacuated, the staff voluntarily locked in some windowless inner room.

"Oh, thank the Lord." DCI Jackson peppered his phony devotion with a few choice phrases never associated with the Church of England. "If it ain't Captain Golliwog."

"Gotta move with the times, Vic. Learn to be a little more PC. My people prefer 'wog' these days." Bhar was too seasoned to let the slur demoralize him. Not long ago, Vic Jackson had been demoted from Superintendent to DI, only clawing his way back up to DCI by virtue of another suspiciously quick arrest. No matter how often he succeeded on the job, the man couldn't seem to open his mouth with saying something mere mortals would be sacked for. Surely if Bhar waited long enough, the Yard's old boy network would tire of protecting Jackson, and his dismissal would come at last.

"I'm surprised the old man couldn't be bothered to show up," DCI Jackson continued. "Top brass is losing faith in him, you know."

"The Hughes case is barely six days old. I refuse to believe anyone with half a brain has lost confidence in the guv."

"I didn't say folks with half a brain. I said top brass, didn't I?" DCI Jackson shook his head. "Never mind. Peer through those rose-colored glasses as long as you can. I've glimpsed the future, Paulie, and it won't be pretty for any of us."

"You've glimpsed the future?" Bhar, accustomed to getting nothing but sarcasm or bluster from DCI Jackson, strained for what he assumed must be a punchline. "Been talking to Riley Castanet?"

"No. Assistant Commissioner Deaver. But never mind, Paulie. I'll leave this in your hands. Just keep whistling past the graveyard," DCI Jackson said, and left.

Bhar found four PCs gathered near Leo Makepeace's office door. Each possessed riot gear—Kevlar vests, helmets, firearms, and clear Plexiglas shields. The leader gave Bhar a curt nod.

"I'm from Hetheridge's team. I take it Mr. Makepeace is still holed up. Has he asked the mediator for anything?"

"Anything? More like everything. A helicopter to Heathrow. A private jet to Switzerland. Immunity from prosecution. And the psychic lady; he's desperate for her. Says she's the only one who understands him. Mind you, she's a nutter, too. Usually in the event of threatened violence in a public venue, ordering civilians into lockdown is sufficient. Not for her."

"I'm not surprised." Bhar remembered how Riley had burst into Hughes's murder scene, promising shock and awe to any who detained her.

"She tried to travel down via the lifts, so we deactivated them. Then she crept down the stairs. She was halfway to the lobby before she was intercepted and escorted back up."

"All to come to Mr. Makepeace's aid?"

The officer nodded.

"Which suite is she in?"

"804."

"Mind if I go up?"

"You'll have to use the stairs."

***

"Deepal!" Riley opened her door wide. "Come in! Now this is service!"

"Service?" He followed her inside the suite. Although far less opulent than Hughes's, it was still top drawer, with a balcony, sitting room, gigantic television, and full kitchen. But either the maid service was inadequate, or Riley generated more chaos than the average lodger. The rubbish bins overflowed. What looked like red wine stained the carpet. Ladies' clothing, including bras and knickers in hot pink and lime green, were strewn about the room. Altogether, it looked like a sorority party's dying throes.

"Yes, the cops were very rude to me. Wait till I call the US Embassy. Heads will roll!" Riley's somewhat dilated pupils, not to mention a whiff of her breath, told Bhar she wasn't on her second or even third drink of the evening. Still, she looked very smart in a black pantsuit cut to emphasize her full bosom and slim legs. Sleek black pumps and a rope of chocolate diamonds around her neck completed the ensemble. Bhar had to admit, Riley was many things, but unattractive wasn't one of them.

"Anyway, the police were smart to send you to apologize. And I'm sure you understand, I was frantic about poor Leo. He texted me fifteen times, threatening to shoot himself, but what did the cops do? Put me under house arrest."

"Lockdown, you mean, and only for your own protection." Surprised by her apparent sincerity, Bhar couldn't resist asking an equally frank question. "Did you really think you could help him? I mean, no offense, but it seems like if you're all that psychic, you could have told Makepeace not to embezzle from the hotel. Or, barring that, not to cover his tracks so poorly."

"Spoken like every amateur I've ever met. Oh! My e-cigarette is charged at last!" Popping a fresh cartridge onto the device, she took a drag. "Much better. Anyhow, being a seer doesn't work that way."

"Convenient. If fortunetelling worked the way everything else in the world does, you folks could be sued for malpractice." Bhar expected Riley to bristle at the statement. Instead she laughed.

"Don't be scared. It's not a death omen."

"What?"

"The black dog. Your aura's spinning like a kaleidoscope. Everything about you is shouting 'black dog,' but it's not a death omen."

Bhar gaped at her. For a moment, he was pleased that someone acknowledged the black dog was real, even if that someone was Riley Castanet. Then the hairs on the back of his neck rose. It was real. The black dog was real.

"I ... I can't believe you picked that up," he stammered.

"No one ever believes me. Not till I prove myself, and then they never stop believing. But seriously, Bhar, most people don't get death omens," Riley continued.

"Why not?"

"Probably because most people don't believe they're going to die. Not really. Even Michael thought he'd live forever."

"But you said you met Hughes because of a death omen. One you misinterpreted."

"Yes, but I'm a psychic. I see all kinds of things, mostly about other people. My own future? Always comes as a surprise. You wanna know more about the black dog?" Riley didn't wait for Bhar to answer. Closing her eyes, she sounded less eerily prophetic and more like a happy drunk. "Change. That's what it means. I know it terrifies you. But change is coming at you from all sides."

"The, er, good kind of change?"

Eyes opening, she released his hand. "What do you think?"

"Right. Er. Fair enough," Bhar said, still shaken. "In the meantime, since you're in touch with his spirit, I don't suppose Mr. Hughes has confided his killer's identity yet?"

"Not yet." Going to the kitchen, Riley opened the fridge. "I knew it. Out of Chardonnay. This house arrest better end soon, or I'll be the next one to threaten violence. Anyway, it's tough, Deepal, settling into the next life. When I ask Michael to talk to me, he always says the same thing. 'Fur.'"

"'Fur?'"

"'Or 'purr.' Which might indicate a killer with an excessive number of housecats. Compulsive gathering of felines is a psychiatric disorder," Riley said wisely. "Mind you, Michael isn't sending me images of cats. Mostly, I get monkeys."

"Monkeys?"

"Big scary ones. Like King Kong."

Bhar struggled to evince no reaction. During a murder investigation, many distinct facts were kept from the general public. In Hughes's case, the diversion of the security camera feed, from the eighth floor to Gorilla Kingdom, had not been shared with the media. Yet Riley was referencing it so artlessly, Bhar was nearly certain she didn't know what she was saying. He saw only two conclusions. Either someone in the hotel— Bob Junkett, Steve Zhao, or the online braggart, Dirk Oakenwood—leaked the news, or Riley Castanet had scored another direct hit.

"When you say King Kong, do you mean—"

The suite's phone rang. Making a grab for it, Riley turned too quickly, turning her ankle and almost falling. When Bhar steadied her, she clung to him.

"Oh, this really is service." Giggling, Riley exhaled e-cigarette fumes directly in his face.

"I'll get the phone," Bhar said, disentangling himself. As he suspected, the call was for him, the officer's report crisp and to the point.

"What is it? Emergency Chardonnay delivery?" She giggled again.

"No. The standoff with Makepeace is over. But that doesn't mean you can go wandering around the hotel again. Stay up here till the all-clear is given. I mean it, Riley! We'll talk again later."

***

At the lobby level, Bhar eased the stairwell door open by a millimeter, afraid a flicker of movement at the wrong time might make some trigger-happy officer's day. When no shots were fired and no threats were issued, he eased into the lobby, head down and hands up.

"All clear?" he asked the nearest Kevlar-suited PC.

"All clear." The man put his Plexiglas shield aside. "Weapon collected, subject in custody."

"Who fired?"

"Makepeace. He really did have a gun in his office." The officer shook his head in amazement. "Antique Colt. Single action Army. A thing of beauty, really. Wild West stuff."

"So he tried to kill himself?"

"No. After the mediator convinced him he was just going to hospital for a mental health eval, Makepeace unlocked the door. Tried to pass over the gun, but his hands were so sweaty, he slipped and fired. If the sarge hadn't been wearing body armor...." The PC drew a finger across his throat. "Nervous little wallys and firearms don't mix."

"No argument there." Hetheridge waited until Makepeace, handcuffed and glistening with perspiration, was led out of his office. As the mediator had promised, Hotel Nonpareil's former manager would go first to hospital, then to a psychiatric unit. Quite possibly, Makepeace, like thousands of inept crooks before him, imagined he could convince a sympathetic doctor that he was harmlessly touched in the head. More likely, he would serve five to ten years at Her Majesty's pleasure.

"Mr. Makepeace! One question!" Bhar called.

The armed officers looked surprised. So did Leo Makepeace, blinking at Bhar several times before understanding broke over his face.

"Wow. Scotland Yard. You weren't called because of me, were you?"

"Afraid so."

"Whoops. Sorry." Makepeace shrugged as much as his handcuffs allowed. "Just so you know, I didn't kill Mr. Hughes. I mean, I hated him. He called me into his suite several times to complain about this or that. Moaned all during the gala. Made every day torture for me. I couldn't have borne it, I think, if I hadn't believed myself about to escape the hotel business forever." He smiled sadly. "But I didn't kill him."

"I believe you," Bhar said, and meant it. "But I have one further question. That antique Colt. How long have you owned it?"

"It's been in my family forever."

"Did Riley Castanet know you had it?"

"Of course. She laid hands on it while she described my past life. She's a real professional psychic, you know."

"Of course," Bhar said, stepping back so the officers could lead Makepeace away.

***

After the hotel staff were permitted to resume their duties, employees were dispatched to every floor to knock on doors and assure all occupants the threat had passed. Bhar took a reactivated lift up to Riley's floor, only to catch her a second time as the doors parted and she stumbled inside.

"Oh, Deepal. I'm not drunk. It's these heels." She laughed. "The tyranny is over! The British are defeated and the hotel bar is open again. What say we get a drink? I'm entitled. Still in mourning for Michael, you know."

"Yes, we all see that. Your devotion to my dead fiancé is remarkable." Equally elegant in black, with the exception of a bright blue scarf across her shoulders, Arianna Freemont entered the lift.

"Ms. Freemont? What are you doing here?" Bhar asked.

"And why are you wearing that?" Riley stabbed a finger at the blue scarf.

Ignoring Riley, Arianna studied Bhar. "You're a police officer." It was not a question.

"Yes, I'm Detective Sergeant Paul Bhar. My deepest condolences on your—"

"Never mind that." Arianna's hair was flawless, her makeup airbrushed perfection. "As to why I'm here, I came to clear out the remaining possessions in Michael's suite. What little Scotland Yard didn't seize as evidence." She indicated the leather tote on her arm, which didn't look more than half full. "I was caught up in the lockdown. And now, not that it's any of your business, I'm meeting a professional contact."

"But that's mine!" Riley shrieked, still fixated on the scarf. "You took that out of his suite, didn't you?"

"I did. It was gift boxed with a note for me." The lift dinged on the lobby level. Back straight and head high, Arianna disembarked. She'd taken only two steps when Riley caught her by the arm and spun her around.

"I was there when Michael passed that scarf in a shop window. It was on a mannequin. See the blue butterflies in the weave? I love butterflies. They're like a totem for me. That's the blue butterfly scarf Michael promised to give me!"

"Riley, stop!" Interposing himself between the two women, Bhar fought to pry Riley's fingers off Arianna's arm. "Surely there's some mistake."

"There's no mistake. Riley's just playing to type." Arianna didn't smile or frown. Her only emotion was in her voice, heavy with certainty. "Sergeant Bhar, there are people in this world who expect to get everything they want. And when they can't get it freely, they lie, cheat, or steal. My uncle was like that, and he wound up dead. Careful the same doesn't happen to you, Mary Ann."

Riley jerked as if slapped.

"Oh, yes. When Michael told me about that brief, tawdry little affair, I hired a private investigator. It didn't take long to get at the truth," Arianna said. "You're Mary Ann Johnston from Valdosta, Georgia. You had three convictions for shoplifting as a juvenile. Went bankrupt as a dog groomer...."

"I didn't—"

"Changed your name, moved to California, and reinvented yourself as a seer," Arianna continued inexorably. "Had two more arrests for shoplifting. Spent six weeks wearing an orange jumpsuit, picking up rubbish along the freeway. I just wish Michael had lived long enough for me to tell him. Then I would have had the pleasure of watching him fire you. And trust me. Your days of wine and roses on Peerless's expense account are almost over."

Riley was pale except for a spot of color on each cheek. Behind her, the lift dinged again, doors opening. Other guests filed out, staring, but Riley didn't move. "Michael loved me. He bought that scarf for me."

"Perhaps." Arianna's mouth stretched in an approximation of a smile. "But in the end, he decided I was the one who deserved it." Her eyes flicked to Bhar. "Now. If you'll let me pass, I'm meeting someone at the bar."

Undone by her effortless poise, Bhar stepped aside. When he turned back to Riley, she'd entered the lift, head down and arms wrapped around her chest.

"Riley?"

"Forget about the drink. Leave me alone."

"Riley, if there's anything—" Bhar stopped, surprised at himself, and the shiny brass doors shut in his face. Had he really almost asked Riley Castanet, psychic fraud and murder suspect, if there was anything he could do?

She cheated when it came to Makepeace and the Wild West. But how did she know about the black dog?

He checked his watch. It was past ten o'clock. Far too late to beg Kyla's forgiveness, and Emmeline would shred him if he tried treating her like a booty call. Even his mum had surely finished writing for the night and gone to bed.

It was likely Hotel Nonpareil's first level bar served a limited menu, even this late. Bhar wandered inside, intent on a pint of bitter at the very least. Clearly the lockdown had unsettled the guests, who'd poured into the bar for a drink and a chance to discuss Makepeace's meltdown. In the far corner, something blue caught Bhar's eye. It was the butterfly scarf.

Arianna Freemont sat at a round table with four others: Sir Duncan Godington, Jules Hetheridge, an Asian man who met Steve Zhao's description and another young man who, based on how transparently he hung on Sir Duncan's every word, might be Dirk Oakenwood.

***

Bhar didn't know what to do. Getting close to the group was physically impossible; he was lucky to find a place at the bar's opposite end. Of course, if he waited long enough, the crowd might thin, allowing him to drift within earshot. But the five of them weren't blind or mentally enfeebled. Someone would notice the policeman in their midst and move the party elsewhere. Probably lodge a harassment complaint, too.

Still. They were right there, all five together, impossible to ignore or walk away from. Arianna had mentioned a business contact. Was that Sir Duncan? With Michael Martin Hughes dead, was Sir Duncan's offer to become Peerless Petrol's environmental czar being reconsidered?

He finished his pint and ordered another. Jules's presence was troubling, but not damning. Each time Bhar dared a glance at the round table, he saw Arianna and Dirk focused on Sir Duncan. Jules and Steve seemed intent on one another.

Suppose Sir Duncan decides to kill Hughes. Hacking Hughes up was too obvious; he knows we're always watching, so poison seemed wiser. The CCTV cameras were the main problem. That flash stuff is cool, but uncertain. No one's used it to pull off a crime like this. Destroying or diverting the eighth floor's camera is much surer. He leans on an admirer, Dirk, to take care of it. But Dirk can't do it, so he goes to Steve, who's already disgruntled over Junkett. And Steve....

A hand fell on Bhar's shoulder. "Hello again, DC Bhar. Long time no see."

For the second time that night, the hackles rose on the back of Bhar's neck. Bad enough to hear Sir Duncan Godington say his name. Now the man had actually touched him.

Turning slowly on his barstool, Bhar managed to shrug off Sir Duncan's hand without erupting. There was nothing he wanted more than to punch the smile off the baronet's face.

"Do forgive me. Too familiar? I've always been a bit touchy-feely," Sir Duncan said.

"I was injured there. Stabbed."

"Were you? Terribly sorry, Constable. So typical of me. Putting my finger right on the spot that hurts."

"Sergeant," Bhar said through his teeth.

"What?"

"It's Detective Sergeant Bhar now."

"Is it? Congratulations. Of course, if it were up to me, you'd be Commissioner," Sir Duncan said. "I'll be happy to write a letter of commendation to your supervisors. It's the least I can do, after everything you've done for me."

Bhar said nothing. His pulse thudded so loud in his ears, he feared Sir Duncan could hear it.

"But past aside, here's what I've come to say. My friends and I can't help notice you sitting all alone, casting longing looks our way. Would you care to join us?"

Bhar's answer, in the calmest possible voice, made the lady sitting next to him gasp. Her male companion gave Bhar a stern look, but Sir Duncan only laughed.

"Right. So if you won't join us, Sergeant Bhar, why don't you run along home? I'm about to finalize a deal with Peerless Petrol. Help their PR department regain the public trust." His smile faded, voice dropping to a whisper. "Then I'll say good-bye to Ms. Freemont, get rid of the boys, and find out what really makes Jules Hetheridge tick."

"What?"

Sir Duncan's gaze never wavered. "Sorry. Tiny joke. She's not remotely my type. But your little Kyla, with the brown hair and the shy smile. Dating her now, aren't you? Yes, I've kept up through Tessa. And I think we both know Kyla's very much to my taste."

For once, Bhar found himself speechless. No joke, no threat, no clever retort. For years he'd believed he hated Sir Duncan. Only now did he realize how bottomless hatred could truly be.

"Nothing to say?" Sir Duncan patted Bhar's cheek, as an auntie might pat a small boy. "Then run along home, Sergeant, before I lose my patience."

***

Bhar decided not call Hetheridge or Kate. It was too late; Kate always had to make time for her home responsibilities, but Hetheridge had been working almost around the clock. Arriving to a dark house, Bhar crept up to his room, not wanting to wake Sharada. There he typed up his notes, emailing them to the case's statement reader. Work, even paperwork, was better than allowing himself to dwell on Sir Duncan's threats. Just as he was about to go to bed, he heard a noise. It sounded like someone rattling the front door.

Seizing a cricket bat, Bhar hurried downstairs. Before he reached the last step, the door opened, the house alarm screeched, and a strange woman wearing one of his mum's new dresses staggered into the house.

"Oh! Buck!" A gale of laughter. "Don't worry, I'll get it!"

The woman blundered toward the alarm's keypad. As Bhar watched, astonished, she input the code with exaggerated movements. Rather like Riley Castanet, trying to board the lift after a great deal of wine. Of course, Riley had been drunk. Never in Bhar's lifetime had his mother taken more than a sip of brandy, and that was only on Christmas.

"Mum?" he whispered, still holding the bat.

Sharada turned. Seeing Bhar in his pajamas, a dressing gown tied around his waist, she burst into a fresh gale of laughter. "Did we wake you? I'm so sorry. But it's good you're up. There's someone I want you to meet. Buck!"

Until that moment, Bhar had been too transfixed by the sight of Sharada inebriated to pay much attention to the figure on the front step. Now that figure entered—at least six-foot-three with gray hair, an extravagant moustache, blue jeans, a pewter belt buckle, and a Stetson he removed the moment he crossed the threshold.

"Hello, son. I'm Buck Wainwright. You must be Deepal." He pronounced it *Deh-pall*.

"Are you an American?" Bhar heard himself quaver.

"Better than that! I'm a Texan." Buck grinned. He was handsome, in a TV western sort of way. Sharada grabbed his arm and squeezed. Bhar involuntarily raised the cricket bat.

"You got my mother *drunk*?"

Buck looked shocked. "It wasn't like that. I'm accustomed to vast quantities of tequila. I had no idea Sherry couldn't handle a few—"

"Sherry!" Bhar roared.

That seemed to sober his mother up. "Buck. I'm sorry. Bringing you home without first talking to my son was a mistake. Could you wait outside, please?"

"Of course." Buck settled his Stetson back on his head. "No disrespect intended, son."

"I'm not your son!" Bhar all but screamed.

"Deepal. Sit down." With a drunk's scrupulous care, Sharada made her way to the sofa. "We have to talk."

"This whole writer's group has been a lie, hasn't it?" Bhar accused. "You've been—what? Going to clubs? Picking up men?"

Sharada, who'd never once struck him, raised a hand as if there was a first time for everything. "How dare you speak to me that way? Of course the group is real. But it meets twice a week. The third night is all mine, to get out of this house and do whatever I like."

"I can see what you like. Where'd you dig up Sam Elliott?"

"Online."

"Perfect." Bhar groaned. "You know this is how lonely women get scammed, right? Bankrupted? Murdered and chopped into little pieces?

"Deepal—"

"Mum, this is madness. I won't have it. You running around with some cowboy stud and acting like a slag—"

He didn't quite get out the word "slag" before she made a noise so high and infuriated, it brought him up short. Her eyes filled with tears, a sight that caused him real physical pain.

More than once in his life, he'd made his mother cry. But never deliberately, and never with such a cruel word.

"Mum. I'm sorry. It's been a terrible day."

"I understand." She sniffed. "But Deepal, I'm not going to live forever. And writing love stories isn't enough anymore. Your father found someone. I need someone, too. I can't base my whole life around you."

"But you have. For, like, thirty-something years," Bhar protested. "I know you have. You've told me, every single day."

"I know." Sharada dabbed at her eyes. "But now it's time for a change."

Chapter Twenty

"It's not fair," Bhar muttered.

Kate, who'd listened to her colleague moan throughout lunch, clenched her fists before answering. "I know."

"I didn't mean to get the guv in hot water."

"You've said that six times now."

"It's true."

"I know it's true," Kate burst out, and was shocked to find herself close to tears. Weeping at work? At Scotland Yard? Talk about the fast track to irrelevancy.

Hetheridge had been in a meeting since half-eleven. It was now almost two. Even Mrs. Snell, that grim-faced office stalwart, had disappeared from her desk, phones forwarded without explanation. Demoralized by rumors in the canteen, and lacking any fresh direction on the case, Kate and Bhar had returned to Hetheridge's office to wait. And, in Bhar's case, self-flagellate.

"I should have figured out a better way to share the info," he said. "Held back on emailing everything to the statement reader. I know it's her job to keep everything current, but the way she worded this morning's update…."

"There's nothing wrong with how she worded the update. The problem was with the people reading it. They saw what they wanted to see."

It was true. Kate had never worked on a case with such an unforgiving timeline, or such unreasonable expectations from above. Bhar's raw report, which included mention of Arianna Freemont's allegations about Riley Castanet—her original name, point of origin, and arrest history—had been spun as proof that Hetheridge's team was fatally remiss. Riley was, after all, still a person of interest, her DNA all over Hughes's suite, her movements during the time of his murder unknown. To add an alias and a string of arrests shifted Riley into the role of prime suspect. The fact these details had been casually offered by Arianna and verified by the Met, instead of the other way round, was the sticking point.

"You don't think they'll demote him?" Bhar asked.

Kate gave a huff of frustration. Not trusting herself to sit and stare at Hetheridge's empty desk, she sprang up, beginning to pace.

"If we could just shore up the case against Sir Duncan," Bhar continued. "I mean, those light flashes that temporarily took out the CCTV cameras. Come on! It wasn't the Tooth Fairy scampering around Hotel Nonpareil, it was him. Arrogant *arse*! Thinks he's untouchable. I should have busted up that little drinking party last night. Arrested every one of them on suspicion of conspiracy to commit murder and—"

"And found yourself up on charges, got yourself reassigned to the Outer Hebrides, and put your mum in an early grave," Kate cut across him. "Look, I've done it. Arrested blighters to intimidate them into talking. But you know that tactic doesn't work on folks with a barrister on speed dial. Which means Sir Duncan, and Arianna, and Jules, for that matter. Might even apply to Hacker One and Hacker Two. Criminals are getting way too legal-savvy these days."

"All right, fine." Bhar sounded guardedly optimistic. "It wouldn't hurt to talk to Steve Zhao, Jules, and Oaken-dude.

See what three small fry had to do with a lovefest between Mr. Green Warrior and Ms. Big Oil Apologist.

"I quite agree." Hetheridge entered the office with a large framed print in his hands. "Sorry I've been off. Mrs. Snell and I met for lunch and had such a smashing time, we were away rather longer than expected."

Placing the print on his desk, Hetheridge looked from Kate to Bhar. "What is it? What's happened?"

"I, er, I fouled up, Chief," Bhar said humbly. Kate, unable to bear such contrition in a man better suited to cockiness, felt obliged to intervene.

"He didn't foul up. He just reported the facts, and someone exploited them. The rumor's all over the Yard. The Hughes case been passed to someone with a reputation for quick results. DCI Jackson."

"Yes, well, these things happen." Hetheridge smiled. "It's not the end of world. You two will continue to investigate, and I'll remain involved. In a more, well, advisory capacity."

"You—you heard?" Bhar looked stunned.

"Around the same time you did, I expect. AC Deaver rang me up with the news this morning. I would have met with you both, but as I said, I'd committed to lunch with Mrs. Snell. Today's her birthday. Though in typical fashion, it was she who gave me the present." Lifting the print, a black and white photograph of a park bench in autumn, Hetheridge moved to the nearest office wall, holding it against a blank space. "What do you think?"

Kate exchanged glances with Bhar. She knew from experience that Hetheridge was cool in adversity. But this acceptance of what amounted to an institutional slap in the face seemed over the top, even for him. Going to him, she took the print out of his hands and set it aside.

"You know, Tony, stiff upper lip notwithstanding... if you want to vent some outrage, now's the time."

He raised an eyebrow, and then looked at Bhar. "Close the office door."

On his feet, Bhar scrambled to obey. Settling into his office chair, Hetheridge tilted back, one foot on the desk. "The fact is, today is indeed Mrs. Snell's birthday. But we didn't leave the Yard merely to celebrate the occasion. We went to talk strategy."

"About the case?" Bhar asked.

Kate made an exasperated sound. "About what's coming next."

"The Hughes case has been unusual. No doubt Bonnie Venicombe exerted what pressure she could, but even after her son Griffin's exoneration, the demands continued. I suspect the point was simple: either to back me into a corner where failure was inevitable, or goad me into overreaching my authority. Given my record, one failure isn't enough. But breaking procedure in desperation? That would have triggered my own early retirement."

"Because you're marrying me?" Kate's voice sounded anguished, even to her own ears.

"Because times are changing. The men—and women— at the top have mostly been replaced. I once told you much of the Met was run by dinosaurs. Well, now the meteor is on the horizon, and our day is almost done."

"You never had any trouble before you announced our engagement."

"No, but if it wasn't that, it would have been something else. Trust me, Kate. You, too, Paul. There's no need to look so downcast. As I told Mrs. Snell...." Hetheridge stopped. "I do seem to be quoting myself a great deal lately. Proof of age, or egotism, or both. But believe me. The old man has some fight in him yet."

Kate found herself smiling. This, perhaps, was trust. Knowing intellectually that Hetheridge was in trouble, that the powers above were lining up against him, yet feeling a curious faith in his ability to make things right. After years of being systematically taught to distrust, and learning the lesson all too well, she felt almost childlike again, realizing she trusted this man. Not because he could bend the cosmos to his will, but because when it came to her, he intended nothing but the best.

"So what can we do?"

"For a start, I'd like Paul to bring Ms. Castanet in for a second round of questioning. It quite likely will turn into an arrest, but Paul, we need you to be as thorough as you can," Hetheridge said. "At present, what we have is mostly circumstantial evidence, and while it's considerable, that doesn't play well with juries who've spent years watching *CSI*.

"Next, we need to look at Sir Duncan again. Make sure there isn't some stone we've left unturned. To that end, Kate, I'd like you to speak to Dirk Oakenwood. Don't wear your engagement ring. See if you can charm him."

She grinned. "It's worth a try. What about you?"

"I'll prevail upon Jules's better nature. I can't pretend much optimism, but it's worth a try. If her connection to Sir Duncan is as peripheral as she claimed, if he befriended her to get close to Steve—"

"Chief Superintendent!" Mrs. Snell called. Without fail, she always knocked before opening his inner office door, but in this case it swung wide without warning.

"Sorry, Tony! Bet you're giving the troops a pep talk. Can't blame you. Got to keep up morale, no matter what." DCI Jackson strolled in, eyeing the décor, the bookshelves, even the drapes as if they might soon be his. "Hiya, kids! Paulie! Didn't I pass you a fortune cookie last night?"

Bhar, who'd described the conversation to Kate in precise detail, affected not to understand. "Did we run into each other?"

"You'll want to work on that memory. I expect better from my subordinates." Turning to Kate, Jackson grinned. "Tell me the truth. You coming back to work after the wedding? Or going for a soft life with the horse and hound set?"

"You know I'll be back," Kate said through clenched teeth.

"Perfect. The prodigal returns. Can't wait." Jackson advanced toward Hetheridge. "So what's on the docket for this afternoon, Tony?"

"I'm sending DS Bhar to re-interview Riley Castanet. Arrest her, if sufficient cause is found," Hetheridge said.

"Yesterday, that would have been a good plan. *Yesterday?* Would have been genius," Jackson said. "Unfortunately, today, it's too little, too late. I'm heading to Grosvenor Towers, where Peerless Petrol conducts their on-shore corporate business, to inspect the murder scene."

"What murder scene?" Kate, Hetheridge, and Bhar all spoke at once.

"Arianna Freemont. She collapsed at the office and died—" He checked his mobile. "In the last five minutes. My team is mobilized. But don't worry." Jackson looked from face to face with pretended magnanimity. "You're all welcome to come along. I'll even let you tour the scene—sometime this evening, after the SOCOs are done and there's no chance of you doing any harm."

Kate made a choked noise of outrage, but Hetheridge interrupted. "Cause of death?"

"Presumed to be poisoning. Apparently, the lady started wheezing on her way to the lifts. Fell over and curled up in the fetal position. Died before the medics arrived." Jackson grinned. "Don't know about you lot, but my money's on strychnine. And with that, looks like I'm off. Don't fret, kids. I'll ring *Lord* Hetheridge the moment the scene is released to secondary investigators."

***

"One of these days, he's gonna fall over and curl up in the fetal position," Bhar muttered after DCI Jackson's departure.

"What do we know about strychnine?" Hetheridge asked. "Besides the fact it's banned, at least in this country. The farmers are always complaining about too many moles."

"Moles?" Kate was impressed. "I didn't realize, in addition to everything else, you're an expert on modern farming techniques."

"My ancestral home in Devon is part farm. Sheep, chickens, some cattle. I would have shut it down ages ago, but keeping it alive means a great deal to the village."

"Sheep?" Kate, a Londoner born and bred, tried to imagine Hetheridge tramping around a pasture in mud-stained overalls and wellies. It was impossible.

"Yes, well, other listed homes have bridle paths and ornamental fruit gardens. Briarshaw has a farm. And moles."

"Briarshaw?" Kate repeated. She'd been under the impression all great country houses had names that ended in "Hall" or "Park."

"Yes. But the matter at hand is strychnine," Hetheridge said. "As near as I can tell, stories about street drugs being cut with pure strychnine are urban legends. Heroin is far easier to obtain than strychnine. Even farmers outside Britain can only get their hands on mixtures created for agricultural use. And no person, no matter how distracted by boardroom politics, would drink something dosed with an industrial preparation like that."

"The plant itself grows in Hawaii," Bhar offered. "Not to mention some third world countries Sir Duncan's lived in. Maybe the killer's poison is homegrown. Of course, that doesn't explain Arianna's collapse...."

"What do you mean?" Kate asked.

"Vic said she curled up in the fetal position," Bhar said. "If that's correct, the murder weapon can't be strychnine. Strychnine causes the opisthotonic death posture. Back arched, head and heels on the floor. The Circe Du Soleil of death."

"I see Peter Garrett's impromptu lecture wasn't wasted on you, Paul. Top marks," Hetheridge said. "So for Michael Martin Hughes and his fiancée, we have a single killer with two methods. Or the first murderer and a copycat, hoping one case of poisoning is indistinguishable from another."

"I wish we could get in there before Vic stomps all over the evidence," Kate said. "See Arianna's body for ourselves. Talk to the witnesses before Vic implants his pre-fab ideas in their heads."

Hetheridge stiffened. He remained still for so long, arms at his side, eyes fixed straight ahead, Kate was alarmed.

"Tony? What is it? Are you feeling okay?"

"Fine." He took out his mobile. "The truth is, and this is for your ears only, we were indeed a touch remiss with Riley Castanet's original name and arrest record. Some PC should have been assigned to uncover Riley's personal details from day one. I fear she was so flamboyantly over-the top, we focused on less forthcoming suspects. I hope the lesson is obvious. No matter how many hours you put in, or how devoted you are, sometimes one small error is all it takes. But you'll be pleased to know," Hetheridge continued as he dialed, "I didn't make the same mistake with Steve Zhao."

"Who are you calling?" Kate asked.

"I told you. Steve Zhao. Before he quit Hotel Nonpareil, he opened his own IT firm, SmartSnap. By the time Bob Junkett prodded Mr. Zhao into leaving, SmartSnap was already solvent. They contract with many major UK businesses. Including Peerless Petrol."

"But what does SmartSnap do?" Bhar, so recently praised, sounded like he'd already lost the plot.

"Provides CCTV camera security that's supposedly infallible," Hetheridge said. "Hello! Is that Steve Zhao? Forgive me, Mr. Zhao, for calling you on your unlisted mobile. It's Anthony Hetheridge. From Scotland Yard. You remember... Jules's father."

Chapter
Twenty-One

B ut is Steve in trouble?" Jules hissed at Hetheridge.
"I assure you, he's not."

"You arrested Kevin."

"Kevin was a drug dealer in possession of an illegal firearm," Hetheridge said. "It was my pleasure to send him away for a time. Especially since doing so separated him from you."

"Dirk's the one who idolizes Sir Duncan," Jules continued, casting a worried glance at Steve, as if her boyfriend were chained to a dungeon wall and not sitting behind Hetheridge's desk, using his computer. "Dirk's the one who was desperate to divert all the hotel's camera feeds. Never mentioned Sir Duncan, just claimed he wanted to make Bob Junkett look completely incompetent. And Steve only helped Dirk tamper with one camera because he didn't want the entire hotel losing its security. Just one, enough to make a point. He can't resist taking the piss, especially with a wanker like Bob."

"I understand. Dirk Oakenwood will be questioned within the hour. Alas, there's nothing we can charge him with. By diverting the camera feed, Dirk left himself open for legal action from his employer," Hetheridge said. "That's about all, but we can try to intimidate him. Get him to roll over on Sir Duncan, unlikely as that seems. In the meantime, Steve has given evidence to the Met in exchange for immunity from prosecution. You needn't fear for him."

"Look, Dad. Tony. Whatever I'm meant to call you. I'm *not* under Sir Duncan's spell." Jules lifted her chin. "I promise I'm not. I don't even like the man."

Gazing into a pair of familiar pale blue eyes, Hetheridge did not believe her. But he'd been wrong before. Perhaps in this case, he was wrong again.

"I mean it!" Jules cried. "I think Lady Isabel is wonderful. When she asked me out to lunch, I was over the moon. Total girl crush. But when we met again, her brother tagged along. I had no warning. I was shocked to see him pull up a chair!"

"Tell me. During the course of that lunch, did Sir Duncan ask about Steve?"

"I'm not sure."

"Jules, please. Think."

"I am thinking! I don't remember anything about Steve! Jeez, if Sir Duncan was interested in anyone, it wasn't Steve. It was you."

"What?"

"He wanted to know how you met my mom. What happened when she … you know. How you met Kate. Details about the wedding. Of course, I disappointed him there," Jules said with a wry smile. "I had to tell him I wasn't invited."

Hetheridge sighed. "That's for the best."

"Why? So I won't mess things up? Scare Kate, maybe, by providing an example of just how disappointing parenthood can be?"

Neither spoke for what felt like a very long time. Finally, Hetheridge said, "I suppose asking you to trust me would be entirely out of bounds?"

"Yes." Jules's lower lip trembled. "Hate me all you want, but I don't trust anyone."

"I don't hate you." Hetheridge touched her shoulder. It was the only fatherly gesture he'd yet allowed himself, and it still felt artificial, like a rehearsal between untalented actors. "Let's defer the subject, eh? To revisit in three weeks, when I return from my honeymoon?"

"I've got it!" Steve Zhao cried from his place at Hetheridge's computer.

"Hacked in already?" Bhar asked.

"I didn't have to hack in. It's my operating system. I can access any SmartSnap camera whenever I want."

"You can't tell me that little detail was ever disclosed in the privacy agreements you signed with your clients," Kate said.

Steve pretended to look shocked. "I'll never tell. Anyway, I have the correct camera and the footage queued up. Wanna look?"

Hetheridge, Jules, Kate, and Bhar faced the desk as Steve turned the monitor their way. As expected, the CCTV camera feed was black and white, shot from on high and jumpy. Yet it showed Arianna Freemont walking toward a lift, staggering in high heels, a hand pressed to her temple. Her breath came fast and shallow; her path was wobbly, disoriented. The receptionist at the desk shot to her feet, hands out, saying something. Never looking her way, Arianna hit the floor nose-first, blood squirting as she clutched at her throat. Before the receptionist reached her side, Arianna had begun curling up, her heaving chest going still.

"Oh my God," Jules cried. Making a choking sound, she backed away from the desk.

"Hey! Jules! I'm sorry!" Steve sounded genuinely contrite. "I didn't think—I should have—*oi!*" he cried as Jules hurried out of the room. Catching Steve by the arm, Hetheridge held him back.

"Let her go. Better she never become desensitized to this sort of thing. We, however, need more. Can you show us what happened before Arianna's collapse?"

"Not really," Steve said. "Whatever caused it must have happened in the executive wing. That's the only place in Peerless Petrol's office space without security cameras. And it's not uncommon." He grinned. "How can the fat cats go on cooking the books and shagging each other if surveillance applies to them, too? Or, as they put it: once you reach executive level, you're above suspicion."

"Fair enough. Can you show us footage of Arianna entering the executive wing?"

"Sure. Give me five minutes." In half that time, Steve procured the correct feed.

"Okay, kids. Here's Arianna, about two hours before she collapsed."

Arianna Freemont carried herself regally on her way to the office. Her suit was navy or black; her heels, at least four inches. Her dark hair was twisted into a chignon, and though it was hard to tell from the ceiling-mounted CCTV camera, Hetheridge thought he glimpsed the sparkle of Hughes's diamond engagement ring on her finger.

"There's the scarf," Bhar said.

"What scarf?"

"The one Riley said was hers."

"You can't be sure it's blue," Kate said.

"No. But I can see the butterflies in the weave."

After Arianna disappeared, Steve leaned back in Hetheridge's office chair as if he, too, were an honorary detective. "But now she's gone. Not to return until she drops dead. You don't think she died of natural causes, do you? Heart attack? Stroke?"

"Not remotely," Hetheridge said. "Can you assemble a montage of footage? Everyone who entered or exited the executive suite today?"

"It'll take awhile, but yeah. Sure."

As Steve worked, Hetheridge went to check on Jules. He found her sitting quietly beside Mrs. Snell's desk, staring at the carpet.

"I'm sorry you had to see that."

"I thought I wanted to." Jules didn't look up. "To face it, to see someone die, if that makes sense. I didn't see mum die. Didn't even see her body. Everyone told me a closed casket was for the best. But you saw her die. Watched her do it."

"Yes."

Jules peered up at Hetheridge, familiar eyes pleading. "Did mum look awful? After... after she did it, I mean."

"No. She was still beautiful," he lied, touching Jules's shoulder again and willing her to believe him. "Beautiful and at peace, I promise."

***

"Here we go again. This is fun," Steve Zhao grinned at Hetheridge, Kate, Bhar, and Jules, who'd recently returned. Only Jules returned the grin.

"I don't mean it's fun someone died," Steve amended. "It's fun trying to catch a killer, that's all. Have a look. I've set all the extraneous stuff to go by at triple speed."

"How can you be sure what—" Hetheridge began.

"Er." Steve looked embarrassed to interrupt, but his intellect seemed to override his sense of propriety. "Watch and see if you don't agree."

Even at triple speed, there was a lot to go through. Men with briefcases, ladies in power suits, administrative assistants threading back and forth, the footage all time-stamped. Finally Arianna reappeared, striding confidently into the executive suite. Back to triple speed for awhile. Then the footage resumed normal speed as a courier from St. Expresso turned up, carrying a tray of drinks in tall containers with plastic tops. He received clearance from the receptionist, but before he could enter the executive suite, a woman in a peasant blouse and long ruffled skirt intercepted him. It was Riley Castanet.

"Oh, no," Bhar breathed.

Even without audio, it was clear Riley took custody of the drinks, sending St. Espresso's courier away. She entered the executive suite, only to emerge fifteen minutes later, empty-handed except for her handbag.

"Where did she go?"

"Back to her office, one floor down," Steve said. "Near as I can tell, she never left the building. She's probably still there, either because she's innocent, or because she's waiting out the investigation."

Jules elbowed Hetheridge. "Told you he was clever."

"On that, you'll get no argument," Hetheridge said. "Steve. Indulge me. Replay the footage of Arianna collapsing. Jules, you may wish to look away."

To his relief, she did. Hetheridge watched, his excellent powers of recollection once again confirmed. Then he looked from Kate, on his right, to Bhar, on his left. "What's missing?"

Neither replied. The answer was too obvious for his question to be anything but rhetorical. Hetheridge, satisfied, punched a familiar number into his mobile.

"Vic? It's Tony. Yes, yes, I know. I understand. That's wonderful. But indulge me in one thing, and if I'm wrong, I promise to write an apology to the entire department. Yes. I know. But please—stop what you're doing and detain Riley Castanet. Then look among her possessions and see if you don't find a blue butterfly scarf."

***

Kate found Riley's videotaped confession hard to watch. She was accustomed to audio interviews; being able to see Riley's face, to watch her hands clench as she played with cigarette after cigarette, was surprisingly hard to bear. In general, Kate had no sympathy with murderers. There was always an excuse: a poor upbringing, an unfaithful lover, a broken promise.

Having experienced all those trials herself without killing anyone, Kate found it difficult to write anyone else a blank check. Indeed, to do so in her chosen profession would have been a terrible conflict of interest. But something about Riley's confession, filmed at the US Embassy's request during extradition talks with the States, worried Kate.

"I didn't kill Michael. I foresaw his death and tried to stop it. I never would have killed him!" Riley insisted on-camera to Bhar, the detective chosen to handle the confession. "But you saw what Arianna did to me in the hotel lobby. She tried to crush me. She tried to take away everything I am."

Once, during a criminal justice seminar, Kate had heard the theory that public humiliation was among the most potent triggers for female murderers. "Slap a woman around and maybe you'll walk away," the professor had opined. "But if you humiliate her in a public place, you risk death by ramming with a car. Poison. Fire. Or bludgeoning while you sleep."

"I'm sorry that happened," Bhar muttered on tape, head down, almost inaudible. "I know you changed your name and your profession in order to start over. But the toxicology report has come back on Arianna Freemont. We know how you poisoned her. Would you like to explain?"

"I couldn't get my hands on strychnine. Yes, I know that's what killed Michael, but only because I saw his body!" Riley managed to simultaneously puff on her cigarette and swipe at her eyes. "I looked it up online, what causes a dead person to freeze like that. If it wasn't drowning, it had to be strychnine. So I thought strychnine would be perfect to kill Arianna. But I couldn't get it, and I knew my days at Peerless were numbered. I didn't have time to keep looking. And my e-cigarette supplier had warned me about the effects of pure nicotine…."

Bhar leaned forward. "You knew it was deadly in high concentrations?"

"Of course." Even as she faced a double murder conviction, Riley seemed incapable of playing dumb. By contrast, she willingly placed her head in the noose, so long as it gave her a moment of authority. She'd even waived her right to a solicitor when that august personage had dared suggest she refrain from mentioning her psychic powers. For Riley, being dictated to was, it seemed, worse than life behind bars.

"When I started smoking e-cigarettes, I used the premade cartridges, which are perfectly safe," Riley continued. "Cut with all sorts of super-harmless stuff. But I wanted more. A bigger high. Better than an unfiltered Camel, better than home-rolled, if you know what I mean. Turns out there are shops in the U.S. that sell pure liquid nicotine. The shopkeepers tell you to wear gloves. Measure perfectly. Keep your mouth shut about the high or you'll ruin it for responsible users. All that bull." Riley blew out a plume of smoke. "I thought they were nuts. But when I realized I couldn't get strychnine, I started searching online for poisons that are easier to obtain. Nicotine came up, and that was already in my gear. All I had to do was intercept the daily latte delivery and empty some of my pure liquid nicotine into Arianna's drink."

"Why do it at the office?"

"It's not like Arianna would have let me into her house. Her or that creepy bodyguard of hers."

"But she didn't question it when you brought the latte to her office?"

"Of course not. She was so arrogant. Figured I came to kiss her butt. Beg to stay on at Peerless, even though Michael was dead," Riley said. "She took the first sip while thinking how to insult me. The second, waiting for my reaction."

"When did you take the scarf?"

"When she started coughing. I didn't say a word. Just unwound it from her shoulders while she tried to breathe, and got the hell out of Dodge."

"How much pure nicotine did you put in the latte?"

"Twice what the internet said would kill." Riley took another deep drag. "Never trust anything the internet says. Not without verification."

Bhar seemed to absorb that. "Let's go back to Michael Martin Hughes. I understand you approached him with the best of intentions. To help him avoid an early demise. I know he hired you, and for awhile you were lovers. But what made you—"

"I've told you!" Riley shrieked. "I didn't kill Michael! But I'm in contact with his spirit, and he told me who did. Sir Duncan Godington!"

"Sir Duncan?" Bhar sounded politely unconvinced.

"I thought he said 'fur' or 'purr.' It was all the damn orange monkeys that confused me," Riley said. "He was trying to tell me Sir Duncan did it, but it took awhile for Michael's spirit to pronounce the name."

"I see."

"No! Deepal, don't say 'I see' like that, I can't take it!" Riley sounded close to the end of her tether. "Michael's spirit showed me the truth about everything. He tried to make a deal with Sir Duncan. All right, not a *fair* deal, but something Peerless Petrol would get behind. Something to make them richer and look environmentally conscious at the same time. At first, Sir Duncan said no. Then, at the gala, he seemed to change his mind. Offered to meet Michael for a private drink."

"Where?"

"In Michael's suite, of course. Michael let Sir Duncan in. Took a leak while Sir Duncan made him a whiskey sour. Can you believe that? Whatever Sir Duncan did to poison him, Michael was in the bathroom and missed the whole thing. He came out, took his drink, knocked half of it back, and started talking shop. Then the pain began, and by the end he couldn't talk at all."

"I suppose after that, Sir Duncan hurried back to his penthouse?"

"No." Riley stubbed out what Kate suspected was her fifth cigarette since the interrogation began. "That's the terrible thing. He sat down on a barstool to watch. Seeing Michael die was a big thrill for him."

"Was it?"

"Of course. While Michael could still speak, he started pleading for his life. Promising Sir Duncan anything. Power. Money. You name it."

"How did Sir Duncan respond?" Bhar asked. On tape, it was hard to tell if he was just playing along or genuinely interested in Riley's story.

"He said real power wasn't Michael's to give." Riley covered her eyes as if reliving a particularly potent vision. "The last thing Michael heard was Sir Duncan saying this: 'Someday, I'll chuck the dosh where it can do the most good and disappear into a jungle forever.' "

"That's what Sir Duncan said to Hughes?"

"The last thing he heard. I don't get it. What does 'dosh' even mean? Lord, fly me back to California where at least I know what people are saying."

"All right. Riley, we've been at this for some time. Why don't I return you to your cell? You can get something to eat, sleep for awhile, and have a go at this again in the morning."

"I'm not lying about the vision. It's true, Deepal. Every word."

Bhar sighed. "Why did you take the scarf?"

"Because Michael loved me, not her. That's all that matters. Love, and the proof of love, even after death. You'll find that out. Just you wait, Deepal. You'll find out."

***

"Oh!" Kate cried, sitting up in bed.

"What is it?" Hetheridge thrashed under the sheets. "What's happened?"

"We made a mistake." Kate threw her arms around him. "Riley's being sent down for both murders, but she doesn't deserve it."

Hetheridge exhaled against Kate's neck. "Sweetheart. Didn't we agree, no police work in bed?"

"But Sir Duncan said it to me. 'Someday I'll chuck the dosh where it can do the most good and disappear into a jungle forever.' I don't know when he said it—during the Halloween bash or at his penthouse. But I'm quite certain he said it. And Riley's an American. She doesn't even know what 'dosh' means. How could she make up that statement?"

"There is such a thing as the unconscious mind. Bits we pick up, without realizing it, and recycle in a way that seems almost psychic."

"We've made a mistake," Kate sighed. "I know Vic's in charge now. The arrest goes in his ledger, and any mistrials or overturned convictions, too. But we've made a mistake. Sir Duncan killed Hughes. For the obvious reason: what Hughes did to the environment. That was bad enough. But when he wouldn't take Sir Duncan's offer at a partnership, to fix it for real, and not just as another moneymaker for Peerless Petrol, that's when Hughes was marked to die."

For a long time, Hetheridge held Kate silently. When he spoke at last, his voice was calm, almost clinical.

"We investigated. We turned over all our evidence to the Crown Court. We performed exactly as detectives are meant to perform. Yes, there was some weak evidence against Sir Duncan, but all of it was circumstantial. The case against Riley is far stronger, particularly since she confessed to killing Arianna Freemont."

"But it's still wrong!" Kate cursed. "If only Dirk Oakenwood had understood what was at stake and admitted what he did...."

"I'm not surprised Dirk kept mum," Hetheridge said. "Sir Duncan has a rare charisma. Once his hooks are in, people will do anything for him."

"And now he has everything he wanted," Kate said bitterly. "Hughes dead. A role as Peerless Petrol's new eco-czar, thanks to Arianna. And yet another murder pinned on someone else. Tony. Everything's going wrong," Kate whispered against his neck.

"Meaning?"

"Maura called my mobile yesterday. Mum called twice yesterday. They're crashing the wedding for sure. Unless they get a big payoff to convince them otherwise."

"Let them crash."

Kate's eyes went hot. Tears weren't far behind, and not the dainty waterworks designed to ensnare male interest. These sobs would be uncontrolled, and ugly. "You don't know what you're saying."

"I do." Hetheridge kissed her mouth. "Forgive me. I never wanted to put you in a position to lie to your blood relatives. Much less appear to choose me over them. But this charade has gone on long enough. I have something to tell you."

Chapter
Twenty-Two

E ven in winter, Wellegrave House was a lovely site for a
wedding. Especially at twilight, the leafless trees wrapped
with fairy lights, the flagstone path illuminated by luminarias,
the walled garden looked magical. Lady Margaret Knolls, never
married and buoyed by the romance of it all, said as much to
her companion, Lady Vivian Callot.

"Admiring your own handiwork?" Lady Vivian asked.

"If I don't, who will?"

"I don't approve of the hour."

"I know," Lady Margaret said.

"Don't approve of the venue, either. Too small. Even
with the portable heaters, it's too cold for this nonsense. And
the garden is filled with hangers-on. I can scarcely count more
than a handful of real guests among the sneaks, snoops, and
spectators hoping for a train wreck."

"There's a tedious policeman at twelve o'clock," Lady
Margaret said. "Jackson, I think. Someone needs to brush the

218

dandruff off his coat."

"I believe it's crumbs."

"Whatever. And look, there's poor old Randy Roddy, drunk in front of his sons. Still taking the loss of the barony rather hard, I fear."

"That lot over by the punch bowl worries me. The bride's, I presume?"

"Of course."

"The toothless one has a photographer dogging her heels. Don't tell me that's poor Kate's mum."

"Of course."

"Why the photographer?"

"The better to sell her story to the highest bidder, I expect," Lady Margaret said.

"But the wedding will already be in the tabloids. I heard the man from *Bright Star* bragging he'd stalked poor Kate all day. Got a mix of flattering and unflattering snaps, to slant the story whichever way his editor prefers."

"Oh, I don't mean the wedding *per se*. I mean the new couple's response to whatever demands the Wakefields make."

Lady Vivian winced. "How horrid. Why on earth didn't Tony hire better security? There's still time to throw them out."

"That, too, would be a tabloid sob story, complete with pictures," Lady Margaret said.

"Yes, well, if I ever marry again, a turnout this grim would break my heart."

Lady Margaret said nothing.

"Dare you continue sitting beside me?" Lady Vivian demanded. Still beautiful at almost seventy, with high cheekbones and an elegant mouth, she looked fetching in a lavender gown with a nipped-in waist. "Really, Peg. If you linger, someone might presume we're a couple."

"We're too old to be a couple. Love is for the young."

"Most of my society friends think you're secretly in love with Tony Hetheridge. That you planned this wedding whilst crying yourself to sleep each night."

"Most of your society friends are idiots."

"They've been remarkably supportive since I came out. Displays of affection. Little notes. Sweet remarks on Facebook."

Lady Margaret groaned.

"I happen to like Facebook."

"I happen to like Jägermeister. But I never brag about it where people might overhear."

"My eldest son, ever concerned for my well-being, warned me you weren't up to a public revelation. He said you'd throw me over rather than become a figure of controversy. Like your friend the bridegroom."

"Tony's marrying a commoner."

"Ha!" Lady Vivian pressed a hand to her chest. "Prince William did it first. But go on, pull the other one."

"I'd rather pull your spleen out through your ear. But the music is starting," Lady Margaret whispered. "Hush."

As usual, Lady Vivian refused to be silenced when her curiosity was aroused. "Where's the minister? Where's Tony? For the love of God, don't tell me they're going to walk down the aisle together, then recite their own abysmal vows?"

"Shh!"

The bride appeared first, a vision in white, veil fluttering. Seeing her, Lady Margaret found it impossible to believe a single tabloid snap was unflattering. Tall and willowy, each step assured, blonde hair an artful tangle of perfect curls, she looked absolutely flawless.

"Who in bloody hell is that?" the old woman by the punchbowl demanded.

"Is that Kate?" Lady Vivian whispered.

"Of course not! Now hush," Lady Margaret hissed, smiling as the "groom" stepped forth to address the confused gathering.

"Hello." Paul Bhar looked surprisingly dapper in evening dress, though Lady Margaret would never give him the satisfaction of admitting it. "I'm not Lord Hetheridge. Which you probably guessed on account I'm taller, younger, and let's face it. Magnetically handsome."

"Oh, for the love of—" The rumpled policeman followed his outburst with an eruption of profanity.

"Speaking for myself, and my good friend, Emmeline, we appreciate all the attention," Bhar continued. "Talk about your fifteen minutes of fame. But now I have a message for everyone from the real couple." Withdrawing his mobile, Bhar began to read.

"Dear friends. We hope, in time, you'll forgive us for eloping. We thought it best. As for making you wait out in the cold, in London, when we were married three days ago in Devon: again, we apologize to anyone who genuinely wishes us well. And if you don't wish us well, but turned up anyway, consider our little joke the price of admission. Please, no matter who you are, come out of the cold, make yourself welcome in our house, enjoy the open bar and live music. The least interesting part of any wedding is the ceremony. Now you can get on with the party, and we can get on with the honeymoon. Sincerely." Bhar looked up with a smile. "Lord and Lady Hetheridge."

"What does this mean?" the elder Wakefield barked at a blowsy woman in a donkey jacket who could only be Kate's elder sister, Maura.

"Kate buggered off three days ago," Maura said.

"I don't understand."

"I do, Mum. Come on, he said open bar."

Satisfied, Lady Margaret turned to Lady Vivian. "Still disapprove?"

"Of course not. A decoy wedding. How romantic." Lady Vivian rose. "Look, Roddy's gone quite purple in the face. I think the ghastly in-laws will forgive Tony and Kate quicker than he will."

"Personally, I hope they're never forgiven and remain boycotted for the rest of their lives."

"Oh, please. None of us with unfortunate relations are ever that lucky."

"Lady Vivian?" a reporter called.

"Yes?"

"Hello. Terribly sorry to interrupt. There's a story you've left your husband and come out as gay. Is that true?"

She lifted her chin, fixing him with the steely glare everyone but Lady Margaret feared. "Yes."

The reporter, who looked all of twenty and hungry for a story, grinned. "So are you playing the field now? Happily single? Dating?"

"She's with me," Lady Margaret heard herself say.

"Oh. And you are?"

"Lady Margaret Knolls, you ignorant fetus."

"Sorry!" The reporter, who seemed to expect verbal abuse, kept right on grinning. "I have a feeling there's more to be told."

"Of course, but that's all you get," Lady Vivian said firmly. And taking Lady Margaret's hand, she led her into the party.

***

Briarshaw, Kate learned, was a house in the British Palladian style. That meant it dated back to the early eighteenth century and was large and square with two supporting wings. The entrance's columns and arches were meant to invoke the memory of classical Greek temples; atop the roof, three figures in Italian marble were affixed, adding to the symmetric effect.

"Ritchie and Henry are having the time of their lives down there."

"I know." Hetheridge put an arm around Kate. From the rooftop, they had a spectacular view of the grounds. At present, they faced the front lawn, as Briarshaw's groundskeeper called an area of scrubby grass dominated by a long pebble drive. On that lawn, Ritchie was exploring on his hands and knees, probably hunting insects. Henry was playing some game of his own invention that amounted to running in circles and shouting a lot.

"First time I've ever seen Ritchie voluntarily ignore the

TV. Or Henry put down a book long enough to run around."

"It's something in the air. I used to love coming here as a boy. Best holidays of my life."

"Is that why you wanted the wedding here?"

"Yes."

Kate smiled. The ceremony, performed on Christmas Day in Briarshaw's chapel, had unfolded beautifully. Poinsettias were the only flowers; a Christmas tree had sparkled behind the vicar. Ritchie's tantrum was brief, Henry found the stained glass fascinating, and Harvey didn't break down in tears until the couple was pronounced man and wife. The instant the words were said, a weight Kate had borne for longer than she could remember had fled at last.

"I adore this house already."

It was his turn to smile.

"These figures on the roof," Kate continued. "Are they saints?"

"I doubt it. To be honest, no one knows for sure."

"Really?"

"Really. The Hetheridge who built this house—Charles, I think it was—wasn't much for writing letters or diaries. I believe he spent most of his time in London, chasing women. But my mother used to say the primary figure in the helmet is Athena, goddess of wisdom."

"Makes sense. What about the other two?"

"On the right, Hestia, goddess of hearth and home. On the left, Artemis, goddess of the hunt."

"Charles liked mythology?"

"Charles liked women. That's the extent of what we know. And he built a splendid home on a fine tract of land. Let's cross to the opposite side."

They did. Facing west, Kate saw two meadows enclosed by ancient stone fences. One was empty; the other housed a collection of sedate woolly sheep. There was a barn, a rose garden, and a small wooded area made dark and fanciful by the setting sun.

"When I was a boy, my brother was the heir. I was the

spare, which meant freedom," Hetheridge said. "He used to tell me, 'All this is mine,' and I laughed in his face. I thought he was the family stooge. I was different. I was going to live my life however I chose. But he died. I inherited. And though I did love this place, I truly did, when I looked around and thought, 'this is mine,' the pleasure wasn't what I'd imagined. Not until now, when I can finally say, this is ours."

Kate looked her husband in the eye. Being precisely the same height, it was easy. "You meant it, didn't you? The first time you proposed marriage, and I thought you were just being gallant, or suicidal. Even then, you meant it."

"Yes."

"How did you know?" Kate whispered, giving voice to the question she'd sworn never to ask.

"Because when I thought of Briarshaw, all I could imagine was offering it to you. My favorite place in the world was nothing, less than nothing, unless you had a share in it, too."

"I love you, Lord Hetheridge."

"And I love you, Lady Hetheridge." He kissed her. "Now let's get back to the front lawn before Ritchie and Henry manage to set it on fire."

THE END

FROM THE AUTHOR

Thank you for reading Something Blue. If you enjoyed this book, please consider returning to the website from which you purchased it and leaving a review.

As many of you know, I'm the author of ICE BLUE and BLUE MURDER, books #1 and #2 in the Lord & Lady Hetheridge series. I'm already at work on book #4, tentatively called BLACK & BLUE. Hetheridge and Kate are married now, but the repercussions are just beginning. Hethcridge's enemies want to cut off his distinguished career. Kate is determined to make the devilishly charming Sir Duncan pay for his crimes. Kate's relatives are scheming to land a big payoff. And Bhar is struggling to deal with two girlfriends, a possible stepfather, and a mystery that hits a little too close to home. Because this time, it affects his beloved mum, the irrepressible Sharada Bhar.

Cheers!
Emma Jameson
5/23/2013

ACKNOWLEDGEMENTS

The author would like to acknowledge the help of several wonderful people: Kate Aaron, Christine DeMaio-Rice, Theo Fenraven, Shéa MacLeod, M.Edward McNally, Tara West, and Mary Ellen Wofford.

A special thanks must be given to Beth Sparks, a wonderful reader who caught many errors in the original manuscript. I am deeply grateful for her kind assistance.

Made in the USA
San Bernardino, CA
09 November 2013